**Also available from Annabeth Albert
and Carina Press**

Better N____ ___

Status U___
Beta ___
Connectio___

Off Ba___
At Attention
On Point
Wheels Up
Squared Away
Tight Quarters
Rough Terrain

Arctic Sun
Arctic Wild
Arctic Heat

Burn Zone
High Heat
Feel the Fire
Up in Smoke

**Coming soon from Annabeth Albert
and Carina Press**

Sink or Swim

Also available from Annabeth Albert

Trust with a Chaser
Tender with a Twist
Lumber Jacked

Treble Maker
____ ___
____ ___
____ ___
____ Fresh
Delivered Fast
Knit Tight
Wrapped Together
Danced Close

Resilient Heart
Winning Bracket
Save the Date
Level Up
Mr. Right Now
Sergeant Delicious
Cup of Joe
Featherbed

SAILOR PROOF

Annabeth Albert

carina
press

carina
press®

Recycling programs
for this product may
not exist in your area.

ISBN-13: 978-1-335-98492-0

Sailor Proof

This edition published by arrangement with Harlequin Books S.A.

For questions and comments about the quality of this book, please contact us at CustomerService@Harlequin.com.

Carina Press
22 Adelaide St. West, 40th Floor
Toronto, Ontario M5H 4E3, Canada
www.CarinaPress.com

Printed in U.S.A.

For Abbie Nicole,
TikTok and viral videos everywhere

SAILOR PROOF

Chapter One

Derrick

It was going to happen. Today was finally the day I was going to deck an officer and thus end any hope I had of ever making chief of the boat, and probably earn myself a court-martial to boot. But Fernsby had it coming, and he knew it, the way he met my eyes as he gave a cocky laugh. He might be a junior-grade lieutenant who had to answer to the other officers, but he wasn't stupid. It didn't matter how much he had it coming, a chief fighting with an officer of any rank over a personal matter was going to be harshly punished.

But it might be worth it.

Fernsby had been goading me the entire long deployment, every chance he got, which considering the close quarters on a submarine was pretty damn often. And now here he was, joking with another officer about winning the first-kiss raffle for our homecoming, knowing full well that I was standing right there. And that he'd be kissing my ex.

Personal matter indeed.

And totally worth punching that smug smile away.

"I hope we go viral. Social media loves two hot dudes kissing." Fernsby smirked as he waggled his eyebrows at the big-eyed ensign who'd been hero-worshipping him all damn tour. And of course he was smirking. First kiss was a storied tradition for most navy deployments, and sailors loved vying for the honor of being first to disembark and greet their loved ones. Usually I was happy for whoever won, and over the years I'd seen more than one proposal as a result of that first kiss.

God, I hoped Fernsby wasn't planning *that*. Bad enough that he couldn't stop ribbing me that Steve chose him over me and that I'd been the last to know Steve was cheating. Watching them be all happy was going to suck.

"I'm gonna get so lucky." Fernsby's knowing gaze met mine over the ensign's head.

An angry noise escaped my throat. "And I hope—"

"Fox. A word. *Now*." My friend Calder appeared seemingly out of nowhere in the narrow corridor and hauled me backward, effectively cutting off my tirade along with a good deal of my circulation.

"Yeah, Fox. Go on with you." Fernsby made a dismissive gesture as I growled, but Calder kept moving, giving me little choice but to follow. He dragged me past various compartments through the mess, where two of our fellow chiefs were playing cards. He didn't stop until we were in the chief's section of the bunking with its rows of triple beds, steering me into the far corner by our bunks and about as close to privacy as we were going to get.

"What the fuck?" Calder wasted no time in unleashing on me.

"It's nothing." I looked down at my narrow bunk. I had the bottom bunk, another chief had the middle, and the top bunk was Calder's. And I was more than a little tempted to disappear into mine and pull the blue privacy curtain. "Fernsby was running his mouth again."

"You sure as hell looked like you were gearing up to slug him. I saw your clenched fist. I'm surprised smoke wasn't coming out of your ears."

Calder wasn't wrong, so I shrugged. "I need to stop letting him get to me. I know."

"Yeah, you do." He shoved my shoulder the way only a longtime best friend could get away with. We'd been lucky, meeting up in submarine school, both getting assigned to Bremerton, and then ending up on the same boat together as chiefs. Calder had a vested interest in me not fucking up, and my skin heated from how close I'd come to doing just that.

"I'm pissed because it looks like he won first kiss and now I have to watch that," I admitted in a low whisper.

"What you need is a kiss of your own," said the guy who probably had different dates scheduled for each of our first three days home.

"Ha. Would be nice, but not happening." It went without saying that I wouldn't have anyone in the throngs of family and friends waiting on me. Simply wasn't how my life was structured, and most of the time I was fine with it. Calder was the one who would have a big contingent of friends and family. And I was well-acquainted with his undying belief that the solution to one terrible relationship was to find another more casual arrangement. "I'm not exactly a rebound sort of guy."

"Everyone knows that about you." Calder rolled his eyes. He was both taller and broader than me, which was saying something because I wasn't exactly tiny. However, his playful demeanor always made him seem younger. "But you should be. And I'm not even talking about getting laid. I'm saying you need to make Fernsby and Steve-the-lying-ex-from-hell jealous by having some hottie there to greet you."

"God. I wish." I let my head thump back against the panel where the bunks met the wall. Unlike Calder, I wasn't counting down the minutes until I could get lucky, but I had entertained more than fantasy about how to pay Steve back. A rebound held limited appeal from an emotional standpoint.

But jealousy? Yeah, I wouldn't mind trotting out someone hotter than Steve, who always was a vain fucker. "But we're only a couple of weeks out from homecoming, and I'm not exactly in a position to meet someone while we're deployed."

Unlike some other deployments, the submarine force had very limited communication access. No cell phones, no swiping right, no mindless surfing of hookup sites. Hell, simply getting messages to friends and family could be challenging, let alone trying to conduct a revenge romance on the down-low.

"Call in a favor?" Calder quirked his mouth. He undoubtedly had multiple persons who would love nothing more than to pretend to be madly in lust with him.

"From who?" My back tensed and my nerves were still jangling from listening to Fernsby brag. "It's not like my contact list is awash in friends with benefits or even friends period."

"You need to work on that whole brooding-loner persona." Calder clapped me on the shoulder, nicer now. "It's not doing you any favors."

"Why be the life of the party when I have you?" I laughed, years of shared memories flowing between us. Any social life I did have, I owed almost entirely to Calder. He'd even introduced me to Steve.

"I do like to bring the party."

"You do." Closing my eyes, I took another deep breath, trying to steady myself. I truly did not want to fight Fernsby even if my fist tended to forget that. "You're right, though. Someone there, even pretend, would make me feel less like a fucking loser."

"Exactly," Calder agreed a little too readily, making my gut clench. Maybe I was that pathetic.

"But I'm not doing something stupid like an ad." I cracked an eye open in time to catch him laughing at me.

"Of course not. You save your stupidity for fighting with officers."

I groaned because he was right. "I'm not the personal-ads type. But who do you know? Surely there's a guy into guys who owes you a favor whom you could loan me?"

I wasn't too proud to borrow from Calder's vast social network.

"Hmm." Tilting his head, Calder narrowed his eyes, the same intense thinking he did when poring over the latest supply manifest. As a logistics specialist, Calder had a solution to almost every problem that could crop up, apparently my love life included. He muttered to himself for a few moments before straightening. "Arthur would do it."

"Ha. Very funny. Try again." I kept my voice down, but my laugh was a lot freer this time. *Arthur.* The nerve. I had to go ahead and sit on a bunk before I lost it laughing.

"He would," Calder insisted, serious expression never wavering. "He owes me."

I shook my head. *Arthur.* I'd known Calder's family for a decade now, including his spindly youngest brother who was some sort of musical genius. And also terminally hopeless. "You want me to use your too-nerdy-for-band-camp little brother to make Fernsby jealous?"

"He's almost twenty-five now. Not so little. He's been out since high school, so no issues about a public kiss. And Haggerty said Arthur's hot now. Kid went and got all buff in Boston."

"Haggerty said that? And you let him live?" Our mutual friend did like them young and pretty. I had vague memories of Arthur having a riot of unruly hair, far redder than his brothers', and big green eyes, but he'd been barely legal last time I'd seen him a couple of years back. And as I'd already been seeing Steve, and Arthur was Calder's little brother, I hadn't looked too terribly hard.

"It was an observation, not a request to go break his heart." Calder kicked my foot. "Come on. It's perfect. Arthur has always liked you, but he doesn't *like* you."

"Hey!" I should have been relieved that Arthur wasn't harboring some giant crush, not indignant.

"Yeah, yeah, you're a catch." Calder fiddled with the strap on his bunk. Everything got strapped down on a sub, even us. "But he's always said he'd never get involved long-term with someone military."

"I don't blame him." This was why I was never doing another relationship myself. Romance and the navy simply didn't mix, especially not submarine personnel. We were bad relationship bets, and I could admit that.

"See? This is why he'd be good for this. He can fake it long enough to get Steve and Fernsby off your back, but it's not like he'd actually date you."

"Of course not."

"Plus all that experience as a dorm RA has him good at shit like signs and banners and cutesy gestures. And he's been back in Seattle a couple of months now. He'd do it."

"I can't believe I'm actually considering this. How are you going to get a message to him anyway?" The last thing I needed was anyone else getting wind of this ill-advised plan. There was no such thing as privacy on a sub.

"Trust me. I've got my ways." Calder's voice went from confident to hushed as voices sounded near the front row of bunks.

"Dude. Did you hear about Fernsby?" asked one of the youngest chiefs, a Nuke with a chipped front tooth and no filter. I couldn't see him or his buddy but his surfer-boy drawl was unmistakable.

"Yep. Fox is gonna be so pissed." The other person had to be Beauregard, who worked with me in Weapons. The Southern accent gave him away. "It's a wonder they haven't murdered each other this whole deployment. If a crew member stole my girl—or guy—I'm not sure I could stand the humiliation."

"Shush." A third voice sounded farther back, and then there was a lot of fumbling around before Beauregard slapped his bunk.

"Okay, okay, here's my new deck," he announced as the three of them exited the quarters.

"See?" I gestured up at Calder. "It would be justifiable homicide."

"It would. But wouldn't revenge be better?"

"I dunno. Fernsby's head would look pretty great mounted on my wall back on base." I groaned as I thought about returning to my little room in the barracks. I'd let Steve keep the apartment, because I was such a nice guy and all. Damn it, I was tired of being nice. Tired of being taken advantage of and pitied and gossiped about. Fuck it all. "Okay. Whatever. See what you can arrange."

"Leave it all to me." Calder straightened to his full height, which came just shy of the low ceiling. "You won't regret this."

"Oh, I'm pretty sure I will." Dread churned in my too-empty gut, but it was a distraction from all the weeks of hurt and anger I'd been stamping down. At least we had a plan.

Chapter Two

Arthur

"This should be easy." I hefted my large cardboard sign out of the trunk as Sabrina laughed.

"Uh-huh." She flipped her cascading bluish-purple hair over her shoulder. She'd prepared for our day on the docks at base with the hair, a shimmery blue top, and a skirt with scales on it. Her whole look gave her the air of a mermaid prepared to lead some poor sailor to his doom. "If this scheme is so easy, why again did you need me?"

"You have a car." We had the kind of ride-or-die friendship built on insults and inside jokes.

"True." After checking her lipstick in a fancy silver mirror, she snapped her purse shut as I carefully removed the bunch of balloons next.

"And you have more social media followers than a minor Kardashian."

"Also true. I'll get you trending." Somehow Sabrina had turned a secret obsession with fashion when we were teens into a successful sideline as an influencer as her alter ego The Makeup Witch with followers hanging on her every post.

"Counting on it." I adjusted my load so that the balloons weren't in imminent danger of escape.

"We'll drown out this cheating loser dude who got first dibs on kissing."

"Your strong opinions on cheaters are only one reason why I love you, Sabrina."

"And my car." She shut the trunk with a gold-tipped finger.

"Yup." I headed in the direction of the community center where the families and friends waiting for the return of the sub were gathering to await buses to the docks. "Anyway, it's a stupid tradition, but like everything else, the navy takes it super seriously. My mom and dad got the honor at least once, and there are a ton of pics of it. It was when he was stationed in Hawaii, and she got flowers and the boat was decorated with a huge lei. It made the *Navy Times*."

"We can do better than some small-time publication." Sabrina laughed as her heels clicked on the sidewalk.

"Everything is small compared to you." It was true on multiple levels because she was big in notoriety and personality as well as stature. Even as we joined the throng of people entering the community center, Sabrina still towered over most of the crowd, commanding far more attention than I ever could, even with my giant sign and balloons.

But the sign that had looked so gaudy back at my place with all its colors and glitter was only one of dozens here. Tons of pretty young women in fancy sundresses toted catchy signs proclaiming how many days it had been since they'd seen their guys, and little kids had smaller signs announcing how much they'd grown. Proud Navy Mom T-shirts were everywhere, and more than one guy my dad's age sported a Navy Veteran hat. The kids raced around the big common room while clumps of people greeted each other with hugs and excited squeals.

"This is something else. They've even got balloon animals

happening." Sabrina gestured at a kids' area set up in the far corner with crafts and a couple of costumed entertainers.

"Yup. When I was little, they had face painting."

"Tell me you asked for something embarrassing that made your big brothers cringe." Sabrina bumped my shoulder.

"I asked for a three-fourth scale viola. I got two music notes and a heart instead."

"You? Ask for something obscure? Never." Her laugh echoed in the large space, mingling with all the other conversations swirling around us. Outside the large picture windows, a row of buses awaited the signal to load up.

"Quit laughing at me," I grumbled as I glanced around to see if any of the uniformed event coordinators were herding people toward the buses yet.

"It's all love, baby." She gave me an air kiss.

In my pocket, my phone vibrated, and I shifted around my armful of stuff so I could fish it out of my skinny jeans. I was waiting to hear about a big freelance job, so I was more eager to check the messages than I might otherwise have been.

But I should have saved my enthusiasm.

Guess what? We caught an earlier flight! We'll probably miss the buses, but we should see you at the docks. Can't wait to see Calder. And you, of course.

And me. Of course. Calder got the bulk of my mom's enthusiasm, as always. And damn it, this was a complication I hadn't counted on. All I'd told Mom was that I was going to greet Calder and Derrick. Calder had sworn me to secrecy on the fake homecoming plan, not that I would have fessed up to Mom under any circumstances. Telling Sabrina didn't count in my estimation because we operated in a judgment-free zone of total honesty. Unlike my parents.

"Fuck," I muttered.

"What?" Sabrina deftly saved the balloons as I juggled things to pocket my phone.

"My parents are gonna be here."

"Oh." She blinked her thick lashes a few times. "This should be interesting."

"Very." There was nothing I could do other than hope they missed the whole playacting-with-Derrick thing. I stepped aside as a pack of dressed-up kids zoomed between us. Then one of the personnel from the community liaison office signaled that it was time to load the first bus. I hurried to make sure Sabrina and I were in that line. Any distance from my parents would help.

"So... Derrick?" Sabrina waited to speak again until we were seated on the navy bus, which was essentially a school bus made over for military use. "Tell me what he looks like so I can help you spot him. Is he gorgeous? Why is it that all the gorgeous guys are the ones who get cheated on? You'd think they'd have better luck."

"Quit trying to write a romance novel, Sabrina." I moved my sign to let a family pass as more people filled the bus. "He's quiet, but when he does talk, people tend to listen. That sort of commanding voice. Tall. Not as tall as you in your heels, but taller than me. Big shoulders. Dark brown hair. And a face like one of those old Hollywood heroes. So, yeah, he's hot. But this is a favor. Nothing more. Honestly, I'm not sure he even noticed my existence previously."

"Aw." She patted my shoulder. "The big bad sailor squashed your tender feelings."

"Save it for your fan fic. I was a kid last time I saw him in person. And even if I wasn't, I don't do military."

"And yet here you are." Gesturing at my sign and balloons, she gave me a pointed look.

"Here I am." I adjusted my balloons so a teen girl with an even bigger bunch could settle in behind us. "As a favor to my brother."

Who had loaned me money on more than one occasion while I'd been in school and broke, but even Sabrina didn't need to know *everything*.

"Uh-huh. And this hot, older, silent man whom you might get to plant one on." Sabrina braced a hand on the seat in front of us as the bus got moving.

"I feel sorry for the guy, that's all." Sure, teenage me had found Derrick beyond attractive, but even then I'd known better than to get a crush on a man in uniform. "He got a bum deal with his ex. I met the guy once when they first started dating. The sort of high-maintenance dude who tries too hard to be hot and comes off fake instead. Terrible voice."

"You can't keep picking men simply because they have the right pitch of baritone."

"You never know when a musical number might come up." I laughed.

"With you? That probability is higher than it should be. I'm still not over you leaving that *fine* hookup simply because inspiration struck for your latest composition."

"Eh. He wasn't that hot. Kinda nasal. And the composition won four awards, which is more than I could say for his kissing."

"And this level of picky is why you're still—"

"Hey, look, we're on base." I could usually handle Sabrina's teasing and give as good as I got, but I didn't need to be reminded exactly how pathetic my love life was right before I went and rescued Derrick from his.

"Oh my gosh, the ships are huge."

It was always fun watching a civilian see the big ships for the first time, and Sabrina's face as the bus turned onto the road that rimmed the docks was no exception. Her wide eyes and slack jaw reminded me of my excitement as a kid, waiting for my dad or uncles to return and taking in all these ships the size of a small city. As always the docks were bustling with activity. Uniformed sailors were everywhere, dwarfed by the giant equipment like cranes and the boats themselves.

The community liaison personnel herded us carefully off the buses and into a cordoned-off waiting area where we had a great view of the Sound and the empty dock space where the submarine would moor. I scanned the crowd but didn't see my parents. Maybe they were stuck in traffic. That would be helpful. I did, however, spot Derrick's sleazy ex right near the front of the barricades, talking to one of the sailors working crowd control. Probably lining up his next hookup.

"Tell me I'm hotter than him," I whispered to Sabrina after discreetly pointing him out. Normally I didn't care at all what I looked like, and clothes were an afterthought at best, but today I wanted to look good in a way I wasn't sure I ever had before. To that end, I'd let Sabrina mess with my hair before she picked out black skinny jeans, chunky belt, and a white pullover shirt with a subtle rib that made it hug my chest.

She gave me an exaggerated once-over. "Much. Lugging heavy instruments around Boston agreed with you."

"I also discovered that unlike the horrors of PE class, weight rooms and cardio machines are excellent at focusing my brain for composing."

"You undoubtedly miss all the cute gym bunnies trying to flirt with you because you're debating C flat versus F sharp." Sabrina shielded her eyes as she directed her gaze toward the water.

"Guilty." I laughed right as a murmur went through the crowd.

"I see something!" a kid yelled.

I'd been here before, on the docks, waiting for a ship to appear on the horizon, but even so I couldn't help the tremor of excitement that raced through me too. The energy was contagious, and few sights were as impressive as a naval submarine arriving in port. Sailors with life jackets over their gleaming white dress uniforms stood up top, waving. More stood up in the crow's nest where a giant American flag hung. Not a single person wavered as the ship moved toward us, their footing way surer than mine would have been. The boat churned through the water as smaller ships, the size of fishing boats or small ferries, moved into position to help guide it into the bay and assist with the disembarking sailors.

Even as the ship docked, the sailors were too far away for me to spot either Derrick or Calder. One of the uniformed liaison personnel directed three young women holding tiny babies to step forward as tradition said that any new fathers would be among the first off the boat. Derrick's ex also got called to the front. Ugh. He was attractive with bleached-blond hair and chiseled features along with a slim body that would have been at home on any swim team, but his entitled attitude ruined any appeal for me.

The crowd whooped and hollered as a brash young lieutenant was first off the boat and gave him a very showy kiss. Lots of cameras flashed and clicked. *Bletch.*

"I'd bet my new eye shadow palette that they're broken up by next week," Sabrina whispered. "Think you can beat that?"

"Oh yeah. That looked fake, even to me," I agreed even as my pulse sped up.

Three teary enlisted men were next, greeting the women with babies as cameras clicked, and the crowd cheered again. Then more sailors were released and the crowd became increasingly disorganized as people jostled to greet them. I still didn't see Calder or Derrick, but then the crowd parted slightly and familiar broad shoulders and hazel eyes moved into view.

Damn. How had I forgotten how swoon-worthy Derrick was? My stomach wobbled as my racing pulse reached Indy-500 levels.

"Derrick," I called out.

Beside me, Sabrina clicked away on her phone camera, but I was only marginally aware of anything other than Derrick's face as he spotted me. He didn't smile, but his eyes went wide and locked with mine. If this had been a movie, the music would have swelled right then, a beautiful crescendo, and I wanted to memorize every note so I could use this moment later. I'd never experienced anything quite like the energy arcing between us.

And then his purposeful strides carried him closer. His gaze intensified, if such a thing were even possible, equal parts terror and excitement in his expression. Or maybe that was all me, the way my legs shook and my back sweat.

I had to swallow hard simply to get enough spit to speak. "Welcome home."

Chapter Three

Derrick

Arthur turned out hot. That was my first thought when I spotted him after I heard my name called. *Derrick*. My actual name, not Fox, not Chief, and outside of Calder a couple of times, I hadn't heard that name in months. And definitely not like that, all eager and excited and *happy*. On the sub, hearing my name inevitably meant that someone needed something right that minute, but the way Arthur said it didn't inspire dread at all.

I'd already been caught up in the energy of the day. Homecoming day was always exciting, even if I didn't usually have someone waiting. The whole crew was jostling about, getting into our dress whites, making sure everything from our cover to the chest candy of ribbons and medals to the gig line was perfectly straight. Getting chosen to be on deck as we came into port was an honor, one that I usually let others, especially those with kids, fight over, since there was still plenty to do belowdecks in preparation and support. As the chief sonar tech, I was responsible for working with the A-gangers from engineering and the operations department to help navigate us in. Adrenaline was contagious, and by the time my department was cleared to disembark, I had enough energy to rival the reactor that powered the sub.

And then I heard my name.

I recognized Arthur's red hair right away. But the rest…

Wow. Arthur had grown hot. Still shorter than me and skinnier, but wiry now, each lean muscle defined under a thin white shirt and tight jeans. No signs of his ever-present too-big nerd-humor tees. Same startling green eyes as before, though, and a new, more chiseled jaw sporting the perfect amount of fuzz. He'd grown into his long regal nose, and the hair that had seemed to have a life of its own when he'd been a teen was sculpted now, this perfectly styled wave that made me want to mess it up. His hands, which had always seemed too big for the rest of him, were clutching a giant sign.

For me.

And for a second—a literal instant when our eyes met and time stopped—I forgot it wasn't real. And in that moment, I wanted it to be. Someone smiling that broadly for me. Had Steve ever been so happy to see me? Hell, I wasn't even sure the poodle my grandmother had let me keep had been that happy. Arthur just radiated pure joy. The kid was one hell of an actor.

"Welcome home." Even his voice was different. Deeper. Sexier.

"Hey," I said because I was simply that brilliant at conversation. I reached an arm out, instinctively going for a handshake, but Arthur shifted his sign and met me partway, coming in for a hug.

A really tight hug.

Damn, he felt good. Amazing really. Solid muscle against me, hair tickling my nose, exactly as silky as it looked, strong arms able to haul me in and hold me tight. He smelled like mint and green tea, two things in short supply on a boat that tended to smell like old socks on a good day. *Sweet.* I inhaled deeply as his lips brushed my ear.

"Calder said to kiss you," he whispered. "And I want to. But you gotta tell me you're good with that first."

Was I good with that? Hot guy who smelled like a concoction I wanted to drink every day for a month wanted to kiss me. And ordinarily, the friendship code would put Arthur far, far off-limits, but here was Calder telling us to kiss. It was a free pass, the sort I'd be a fool to turn down.

I wasn't a fool.

And what harm could a peck do?

"Yeah." My voice was a rough whisper, and I didn't have a chance to brace myself before Arthur was sliding his mouth over from my ear to mouth. A double shot of tequila would have had less punch than the first brush of contact.

And okay, not a peck.

We were kissing. Arthur and I, which should have been weird but somehow wasn't. At all. Someone whooped behind us, but almost all of my attention was riveted on Arthur, like I was on watch and every sense was heightened lest I miss something vital.

Like how soft his lips were. Full too. Or the bristle of his scruff against my cheek. I'd done a submarine shave that morning, not my best job, but close enough that the rasp of beard felt electric. Our chests were pressed so tightly that I could feel his heart pounding. Or maybe that was mine, blood zooming to places that had been in deep freeze for months.

"Wow." Arthur pulled back, leaving me dazed and still clinging to him.

"Damn." The statuesque purple-haired woman he'd been standing with laughed loudly and thumped Arthur's shoulder. "Is that the best you can do? Your man has been at sea how many months?"

Your man. If only. If he were actually mine, we'd be racing across base, a mad dash to find a room with a door. But he wasn't and all we'd ever have was this moment. A potent mix of want and resolve raced through me as suddenly I was determined to make this count.

I pulled him back to me, and this time when our mouths collided, I was ready. Ready to taste. Ready to absorb every single detail. Ready to seize control and kiss like the world might be ending.

And it could have. Not sure I would have noticed. Everything faded away. The crowd. The docks. The balloons Arthur had been clutching and his sign both as his strong hands clung to my shoulders as we kissed in earnest. He tasted like he smelled, sweet and minty, and his tongue against mine was like floodlights coming on.

"Welcome home," Arthur breathed against my mouth as the sound of applause gradually pulled me back into awareness of our surroundings. Applause. Whoops of laughter. Clicking cameras. But still I couldn't seem to look away from him.

"Your balloons escaped." Arthur's friend was laughing harder now.

"So they did." Arthur turned his gaze skyward where the colorful balloons were racing to the heavens.

"And posted! Man, this video is *so* going viral." The friend made a triumphant gesture.

"Wait. Video? Viral?" Shaking my head, I tried to clear my muddled brain, but before I could I heard my name again, more urgent this time.

"Arthur! Derrick!"

Stomach cramping, I slowly turned my head, like that could delay the inevitable. Sure enough, though, Arthur's parents— two people I had mad respect for, especially his retired master chief father—strode toward us with huge eyes.

"Your parents came?" I whispered to Arthur as I released him.

"Not part of the plan." He shrugged like this wasn't a huge

fucking problem. "It was a surprise to me too. Mom texted earlier, but I was hoping they'd miss…the excitement. Oops."

"Yeah, *oops*. You could have said something."

Arthur blinked. "Exactly when?"

He had a good point, so all I could do was sigh.

"What is this?" Arthur's mother, Jane, didn't seem angry, more perplexed with a furrowed forehead. *Me too, Jane. Me too.* This was fast becoming a clusterfuck. I really didn't want to confess to the petty jealousy that had led to me agreeing to Calder's crazy plan, but maybe—

"Damn. Way to go, Fox."

Oh fucking hell. Kill me now. Seriously, a lightning strike would have been welcome because Steve and Fernsby were right there. And yeah, that was the whole point, for them to see the kiss I was still reeling from, but now I was trapped.

"Hey, Mom." Arthur didn't even spare a glance for Fernsby or Steve, doing an impressive job of actively ignoring them.

"You and… Derrick?" Jane continued to tilt her head like we were a mystery to figure out.

"Yup." Arthur answered before I could. "Surprise. I didn't tell you—"

"No *surprise* there. You don't tell me much these days." Jane's mouth twisted. As always, her husband was more of a silent presence, but he too looked befuddled and also distinctly uncomfortable. "But how long has this been a thing?"

Arthur gave an easy shrug. "A while. We didn't say anything because Derek was still on the rebound from his total snake of an ex. But, I wasn't going to miss the chance to welcome him home."

Oh, he was good. Exactly enough vague truth there to be convincing, and he managed a dig at Steve to boot.

"Calder? Did you know about this?" Jane asked as he strode

over, trio of friends trailing behind him. "Derrick and Arthur?"

"Oh yeah." He was as good a liar as Arthur. "Isn't it great?"

"Uh-huh." Jane's eyes were too wide and her mouth too tight. "Great. We made reservations at your favorite place for an early dinner. Arthur, you and Derrick will come."

Bad idea. I glanced at Calder, hoping he'd give me an out of some kind, but he just grinned, enjoying this way too much. Deceiving Steve was one thing, but the Eulers were good people. They didn't need to get unwittingly roped into my fake homecoming plot.

"I'm not sure I'm hungry," I hedged.

"Liar." Calder chuckled and bumped my shoulder. "We all know you can't wait to get alone, but you can do dinner."

His father went distinctly pink at the mention of Arthur and I being *alone*, and my sputtering noise wasn't much better.

"We'll be there." Arthur linked arms with me as if I might be about to flee into the crowd. Which, honestly, might be the better option than dinner with the Eulers, but I still nodded. He stretched like he was going to kiss my cheek, but instead whispered in my ear, "Trust me."

The absolute worst thing was that I might not have a choice.

Chapter Four

Arthur

Derrick didn't want to trust me. That much was clear from his stiff posture and guarded eyes. He kept casting me wary looks, and his crappy acting wasn't doing our ruse any favors. Thus, I was only too happy when he said he'd need to change out of his dress uniform before eating, which gave us the perfect opportunity to temporarily ditch my parents. Derrick and Calder both had on-base housing that was apparently walking distance from the docks, but first I needed to find Sabrina, who had disappeared somewhere around the appearance of my folks. I scanned the still-crowded docks area as Derrick continued to act like another two hours with me was a capital punishment.

"This is a bad idea," he muttered as we walked.

"Probably." I refused to let him bring me down. Best kiss of my life, and Derrick's ex had looked ready to floss with barbed wire. Total win.

Derrick huffed like my good cheer was another burden. "Then why do it?"

"Because your ex was standing right there," I patiently reminded him. "It was either agree to dinner or announce that my bigger priority was to get naked and climb you like a tree, which considering my parents were also right there, I figured you'd prefer the dinner option."

"Thanks." Derrick blushed, a legit dark pink color, at the word *naked*. Throwing the big bad chief off his game was too much fun, and I had to restrain myself from making even more blush-worthy suggestions.

But I could be adult, so instead I patted his arm right below his stripes. "Look, this way we seem like a happy couple a little longer. No harm in that."

"I don't like lying to your parents." He quirked his mouth and looked out over the Sound.

"Next week, I'll conveniently mention to Mom that we didn't work out because of my thing about dating military men. I'll say I can't do another deployment and that will be that. They never need to be bothered with the truth."

"I still don't like it, but okay." Pausing by a crane, Derrick leaned against a guardrail. "That plan makes some sense, and it's a story I can use with Fernsby and Steve if one of them asks."

"See? Benefits all around." I gave him an encouraging grin as I spotted my favorite mermaid talking to a young ensign. "Oh, there's Sabrina."

I waved, and she returned the gesture before striding toward us, wielding her phone like it was a light saber. "My post is already in triple-digit likes and has tons of shares."

"Your what?" Derrick's frown deepened.

"Sabrina is my secret weapon." I pulled her in for a fast hug. Derrick could be a bit more appreciative of our efforts. "I wanted to make sure our kiss got more attention than your ex's. Sabrina's got the followers to make that happen."

I liked to think we'd made a nice spectacle with our kiss. And what a kiss. *Damn*. Not that I had oodles of experience, but Derrick could kiss. Kissing him was like my playlist landing on a top-ten all-time great song, both familiar and awe-inspiring at the same time, making my insides all bubbly. If I'd been scripting sound effects for the moment, I would have gone for something bombastic or maybe the roar of a runaway train.

"I just wanted to make him jealous." Derrick groaned. "Not go viral."

"Well, judging by the look on both of their faces, you totally succeeded. And that kiss deserved to go viral." I couldn't help my dreamy sigh. Whatever. It wasn't like I was getting a second shot at those lips, but I wasn't going to dismiss how damn good it had been either.

"Yes, it did." Sabrina made a show of fanning herself with her phone.

"So, we're having dinner with my parents," I addressed Sabrina, who kept glancing back at the sailor she'd been talking with. "You can come."

"Actually, I was just walking over to ask you how you feel about the ferry and the bus." She had the grace to look sheepish before returning to eye-fucking her new friend. "I have...plans."

"You were going to ditch me?" I faked horror because this was hardly unprecedented, and I'd mainly needed her to get the sign and balloons here. And her social media rep didn't hurt either.

"You seem in perfectly capable hands." Sabrina gave Derrick a very obvious once-over.

"Ha. But okay." I laughed as Derrick turned all pink again. "I'll find a way back. Go get lucky."

"Oh, I will," she drawled before making her way back to the ensign.

Derrick waited until Sabrina was out of earshot to speak. "She seems...fun."

"She's a force of nature." I followed him as we resumed our walk toward the barracks. "We met in high school when Dad was stationed here before his retirement. We were band geeks together, but you'd never know it now."

"Nope." Chuckling, he strode purposefully toward one of the buildings. "Calder and I were just laughing about that the other day—how that one band camp sent you home."

"It was one camp." I frowned as we stopped by the door. I didn't want to sound too pouty, but I also liked to think I'd moved beyond my hopelessly nerdy past. "Do you need me to wait here while you get changed?"

"Yeah, probably easier than trying to get you signed in as a visitor. I'll be fast."

"Sure." My tone was more clipped than it needed to be.

"Hey." Derrick reached for my arm. "I didn't mean anything by the band camp crack."

"It's okay," I said even though it wasn't. "My brothers got tons of mileage out of me being too geeky for the band camp crowd."

"I can do better than your brothers." Derrick really did have a nice laugh, deep and rich. Sabrina was right. I was a sucker for a good voice. And the smile lines around his eyes didn't hurt either. "And thank you, by the way. I do appreciate...all this."

"You're welcome." In a slightly better mood now, I waited under a tree while Derrick went into the barracks. He and Calder were among some more senior enlisted personnel who had single rooms in the barracks and got additional perks for being mentors to the younger service people in the housing. I had fun people-watching with all the fresh-faced recruits coming and going from the building in the short time Derrick was gone.

He returned in civilian clothes—jeans and a gray shirt with

buttons that made his hazel eyes appear more green than gold. I didn't have much chance to ogle him though before Calder and two of his friends arrived. After Calder too changed, we ended up all riding together to the restaurant in Silverlake, and somehow I ended up in the middle of the back seat, squashed against Derrick, who smelled like the sexiest pine forest ever and who was solid and warm.

My body hummed with wanting to kiss him again. Preferably without an audience, just to see if he really was that good at it, if things between us could be that magical, or if it had simply been the moment. Would it have the same rush without the revenge motivation? Given that simply sniffing his aftershave had me half-hard, chances were good that a repeat kiss would be even better.

But also, not happening, so I might as well enjoy being pressed up against him. And at least I'd get to sit next to him at dinner and maybe avoid the whole Mom inquisition thing. Speaking of, she started waving at us as soon as we entered the place, which was an upscale brewpub with a huge drinks menu, but also steaks and some twists on bar food classics.

"We're over here," Mom called out.

"Damn. Four tables." Calder led the way over to the bank of tables pressed together, where yet more friends and family waited, including one of my other brothers and his family who had apparently driven up from his base in Tacoma.

"Ollie! How the hell are you, man?" Derrick had a hearty handshake for Oliver, who was slightly younger than Calder but older than me. My mom kept beaming at Oliver's kids. She'd been so happy when he got transferred to this coast after stints in Florida and Georgia.

Not surprisingly, most of the conversation at our end of the table revolved around duty stations and deployments, Oliver and Calder swapping stories with occasional input from Derrick or one of Calder's other friends. They spoke a language of acronyms and military slang that made my head hurt. Like my dad and uncles before them, Oliver and Calder were singularly focused on advancing in rank, and honestly, their conversation was almost as boring as when the topic shifted to all the sports happenings Calder and Derrick had missed while deployed.

Ordinarily I'd distract myself with the kids, but they were at the opposite end of the table on various tablets and phones until the food arrived.

"You okay?" Derrick asked in a low voice after the server set our burgers in front of us, and the rest of the table was distracted by eating.

"I should be asking you that." I waggled a fry at him. "You're the quiet one. My family's a bit much, even when it's only some of us like this."

"I know. It's weird, but I kind of like the chaos that comes with visiting your folks." Derrick had such a fond smile that I regretted not visiting more often during the latter part of college and graduate school. Maybe family gatherings would have been more tolerable with him around.

"You're welcome to them," I joked.

"I wish." A shadow passed across Derrick's eyes, and I wanted to ask more about his past, but before I could, he frowned. "I still don't like ly—"

"Shush." I sent him a message with my eyes to not blow our cover.

"Sorry."

"It's okay." I dragged another fry through a puddle of ketchup before glancing down the table. "I just want to savor my mom looking at me like I might have done something right for a change."

"That can't be true." Unlike my brothers, who always tore through food after a deployment, Derrick took small bites, like he was trying to make the burger last, making me wonder what else he hadn't had lately that he might like to take his time with.

I shifted in my chair. "Believe it. I'm the odd kid out."

"Nah. Calder's always talking about how smart you are. You've got some kind of graduate degree, right? Your folks have to be proud of all your school success."

"Master's, yes. But they don't feel video-game music is a viable career path." I took a bite of my own burger to avoid sighing dramatically.

"Isn't it?" Derrick sounded way more curious than most of my family. "I mean it must be. Some of my buddies have playlists of nothing but game soundtracks. It's kind of cool that you want to do that."

"Yup. It's big business." I preened under the praise. "And while my heart is in doing my own scores, I also do freelance work cleaning up other people's arrangements and other sound projects on a piece-by-piece basis. I'm still establishing my rep, but an indie game from some friends did really well, won me some awards."

"That's great." His smile was so warm that the temperature in the room seemed to climb a good ten degrees.

"Yeah, well, awards don't pay rent, but it's a start. The sporadic nature of the work gives my parents hives."

"I bet. But some things are more important than a good pension."

"Exactly." Our gazes linked, and something new zinged between us. Not the sexy energy of the kiss, but something perhaps even more powerful. Understanding. I felt seen in a way I almost never felt at family things.

And of course, my mom chose exactly that moment to plunk down in an empty chair on the other side of me, making the rounds the way she always did at big gatherings.

"You two are so cute together." She smiled encouragingly at us both. "I want to hear everything."

No, she really didn't, but I still nodded. "Thanks."

She adjusted her glasses as she continued to study us like we were an interesting science exhibit. "About time you had a *good* boyfriend."

"Yep," I agreed, even if my definition of *good* was far from hers. If only this particular boyfriend wasn't a big fake. Knowing I'd have to hear her sigh when I told her about our "breakup" had my back tensing, even more so when she leaned toward Derrick, a certain gleam in her eyes.

"I have a question for you."

Chapter Five

Derrick

The back of my neck had started prickling the moment Arthur's mom sat down with us. I wasn't going to like whatever this question was, and my stomach did the same gnawing thing it did whenever one of the sonar reports came back with an error. Our chief of the boat was huge on everything running on "automatic." It was his favorite phrase, and one I used with the sailors under me too. Automatic was good because it meant nothing unexpected was gumming up the works.

However, not a damn thing about this whole damn enterprise with Arthur was on automatic. New complications kept coming up, and unlike on the sub, I felt woefully unprepared for the challenge of playing Arthur's fake boyfriend.

"What's the question?" Arthur's tone was a little more demanding than mine might have been. Jane had always been good to me, and the whole Euler family in their sitcom-y perfection with the happy parents and four rowdy boys and huge extended family was fun, like visiting a theme park of what a family was supposed to be like.

"So, you know our family reunion is coming up." Jane turned toward Arthur, who was already frowning. She tapped his arm in a gesture that was somewhere between motherly and commanding officer. "You'll be there. And you should bring Derrick."

"Uh…" Arthur and I made near identical horrified noises. I'd been to the Eulers' home in Anacortes for various holidays and gatherings, but I'd only heard stories about their big, over-the-top extended family reunions that happened most years.

"I think you should both come." Jane's smile never wavered. "Aunt Maureen is already texting me about you two."

"How does she know?" Arthur frowned.

The gnawing in my stomach increased and I pushed my plate aside. This thing was fast spiraling out of control.

"Your video is everywhere. It made Maureen's social media feed because it's trending. Your cousins follow the makeup video crowd like your friend Sabrina, but Maureen said your welcome home kiss is so viral it's even in her military family groups and other places."

"Good." Arthur beamed wide enough to risk straining something, then sobered. "I mean, that's neat. Inspiring others and all."

His happy reaction gave me pause. This whole time he'd seemed rather laser focused on getting our kiss viral and on outside reactions to it with no sign that he himself was thrown for a loop by it as I was. Maybe it hadn't been that spectacular for him. Maybe he did things like this a lot. But I was still rattled, even now, hours later, and I didn't like it.

"How does going viral relate to the family reunion?" I asked.

"Well, everyone will want to see you," Jane said like this should be obvious. "Also, it's fun. You should come. Arthur could use the company."

"I'm not sure about getting leave," I hedged.

"Calder said most of your crew has a couple of weeks off

after you finish the return-to-port duties." She nodded like a poker player who knew she had the winning hand.

"Did he, now?" I glared right at Calder, who had turned toward us at the sound of his name. It was true that our commanding officer and the chief of the boat had both been bugging us about scheduling our leave, stressing the importance of R&R after a long deployment. But that didn't mean that I wanted to extend this ruse any longer than we absolutely had to.

"Dude. You're not going to be able to go anywhere on base without people talking about this anyway." Calder shrugged. "You might as well come."

Oh fuck. I hadn't even thought about that. If the kiss was viral, that meant that I was probably the subject of the thing I hated most—base gossip. God, I did not want to spend weeks waiting for it to die down, knowing people were talking as soon as I left a room. The whole point of this thing had been to avoid the pitying looks and whispers I'd had ever since Steve and I imploded.

"Yes, come." Jane patted my arm. "It would make me so happy. Arthur doesn't call nearly enough these days, and knowing he has someone *responsible* at last is giving me such joy."

"Mom. I'm not a westie puppy looking for a good owner," Arthur grumbled.

Meanwhile, my jaw tensed. I didn't like the idea of disappointing Jane, who had always made me feel so welcome. And it didn't matter whether it was now or next week when Arthur shared news of our convenient breakup, she was going to be bummed, and that sucked.

I needed an out, and no one was giving me one, including my best friend.

"I need to check the leave calendar before I can consider

the invite. Calder, I think I left my phone in the car. Come with me to look for it?" I gave him another hard stare until he nodded.

My phone was perfectly safe deep in my pocket, but I needed an escape. Once we were outside and out of view of the windows, I whirled on him. "Way to help me out."

"You need a vacation." Calder leaned against the car. "Senior Chief says it. The commander says it. But you don't listen. Knowing you, you're planning on turning your leave into another mentorship or other opportunity at the base. You can't work all the time."

"Says the guy who wants to advance as much as me." I didn't bother disputing his prediction, which was correct, but I didn't see the problem.

"Maybe. But I know how to relax."

"And joining your family reunion is how you want me to relax? Are you *trying* to set me up with Arthur?"

"What? No way." Calder laughed. "Arthur's not into you in that way, and I'm assuming it's mutual. But you saw how happy Mom was about this development."

"There's no development." I tapped the car for emphasis.

"I know that. And you know that. But she doesn't. And it's wonderful." Grinning, Calder continued to lounge against the door. "All her focus is on Arthur, and I haven't had to field a single question about who I'm dating or hear not-so-subtle hints about grandkids. Fucking awesome."

"I'm not coming along simply to get the heat off you." I paced in front of him.

"No, you'll come because it's fun. This year they're taking over this family camp near Port Angeles on the Olympic Coast. Kayaking. A little lake for swimming and paddleboats. Volleyball. You do remember how to let loose, right?"

"I don't like lying." Pivoting on my heel, I gritted my teeth.

"It's not *lying* as much as just being Arthur's roomie for the event and getting to hang out with me and Ollie and everyone else."

"I'm still not sure…"

"Thinking about how jealous Steve will be at your vacation photos should be incentive enough, but I'll swap bunks with you for the next deployment." Calder knew that I hated being on the bottom bunk, hearing the creaks whenever one of the other two shifted in their sleep, and the top bunk had marginally more space and privacy. And making Steve jealous spoke to my petty side, which I probably needed to stop indulging.

"I'll think about it." The offer was tempting but still probably not worth carrying out a fake relationship. "Not sure how many more kisses I've got in me, though."

"That bad, huh?" Calder chortled, and hell if I was going to tell him he had it all wrong.

"Something like that."

"It's a family event." He clapped me on the shoulder. "Not even the newlywed cousins will spend the whole time making out. Just treat him like any other buddy. Easy."

Easy. Yeah right. Nothing about this whole thing was easy, including how my body still hummed with the memory of how soft Arthur's lips were and how he'd tasted. No way could I pull this off for days on end.

Chapter Six

Arthur

Alone with my mom was a dicey proposition. I loved her more than all my instruments combined and I'd swim across the Sound for her, but somehow the last few years I never had good answers for all her questions. No matter how much I achieved, I still felt like something of a disappointment.

"I've always liked him." Mom glanced at the door to the restaurant, as if that might make Calder and Derrick hurry up. Ha. I had a feeling Calder was getting chewed out for not giving Derrick a suitable excuse for the prospect of being saddled with me in the middle of nowhere for a week.

"Me too." My sigh was genuine because he truly was a very nice and likeable guy, but that didn't mean I was okay with my mom acting like he was the best decision I'd ever made. "You know I've dated before."

She made a dismissive gesture. "Musicians. You need someone stable. Solid."

"Musicians are great people. And stability is overrated." My voice was even firmer than usual thanks to that moment I'd shared with Derrick earlier when he'd seemed to understand why someone might choose music. I was so tired of being the odd one out in this family of do-gooders and public servants.

"All I'm saying is that I'm happy for you." She patted my

hand. "Very happy. And I want you to both come to the re-union. It will be fun."

"Your tenacity and inability to take no is why opposing counsel fears you." It was also why she'd managed to graduate at the top of her law school class while being over forty with four kids, and why she'd never given up on her dream of being an environmental attorney even with move after move thanks to the navy.

"Come on, Arthur." She laughed but there was a weariness there too. "You're not literally allergic to the outdoors."

"Not *literally*. But we've never been friends either." I kept it light, trying to ignore the heaviness in my chest from knowing I was testing her nerves yet again.

"Bring Derrick, and I'll make sure you get one of the more private cabins."

"Oh?" I sat up straighter. This was an unprecedented offer, one I needed to hear more about. "No sharing with the nephews?"

"Nope." Her grin was easier now because she knew she had me. "A couple of the private cabins have renovated bathrooms too."

"Awesome." *Great.* Now I had a serious incentive to talk Derrick into going, and judging by his face when he and Calder had left, that wasn't going to be easy. Sure enough, he came back into the restaurant with his muscles all tense like he was trying to outrace a rainstorm and failing.

"Find your phone?" I asked after Mom had been called away to deal with something involving the kids. I knew perfectly well that his phone had been in his pocket because I'd felt it when we'd been squashed together in the back seat.

"What?" Derrick blinked before his eyes went wider. A flush spread across his cheeks. "Oh. Yeah. We did."

"Did you find out about leave?" I kept my voice down,

letting the other conversations swirl around us. Calder was back talking with his friends, and I had Derrick all to myself.

"I'll have to look into it." He was surprisingly cagey, not the outright refusal I'd been expecting at all.

"That's not a no." I bumped his shoulder.

"Do you actually want me to come?" He peered at me intently.

His intense gaze was freaking me out, making it hard to be anything other than honest. I shifted in my chair. "If you come, I get a private cabin and don't have to bunk with the older nephews."

"Don't like being a built-in babysitter?" Derrick laughed. God, I could listen to that sound all night. As it was, I was going to drive myself nuts trying to capture its essence in a future composition.

"Nope. Don't get me wrong, I love kids." I glanced down the table where Ollie's younger two appeared to be having some sort of heated conflict, with my mom and their mother functioning as intermediaries for peace. "And I always help out with the kid activities. But I'm almost twenty-five. I'm ready to be done with the kids' table, so to speak."

"So I'm your ticket to cushier accommodations?" Stretching, Derrick sat back in his chair.

"And better sleep." I grinned at him because he still hadn't said no. "None of the kids seem capable of actually staying in their beds. Someone else can get up with them at dawn."

"Not sure anyone's ever wanted to spend the night with me to improve their *sleep*." Derrick grinned back. Was he flirting? Was that why my pulse was speeding up and my brain was full of sexy thoughts? I couldn't tell, which made my back tighten even as my body hummed.

"Well, I know how to proposition a fellow. Come and you can have my share of the s'mores." I held his gaze, testing. He blushed but didn't look away. Interesting. Very interesting. I was woefully short on practice for flirting, despite Sabrina's and others' tireless lessons. However, Derrick didn't seem entirely disinterested, even to my novice eyes.

Derrick's mouth twisted, making his grin a little crooked and a lot more endearing. Damn. I wanted to kiss him again. Right there. No way could we survive rooming together on the island. But on the upside, maybe I'd get my wish for more kissing, bad idea and all.

"Calder says if I come, we can swap bunks." Ah. There it was. His reluctance to say no to the invite had nothing to do with me or even with wanting to help me out.

My posture stiffened but I kept my voice free and easy. Whatever motivated Derrick to come, I was good with, even if part of me wished that I was incentive enough. "Whoa. Calder never gives up the top bunk for anyone. Ask Oliver. What's his deal?"

Derrick shrugged. "Says he likes not being the focus."

"Ha. My mom needs to learn to be happy with fifty percent of her offspring happily coupled."

"She just wants what she thinks is best for you guys." Frowning, Derrick took a gulp of water. "She's a good mom."

"She is, yeah." It was nice that Derrick was such a fan, but he wasn't the one who had had to grow up as quirky youngest Euler brother. However, I was more curious about Derrick's own family situation than trying to educate him on the realities of mine. "Is your mom going to be mad if you spend your leave with us?"

"No. No mom. I was raised mainly by my grandmother and she died when I was in basic training. So it's been just me for years now."

Aw. I could practically hear Sabrina's sympathetic noise. And I too was not immune from wishing I could hug Derrick. Wait. I could. Everyone here thought we were a couple. *Fantastic.* I threw an arm around his shoulders.

"Well, then you definitely need to come. Euler Family Camp is an experience like no other." My family might drive me up a wall, but they were mine, and I knew damn well we were pretty lucky compared to some.

"Maybe," Derrick whispered. He didn't move away from my embrace either. "We could fess up first—"

"And miss our shot at better accommodations?" Enjoying his nearness, I gave his broad shoulders a little squeeze. "I think not."

"Okay." Derrick huffed out a huge breath, but I just grinned at the novelty of having gotten my way.

"Was that a yes?"

He gave me another crooked grin. "It's an 'I'll talk to the senior chief tomorrow, find out my leave situation for real' very strong maybe."

"I'll take it."

"Good." Our gazes locked again, moment stretching out, a new bargain having been struck, but also something else. An easiness that hadn't been there before. I wondered what he'd do if I went in for a fast kiss right then. Just a—

"Are we ready?" Calder seemed to finally remember we existed, as people started getting ready to leave. "Arthur, we're dropping you at the ferry?"

"Yup." Sighing, I dropped my arm before standing up. Playtime over. Back to the real world, where Derrick wasn't remotely mine and no further kissing was happening.

Once all the goodbyes were said and the bill settled, we ended up back in Calder's car, squashed together in the back seat again. Derrick still smelled amazing, and my urge to kiss him was still there, but I was good, didn't even sniff him or lean into his solid body.

"Are you going to be okay doing the ferry and bus?" Derrick whispered to me as Calder and his friend debated where they might go for a drink after dropping me off.

"Of course. I've done it tons of times." Which he probably knew, so I wasn't sure why he'd be concerned. *Unless...* I pitched my voice even lower. "If that's you wanting an excuse to not go back to the barracks or out for drinks with Calder's crowd, you could come with me. Keep me out of trouble."

"Come with you?" Derrick sounded more confused than intrigued. "Why?"

"No reason." I kept my tone light. No sense being disappointed. It was my own fault for even making the offer. "It was just an idea. I've got a shared place, but it's larger than the barracks' rooms and we've got a big TV."

"Thanks, but I should probably get back." If he was tempted, Derrick sure wasn't showing it. Who knew, maybe he was looking to go out with Calder and his friends, maybe pick up an actual hookup, not a fake arrangement.

"I figured." I narrowly avoided sighing. "Guess you'll let me know about the reunion?"

"You'll hear from me." He chuckled, a warm sound that washed over any lingering wistfulness I felt over him turning my offer down. And now I wasn't sure what to hope for. I liked the idea of him coming, but not if it meant setting myself up for a hopeless crush on the last guy I should be longing for.

Chapter Seven

Derrick

"This is a terrible plan." I greeted Arthur at the ferry station with the complaint because it saved me having to figure out how exactly one greeted a fake boyfriend. None of our target audience was around—just the usual ferry traffic, people heading for boats and buses. But was I supposed to keep the act going at all times? I wasn't sure, and I particularly didn't like the part of me that was demanding I greet Arthur with a hug or something more.

Back tight, I ignored those impulses and led the way to my car. I'd been up early to go claim it from the buddy who lived off base and who stored cars for a few of us when we were deployed. I'd taken it for a wash and oil change, and now it gleamed in the summer sun.

"Oh, come on. It's a great plan." Arthur threw his over-loaded bag in the back seat. He was back in more familiar attire—a T-shirt featuring woodwind instruments duking it out with horns and loose jeans with messier hair. But still hot. Damn it. "And no more grumbling. It's a gorgeous day for a drive, and you've got a sweet ride."

He whistled low as he circled the car, blatant appreciation for my classic Dodge Challenger in his eyes. The red finish with black details really was eye-catching, and driving the car always lifted my mood.

"Thanks. Did a lot of the restoration on it myself." Because I was deployed so often and had lived mainly on base, I didn't need a commuter car. Indulging myself in a classic a few pay grade promotions ago had been a rare splurge for me, and Arthur's appreciation of my hard work made my chest warm.

"And thanks for not making me ride with Calder and his crew." Arthur opened the passenger door but didn't seem in any hurry to climb in.

"What kind of boyfriend would I be if I made you ride with your brother?" I managed a smile for him. Might as well get in the habit. The decision to drive myself had been far easier than the decision to come in the first place. I liked having my own wheels, my own way to leave an event, and Calder was bringing two friends from base. No way did I want to be stuffed in the back seat again with Arthur practically in my lap. There was only so much temptation a guy could take.

"Are you the kind of boyfriend who parts with the car keys?" Grinning impishly, Arthur tilted his head.

"Not a chance." I jangled my keys as I headed for the driver's door.

"I'm just saying, you probably haven't driven in months." He wasn't wrong, but I merely snorted. No matter how long I'd been at sea, I never forgot the pleasure of an open road and the purr of a well-tuned engine. And even Calder didn't get to drive my baby. Arthur, however, was determined. "I could help you out with that. My brothers made sure I could drive a stick."

"Good to know." I pointed at the passenger seat. "Get in the car, Arthur."

"And no kiss hello? I'm wounded." Laughing, Arthur slid into the seat. Despite his leaner stature, he had the same long limbs as his brothers and moved with a surprising grace given how distracted he could be at times.

"I think I've had enough PDA now to last a lifetime." I waited for Arthur to buckle up, then backed out of the space and headed north. I kept my voice light, but I wasn't kidding. The last few days had been endless jokes and teasing about my viral welcome home, and if I hadn't already regretted the deception, all the attention would have done it. And honestly, the gossip was a huge reason why I'd messaged Arthur that I was in for the reunion. The trip couldn't be any worse than sticking around base.

"That's just a shame." Arthur used an exaggerated scolding tone as we sped past the outskirts of the base.

"How do you figure?"

As I stopped for a red light, he winked at me. "You're too damn good at kissing to keep it all to yourself."

"Think so?" The back of my neck heated.

"You looking for compliments?"

"Nah," I said, even if I kind of was. He'd seemed so singularly focused on the audience that it was nice to know that the actual kiss had been tolerable for him.

"Seriously, though, how bad was the teasing on base?" Arthur asked.

Bad. My buddies were crass and mouthy on the best of days, and having something to rib me about made them even more so, and that didn't even start to account for the random comments from people I barely knew. "Nothing I couldn't handle."

"At least tell me that your snake of an ex drunk-texted you all salty." He sounded all proud of himself. Outside, the traffic finally thinned out as we made our way toward the canal bridge that would take us onto the Olympic Peninsula.

"There might have been a text." I couldn't hide my smile, and Arthur predictably chuckled. Steve jealous was a nice ego boost even if he had insinuated that Arthur was too young for me. Like he had room to complain. I hadn't bothered with a reply.

"Knew it." Arthur's tone was triumphant before he shifted to more curious. "Would you have him back if he and Lieutenant Idiot break up?"

"Nope. Fool me once and all that." Steve had lied. And lied again. And been an ass about the logistics of the breakup. And now seemed to delight in rubbing his thing with Fernsby in my face. "I'm out on relationships."

"Other than the fake ones." Arthur shifted in his seat, almost like he was worried I might change my mind and turn the car around.

"Other than playing pretend. Don't worry. I'm not going to leave you stranded or something. When I give my word, I follow through."

"I know. Your trustworthiness is why my mom likes you so much." Arthur sighed and stretched, looking out at the canal and the mountains beyond the wide body of water. "And see, this is nice. We can enjoy the drive, and there's none of that tension about if we'll last as a couple and what we're gonna do later and all that."

Speak for yourself. He might not be nervous about things like sleeping arrangements and being alone, but certain parts of my body were already tense and we weren't even to the part with a space with multiple flat surfaces and a door that locked. But he didn't need to know how his mere nearness affected me, so all I said was, "Yeah."

"So where was our first date?" Arthur demanded.

"Excuse me?" Blinking, I kept my eyes on the road even though I really wanted to know what the heck he was after and if he was joking.

"We need a good story," he explained with more patience

than I probably deserved. Fake relationship. Right. Yet more details to manage. "People are going to ask, and if our stories don't match, the gig is going to be up."

Being found out might put an end to this fake relationship nonsense, but it would also be all kinds of humiliating. I'd had enough embarrassment for the decade thanks to Steve and then the viral kiss, so it was better to have a ready lie. "Okay. We went with Calder for food—"

Arthur cut me off with a pained groan. "Derrick. I'm twenty-five. Not fifteen. We most definitely did not have a chaperone. And surely we can do better than *dinner.*"

"Dinner is a no-go?" I didn't have the most experience with dating, but dinner seemed pretty standard fare.

"It's boring. And lacks romance. After that kiss, everyone's going to expect some swoony story, not burgers and the latest big-studio action flick."

Well, then. Maybe Arthur had unwittingly explained why my relationships had never worked out. But rather than confess my lack of a romantic soul, I drummed my fingers against the steering wheel.

"Okay, King Romance. Let me think how I'd impress a discerning date like you."

"Hey, who says you're the one doing the asking?" He yawned like my lack of game was just that dull. "Maybe I had tickets to a classic car show last time you were stateside."

"Not a bad idea." That he knew me well enough to suggest something fitting made me feel that much guiltier for tossing out dinner with his brother.

"Would you have said yes?"

"Uh…" I made a strangled sort of noise because I could picture it only too well. Us at some family event, me there with Calder, us making small talk, him making the offer. And me far more tempted than I would have ever thought a week ago.

"I don't mean for *real*." His sigh was so dramatic that I didn't have to glance over to know he was rolling his eyes.

Yes. I would have said yes. And probably set about a path to tanking one of my oldest friendships. But even with his reminder this was all fake, I could still see the scene, taste the tang of temptation.

"Sure. It sounds fun." I tried to match his casual tone. "But how about…" I wanted to impress him the way he had me, wanted to be more than some stodgy fun killer with zero romantic bones. "The zoo has these annual outdoor concerts. The music might not meet your fancy college standards, but maybe we took a takeout picnic. Something chocolate for dessert."

"You remembered I like chocolate?" His little pleased chuckle went straight to my groin.

"That and you'd probably be more impressed if I took you to some obscure tuba or didgeridoo concert, but we better pick something that I know for sure actually occurs. The fewer holes in our story the better."

"Yeah. Okay. I like it." Arthur slapped his thigh. "First date was the zoo concert. Second was a car show. And third was none of their business."

I coughed. And coughed again, oxygen suddenly in short supply.

"Careful there. Work on not having a horror movie recoil at the idea of sex with me."

"I wasn't—"

"It's okay. Just stick to the story and we'll be fine."

I wasn't so sure, but I let the conversation drift off rather than end up in even more uncomfortable territory. No good could come from telling him it wasn't horror that stole my breath but rather sudden, swift desire. Damn kiss, lurking near every conversation.

We continued our drive north, but it didn't take too much silence before Arthur wiggled around in his seat again. The guy's need for perpetual motion made me smile even as I wished he'd pick a position and stick with it.

"Does your stereo have a connector for my phone?" he asked.

"It should." I'd installed a nice stereo a few summers back, a modern one with GPS and an interface for my phone. "Feel free, but please tell me you're not still in your Austrian Funeral Dirge phase."

"That was one summer."

"And then there was the phase where all you listened to was obscure ancient computer stuff."

"Eight-bit chiptunes. Classics. But no worries, I'm not subjecting you to those."

"I'm still nervous." I laughed, this lightness between us both welcome and kind of weird, how easy it was to be around him.

"Don't be. I made us a special playlist last night."

"You probably make a playlist for getting groceries," I teased as we took the Hood Canal Bridge with its spectacular view of both the canal and sound.

"Guilty." Arthur fiddled around with his phone and the stereo until a vaguely familiar seventies ballad filled the car. "And I had fun, trying to figure out what music a silent, brooding sailor might like."

"You could have asked me." We'd texted a few times in the lead-up to today's journey, mainly practical stuff, but I wouldn't have minded some conversation. Hearing from him made my chest do a little skip, and I couldn't decide whether it was anticipation or guilt over the continuing deception.

"Now, what's the fun in that?" Arthur hummed along with the music, perfectly in tune. He'd always been more obsessed with instruments and digital music, but his singing voice was quite pleasant, and I let one song bleed into another until I had to laugh.

"Does every song involve water in some way?"

Arthur made a happy noise. "You guessed it. Yay."

"You're easy to please." I shook my head.

"You have no idea," Arthur muttered as the song changed to one I knew, an oldie that had been in a movie my grandmother had loved, and I sang along. Our voices mingled nicely. We weren't going to win any music reality shows as a duo, but he was fun to sing with.

"You're good," he said as we finished.

"That's what I hear." I waggled my eyebrows at him, loving his easy chuckle.

"Did you ever do choir? Like high school?"

"Nah. I'm not really the performing type. I'd sing along with my grandma and the radio, though. She had a nice voice and could play piano. Made me take a couple of years of lessons." I groaned at the memory of her hawk-nosed, exacting music teacher friend who had made me do scale after scale. I'd preferred her other friend, Flora, the cranky loudmouth who swore worse than any sailor in my crew and who spurred my love of classic cars.

"Lessons are the worst." His voice was sympathetic. Outside, the landscape was much more rural, endless acres of evergreen trees, and we weren't even to the mountains or the national park yet.

"Says the guy who taught himself a half dozen instruments. We're not all geniuses like you."

"Not quite genius, but at least my fake boyfriend has a high opinion of me." Arthur sounded happy, like all the sunshine and gorgeous scenery was working its magic on him, making him all punchy and adorable.

"Ha. You're impressive and you know it." I let his ego have

the win, but his tease also reminded me of something I'd wanted to ask him on the drive. "Speaking of the fake-boyfriend thing, though, how do you want to play this?"

"What do you mean?"

"We covered the backstory, but what sort of boyfriend are you wanting me to be? Distant? Attentive?" I tried to keep my voice casual. This was strictly data collection so that our ruse didn't fail the first night of the reunion.

"My preference matters?" Seeming surprised, Arthur shifted around in the seat again.

"Well, yeah. You're stuck with me for a week. Seems like you should at least get a fake-boyfriend experience you enjoy."

"Awww. You're sweet. Just be yourself." Arthur's voice was warm, but he maybe had too much confidence in me. "What sort of boyfriend are you normally?"

"Uh." I made a sputtering noise as we slowed for a curve. I took a minute to handle shifting gears, while I searched for an answer. "Other than Steve, I don't have a ton of relationship experience, and clearly I fucked that one up, so maybe you could help me out here, tell me your ideal boyfriend traits."

"Whoa, whoa." Arthur threw his hands up. "You didn't fuck up. You're not the one who cheated and lied, and whatever my opinion might be on how much deployments suck for relationships, he signed up for that sort of separation when he decided to be with you."

"I don't think anyone is truly prepared for deployment. It's hard on even the strongest of couples."

"As I well know."

"And… I maybe wasn't the most attentive when we were in port," I admitted. If I couldn't be honest with my fake boyfriend, who could I be? "He complained about me taking on extra responsibilities that weren't strictly job requirements. And he said I wasn't as fun as he'd thought. He was really social, liked going out and parties, and I think staying in with me started to chafe."

Memories made my jaw clench, and I looked straight ahead, at the rolling terrain, not at Arthur.

"Then he should have spoken up." Voice firm, Arthur tapped the dash for emphasis. "Like an adult. No sneaking around."

"Yup." Damn but it was nice to have someone on my side instead of dishing out well-meaning advice that inevitably made me feel worse. "And I'm sorry. You don't need to hear all my pitiful relationship drama."

"I don't mind." Laughing lightly, Arthur finished with a big yawn. "And for the record, I'm no prize either. I get lost in composing and forget to eat, let alone remember dates to hang out. I once totally forgot I had someone over."

"Oops."

"Yeah. It's not that surprising that I haven't had the most practice with boyfriends either."

"Ha. We're a pair." If I was going to be hopeless at relationships, it was at least nice to have company.

"Hey! How about we use this week as practice?"

"Practice?" My voice came out wary even as my brain jumped ahead to all sorts of sexy things I'd like to *practice* with him.

"Yeah. Be better boyfriends. The kind we'd like to be when it counts."

"Huh." Not that I was ever traveling the long-term relationship route again, but Arthur made a certain amount of sense. It might be nice to get my confidence back, stop beating myself up for my shortcomings. "That's not a terrible idea."

"I do have good ideas. You just have to trust me more."

"Working on it." Considering that the last time I trusted him I ended up with a kiss I still hadn't recovered from and a fake relationship that kept getting more complicated, I was still a little skeptical of this plan. Being nice to Arthur was hardly a chore though, so perhaps Operation Be a Good Boyfriend wouldn't be that hard.

"Okay, so I'll try not to forget you exist—"

"Pretty low bar." I had to laugh and Arthur joined in.

"Hey, I'm starting small. And you can practice spending time with someone instead of work, work, work. Easy."

If only. The spending-time-together part wasn't going to be difficult, but I still doubted our ability to pull this thing off unscathed.

Chapter Eight

Arthur

I had the best ideas. Learning how to be a good boyfriend by using Derrick as a test case was going to be amazing.

Or fail spectacularly.

Or intensify whatever low-grade crush I was already nursing for Derrick.

Whatever. It would be fun finding out, and I was greatly enjoying our drive to the camping resort even if Derrick wasn't parting with the keys to his sweet-ass ride and had a strict no-drinking-in-the-car rule when I suggested stopping for soda.

"What's the absolute worst thing a boyfriend could do?" he asked, continuing the discussion we'd been having about pet peeves around relationships. It was fun and slightly silly and might help me be a better fake boyfriend, but also I liked talking with Derrick, no matter the topic.

"Hmm." I took a second to think because unlike a lot of my friends, Derrick seemed to want actual answers from me, not simply fast one-liners. "Ignore me. Which I know is rich coming from me, but I don't like being ignored in plain sight, that invisible feeling."

"I get that." Derrick nodded solemnly, and it made sense that he'd understand because he tended to fade into the background at events himself.

"What about you? What's your deal breaker? Other than cheating, obviously."

He groaned. "Cheating is only cheating if it's a deception. Had Steve simply told me he wanted an open relationship, I probably would have agreed. Not gonna say I'd love it, but I'd deal. I know several couples with nontraditional arrangements. Everyone copes with the separations and stuff in their own way. All I wanted was for him to talk to me."

"So lying and bad communication skills. Got it. My other deal breakers are petty in contrast, but I can't do an awful voice or laugh."

"Like this?" Derrick did a terrible imitation of a thick New England accent, adding a braying laugh at the end.

"That." I was laughing so hard that speaking was difficult. "Add terrible musical taste to my list."

"I can't blast bubblegum pop in our cabin?" Derrick made me laugh even more.

"Not if you want to live." I took a moment to catch my breath. "Oh, and I don't like being made fun of. That's another deal breaker for me."

"I know. And I'm sorry again for my band camp crack the other day. Was school really hard for you?"

Outside, the scenery was peaceful and calming, endless green trees and scenic vistas, a contrast to my churning brain. "School. Brothers. Cousins. It's never easy being different. I found my people in college and grad school, but I still don't like being the butt of jokes."

"I hear that." Derrick shot me a sympathetic glance before returning his eyes to the road. "I mainly kept my head down in school, didn't come out until later. You're kind of to blame for that actually."

"Me? How so?"

"I had met Calder and he was talking about bringing me

home for some holiday dinner, but he gave me this whole lecture about how his little brother was gay and he was bi, and if I had a problem with either of those things, I could just plant my ass on base. So I told him the truth and never really looked back after that." The way Derrick pursed his mouth said that it hadn't been quite that simple, but I was still strangely proud that I'd played some small part in his journey.

"Nice. I like inspiring you. Calder drives me nuts, but he's always stood up for me when it truly counted." The warmth in my chest faded into chilly dread as another thought occurred to me. "And you and him never..."

My stomach churned at the mere thought of them getting it on. Swallowing hard, I stared out the window at the increasingly mountainous terrain.

"God no." Derrick's laugh was harsh. "The only thing worse than one of your lieutenants stealing your person is a bad breakup with a crewmate. We never vibed in that way, thank fuck because intra-sub romances are destined to implode, usually spectacularly and with collateral damage."

"See, this is the good thing about fake relationships." Not wanting to reveal how relieved I was that he and Calder never messed around, I forced a more joking tone. "We get to decide our own no-drama exit strategy right now. Two years from now, we'll run into each other and it will be a funny memory."

Even as I said it, I hated the idea. I didn't particularly want to see Derrick parading someone new around. Oh, he said he was done with relationships, but I didn't buy it. No one who kissed like him was going to stay single forever.

"Yeah." Derrick didn't sound any more enthusiastic than I was.

Needing to lighten the mood, I turned the stereo up as one of my more iconic song picks came on, an overwrought eighties ballad, and I sang along in overly dramatic fashion until Derrick joined in.

We continued singing and sharing relationship pet peeves until the GPS bleated at us to take the turn for Lake Crescent, which had several different camps and retreat centers around it, including this one.

"Prepare for chaos now," I warned. My muscles were tight from two hours in the car, and I was ready to stretch my legs, but not necessarily ready for my family's onslaught. "Do you want a code word for if you need a break from all the social-izing and pointed questions?"

"As far as they know, we've been dating a short time. Surely they're not going to give us a hard time about a wedding or kids?"

"I saw that shudder, Derrick." I laughed as the lake came more into view. I'd been here before, but the green-covered mountains hugging the blue water never stopped being impres-sive. "And you clearly haven't been around the Eulers much. We'll have to hear a half dozen opinions about small versus large weddings by dinner, at which time they'll move on to the merits of adoption versus surrogacy."

"Can't you tell them it's too early to say?"

"You try that." My mother and aunts weren't the type to give up easily. "They might listen more if I say they're not getting invites to any hypothetical events if they keep it up."

"Ha. Bribery. I like it." Derrick took the turn for a small bumpy lane that led to the family camp on the shores of the lake, a mix of larger buildings like the dining hall and meet-ing space and smaller cottages and cabins, all with a quaint early 1900s vibe, weathered clapboard and faded colors, but well-kept, with little paths between the buildings. The view of the lake, even from the parking lot, was nothing short of stunning and was so captivating that I almost forgot to be nervous about the reunion. But then Derrick bumped my shoulder after he finished parking. "Showtime."

"Yeah. Better get our happy couple faces on," I joked as we exited the car and grabbed our bags.

"I draw the line at making out in the check-in line, but feel free to act like you can't wait to be alone." Discovering that Derrick had a robust sense of humor was one of the highlights of the day for me and wasn't helping my efforts to avoid a giant crush on the guy. Silent, he was easier to dismiss, but this joking, conspiratorial Derrick was almost as dazzling as the scenery around us.

"Better alone than drafted for a volleyball game." I laughed rather than admit how damn easy it would be to pretend like I wanted to jump Derrick.

"Fair enough." Derrick strode across the lot, confident movements like he'd been here before. Much as I didn't want a military partner, I did have to admire their decisiveness and swagger. Fuck. Even the way he squinted at the sun was sexy. I had it bad and this was only day one.

"You made it!" Clipboard in hand, my mom was out in front of the large brown historic building that housed the dining facility among other rooms.

"We did." I greeted her with a hug. "They put you on welcome duty?"

"I volunteered." Her grin made her look far younger, more like the mom of my childhood and less like the big-time lawyer she was now.

"I'm not surprised." I smiled back. Maybe this week wouldn't be so terrible.

"Speaking of chances to help out, check your messages later. I had a great idea for the kids." Mom's assertive tone made my optimism of a second earlier flee. Past great ideas had led to costumes and paint spills among other disasters.

"Does it involve bunking with them?" I narrowed my eyes.

"Nope, no bunkhouse for you." She dangled a key card from her pale pink nails. "I helped Maureen do the cabin assignments. You'll love yours. Renovated bath and fresh paint. Feels very airy and spa-like."

"Awesome." I snatched the key before she could change her mind.

"Thank you." Derrick was far more gracious than me, and he too had a hug for Mom. "I'm sure we'll love it. And thank you again for inviting me along."

"Of course." She gave him a fond pat before releasing him. "And Arthur, keep this one around, okay? I do love a well-mannered man."

"Grandma!" Oliver's brood came racing up the path, saving us from further instructions, and I deftly stepped aside as Mom was swarmed by kids.

"I think we'll go find our place." After waving at Oliver and his wife, I motioned to Derrick so we could make our escape.

"Don't miss dinner!" Mom called as we set off down the path to the single cabins, which lurked farther into the trees, away from the main buildings, little pale gray boxes along the lakeshore, each with a teeny porch and welcoming planter. Little stone chimneys added to the quaint appeal. Ours was toward the end of the row, and its cheerful facade had me back to thinking that this wouldn't be so bad.

"This is cute. Tiny, but cute." Following Derrick onto the porch, I shifted my bag so I could work the lock.

"Let's put our bags down before they summon us for dinner." Derrick waited for me to open the door.

"Good id—"

Derrick's low groan cut me off. "Oh fuck. There's only one bed."

Chapter Nine

Derrick

Why the fuck hadn't I thought about the possibility of the cabin being far smaller than a traditional two-bed hotel room? I was known for my ability to think ahead. Being able to spot potential problems had kept me and my fellow sailors alive on more than one occasion. And yet, here I was, completely flummoxed by the sight in front of me.

I stood rooted to the doorstep, like that would help. But Arthur hadn't been kidding about the cabin being tiny. The interior appeared to be one room. One room dominated by one bed that wasn't even particularly large. The bed was on the far wall with two high-back chairs and a small table in front of the fireplace. Floor space was at a premium too. I slept months at a time on a submarine. Sleeping on the floor would be nothing, but there wasn't a readily apparently spot where a person could bunk down without rolling into the fireplace or risking a foot to the face.

"I'm going to check out the bathroom," Arthur announced, as decisive as I typically was. After dropping his bag on one of the chairs, he opened a door, which turned out to be a post-age-stamp-sized closet.

"Not exactly promising," I muttered. "Not enough space there either."

"You're not sleeping in the closet." Arthur opened the only other door, which led to a surprisingly spacious bathroom with an old-fashioned slipper-shaped tub complete with claw feet taking up all of one wall. "Damn. That thing is huge. Maybe I can just sleep there."

"You're not sleeping in the tub." I could be firm too.

"Why not? Just give me a pillow and a blanket. It wouldn't be the worst thing. Hell, we could both fit in there." Arthur grinned while I had had to grit my teeth over the parade of images of us sharing that tub, all squished together, soapy and slippery and—

Snap out of it, Fox.

"No one is sleeping in the tub." I glared at him because I hated that he'd provided fuel for my next six months of fantasies. And underscored the fact that we couldn't share space this small without something spontaneously combusting. "What if we told—"

"I'm gonna stop you right there." Arthur held up a hand. "If we come clean, you'll be fine. Mom loves you. You'll bunk with Calder and his friends or keep this cabin. But me? I'll be in the doghouse for lying *and* I'll be stuck on nephew-wrangling duty for the next decade."

"I see your dilemma." I scrubbed at my hair, seeking an out. I didn't want Arthur in hot water with his family, but that one small bed loomed large as we both turned back into the room. "We could fake a fight. You could blame me for the argument and kick me out to sleep with Calder's crew."

"And spend all week with everyone trying to get us to make up?" Groaning, Arthur paced away from me. Eight paces and he was across the cabin and needed to spin on his heel to avoid hitting the window. "Dude. You don't understand the risk of a spontaneous flash-mob musical number with these people. You'll have apology suggestions by the dozens."

Fuck. More public humiliation. No thank you. No audiences. "Hmm. Meddling relatives or risking singeing my hair in the fireplace. Choices."

"We're adults." Arthur came back to stand directly in front of me. "We can share a bed without having sex. Hell, half of that bed is probably still bigger than a sub bunk."

"Yeah." My voice was weak and soft as damp tissue paper. All he'd had to do was mention sex and that bed, and my brain was only too happy to gallop ahead, replacing lewd thoughts about that tub with images of us rolling around on the bed, messing up the pristine white bedding.

"Or we could just have sex." He poked me in the chest, and the glancing pressure felt like a torch, spreading warmth and light all through my torso, making me more than a little light-headed.

"What?" I gulped. No way did he just say that.

"It's on the table," he said as patiently as if we were discussing dinner entree options. "We're both consenting single adults, and everyone will think we're doing it anyway."

Damn logic. He wasn't wrong. But no way could we go there. "It is *not* on the table."

"Suit yourself." Shrugging, Arthur stalked over to the bed and flopped into the center. "It would probably be anticlimactic anyway."

"How do you figure that?" Agreeing would have been smarter, but my ego did not care for how easily he assumed that sex between us would be bad or not worth the hassle.

"A kiss that good…mmm." Sighing dreamily, Arthur made a noise that was probably illegal in three states. "No way would the sex live up to it."

"It most certainly…" My own resistance had nothing to do with worry over it being mediocre and everything to do with concern over it being far, far too good. "Wait. You are not goading me into sex just to prove that it wouldn't be a disaster."

"Admit you're tempted." Giving me the most mischievous of grins, he patted the bed next to him.

My feet flexed inside my shoes, and I had to fist my hands to keep from shuffling forward.

I *was* tempted.

I really was.

"Dinner!" A yell sounded from outside before a gong rang.

"They have a literal dinner bell?" I laughed because the alternative was to weep from how damn close I'd come to joining Arthur on the bed and how pissed I was at the interruption when I should be grateful.

"Yup." Arthur sat up. "Let's deal with the sleeping arrangements later, okay?"

That was the worst idea ever. Dinner would be the perfect time to try to work out something less likely to destroy my willpower. But instead, all I said was, "All right."

Chapter Ten

Arthur

"Introduce me to your new man," Aunt Sandy demanded as she passed our table on her way back from the dessert buffet. Fork in hand, she settled into an open chair at our table. She shared my mom's habit of circulating throughout a meal, collecting all the best gossip. It was a wonder it had taken her this long to make it to us.

"Aunt Sandy, this is Derrick." I'd made so many introductions that I doubted even Derrick's impressive brain was keeping track of names. The dining hall was full of relatives and friends, a lively group, and I too was struggling to keep up with all the newcomers and changed hairstyles and kids who had grown half a foot since I saw them last.

"You look familiar." Her eyes narrowed, revealing the same shrewdness that had made her an excellent flight nurse. She was a double relative as she was my mother's sister who had also married a Euler cousin.

Derrick extended a hand across the table. "I'm also Calder's friend."

"That's where I saw you before." Like my mom, she had short, fading red hair laced with gray and white. She had a firm handshake for Derrick before returning to her pie. "And of course that video that Maureen sent around."

"That did make the rounds, didn't it?" I was getting tired of hearing about the video. Now that it had served its purpose and made Derrick's ex jealous, I was way more concerned with the prospect of getting some real, *private* kisses than with the idea of going viral again.

We could just have sex. For the millionth time during dinner, I mentally slapped myself. *Smooth. So smooth.* There were a ton of ways that I could have seduced Derrick and probably had better results than making it sound like a choice between a movie and a video game as after-dinner entertainment. But instead I'd blurted that out, and he'd predictably shot me down, and now we'd spent the whole meal weirdly tense and formal, that one bed undoing all the fun and easiness we'd found on the drive over.

And what was worse was that I'd wanted him to say yes, bad idea though it inevitably was. If we were going to practice good-boyfriend behavior, hooking up this week made a certain amount of sense. Lord knew I could sure use that sort of practice too. Moreover, I simply couldn't get that kiss out of my brain.

"You're aiming high, Arthur." Aunt Sandy shook a long finger at me. "I like it. Calder must be having kittens though."

From across the table, Calder winked at me. He was clearly enjoying the attention being on me a bit too much. The family opinion seemed to be unanimous that Derrick was too good for me. All the approval was unsettling, as was the implication that someone like me would need to work extra hard to keep Derrick.

"That's one way to put it," I said mildly, giving the man in question a hard question. "Did Kelly come?"

It was a deliberate change in subject, but I did like Sandy's daughter, who was married to a woman who worked as a social worker for a veterans support organization. They had two little girls who were a nice change of pace from the seemingly endless stream of boy babies in the family.

"Kelly's family will be late." Sandy frowned. "She got called in to work an emergency shift, so they're leaving Olympia first thing in the morning."

I made a sympathetic noise. "That's too bad."

"Eh. That's the life of a nurse. We're so proud of Kelly's acceptance into a master's degree program too. She'll do so much good as a nurse practitioner."

"I bet." I nodded, but my spine still stiffened. *Do good.* It might as well be the family mantra. I swept my gaze around the room. Soldiers. Firefighters. Nurses. Paramedics. And, of course, a huge contingent of sailors. And every last one of them served the greater good.

And then there was me.

"You should think about going back to school as well." Aunt Sandy had clearly been talking to Mom.

"I already have a master's." I worked to keep my tone level. No sense pissing off one of the aunts on the first night.

"Yes, but not in education. You'd be such a good music teacher." She patted my hand encouragingly. The family was obsessed with finding me my "calling." Too bad I'd already done exactly that.

"I'm pretty happy doing what I'm doing. Just landed a big job for later in the month."

"That's excellent." Derrick played the part of the supportive boyfriend to perfection, leaning forward, eyes all eager. "Tell us about it."

"My friends are doing an expansion pack for their award-winning game, and I'll be doing the score for the new level. It introduces a fun new mechanic, and I'm looking forward to the work. Hopefully, it leads to more jobs for other games."

"I'm sure it will." Derrick threw an arm around me, easy as

if we did that all the time, easy like the tension in our cabin never happened, easy like he truly was that supportive. If only.

"Aw. You're so cute together." My mom arrived at our table, wearing a visor from our last reunion and toting her clipboard and a pen.

"Thanks." I forced a smile. We were cute. I might as well try to enjoy it. "You've got a clipboard. Should I be worried?"

Mom didn't laugh at my tease. "Did you check your messages?"

"Uh…"

"I'm betting they had better things to do before dinner." Aunt Sandy laughed a little too loud.

"Indeed." Mom had the grace to blush. And honestly, I wished they were right. Making out would have been a far better use of our time than debating who was going to sleep in the tub. Mom dragged a chair over next to me. "I had an idea for awards night on the last night of camp."

"Yeah." My face scrunched up. I wasn't a fan of the annual awards, which celebrated both recent accomplishments outside of camp like promotions, but also silly stuff like fastest canoe time, best hiker, and other awards I'd been destined to never win as a kid.

"I want to add a talent show for the children. With prizes, and I brought some cheap trophies."

I couldn't hold back my groan. "Of course it would have to be a competition."

"Well, prizes make it fun." She beamed, clearly in love with her big brainstorm. "And you could get them to do some sort of group musical number too. Something cute."

"But with a winner. Everything needs a winner." I tried to hide my bitterness behind a tease, but judging by Derrick's frown I hadn't entirely succeeded.

"Winning is—" My mom continued earnestly before her eyes narrowed. "Wait. You're joking."

"Yup. Sarcasm, Mom. But I'll do it." If I didn't, someone else would, someone who shared the family obsession with crowning winners. Better to go along with the idea, try to subvert it from the inside, and if I was lucky, rehearsals might keep me from horrors like volleyball and horseshoes.

"You will?" Sitting up straighter, she tilted her head like she'd expected a lot more resistance from me.

"If there's one thing I'm good at, it's picking songs and scripting award shows." I made my voice all cheerful. It wouldn't do to let on that I had my own agenda behind agreeing. "All that RA experience should be good for something."

"Excellent." She reached between Sandy and me to squeeze my shoulder.

"I can help," Derrick volunteered, clearly making a bid for more good-boyfriend bonus points. At this rate, no one I brought around in future years would ever measure up. As it was, finding something to top that kiss was going to be a challenge and a half. I should have thought this through more.

I nodded, though, because that was what a besotted boyfriend would do. "Thanks."

"Even better." Mom beamed at both of us before standing. "Now, I better catch Maureen before we transition to the fire circle."

"I'll help with rounding people up," Aunt Sandy said as she too left the table.

"You don't actually have to help," I whispered to Derrick after they were both gone.

"I don't mind." He shrugged, expression hard to decipher. Probably he was simply doing what we'd talked about in the car, practicing being an attentive partner. Which meant I should probably release him from the obligation, but before

I could, Calder came around the table to stand at Derrick's other side.

"Hey, man, come grab a beer with us before the campfire." Calder knew perfectly well that I wasn't a drinker and that I'd rather be roasted like a marshmallow than hear more military talk, so it wasn't surprising when he didn't even glance at me. Derrick did, however, darting his eyes toward me as his mouth quirked.

"Is—"

"Go ahead." I made a dismissive gesture. He'd racked up enough good-boyfriend karma for one evening. "It's okay. I should probably come up with some sort of sign-up sheet for the show, see which kids are interested. You go enjoy your drink."

I didn't see Derrick again for about an hour as I found some paper and a pen in the resort office and set about talking to different families, signing up eager kids and persuading those more reluctant or shy to give it a try. Meanwhile, snippets of songs kept parading through my head, possibilities for a musical number that might have meaning beyond another opportunity to crown a winner.

At the fire circle, which was located in a clearing between some of the larger buildings, Calder's crew was already there, Derrick included, beer in hand. Shoulders loose and relaxed, he looked content. No sense in me dragging him away from his friends, so instead I assisted in handing out the ingredients for s'mores and settled for catching glimpses of him in the flickering firelight.

"Your guy seems nice." Ingrid, a cousin around my age, smiled at me as she helped one of the kids load marshmallows onto a stick.

"He is." I looked over at him again, chest going warm

and tight at the same time. He was nice. So nice. But he wasn't mine.

"You're not fighting, are you?" Ingrid asked.

"No, of course not." I managed a return grin. The last thing I needed was that rumor. "He's hanging out with his friends."

"And you get him all to yourself later anyway."

"There is that." Damn it. I'd managed to avoid thinking about the one-bed situation for an hour or so, but now those thoughts swarmed my brain. I kept replaying my clumsy come-on, including the brief second when I'd thought Derrick might be about to agree. Hell, sleeping in the tub might be good for me, let me cool off this obsession with him. After all, no matter what, we were *not* going to share that bed.

Chapter Eleven

Derrick

One bed. As I listened to Calder and his friends recount some tale about life on a different sub, my brain kept wandering back to that little cabin and the single bed waiting for us. I wasn't ruling out sleeping upright in one of the chairs. I'd made do with worse. And anything to avoid the temptation that was Arthur. The firelight kept reflecting off his hair, making it gleam like polished copper. But what truly captivated me was his smile, and I couldn't believe I'd never noticed it as much before. But he had a smile for everyone—the baby riding in a striped sling, the dad toting said sling, the little girl asking for seconds on s'mores, his mom bugging him about his sign-up sheet for the talent show, and more. They all got a brilliant Arthur smile.

But when he glanced my way, he frowned, and I hated that. The one-bed thing was undoubtedly wearing on him too, and I wished I knew what to do to earn one of those smiles for myself. He'd been so free with them in the car, and I wanted to get back to that place.

"Hey, we're going to play cards after this." Calder clapped me on the shoulder as the crowd at the campfire started to disperse, camp staff handling the fire extinguishing, parents rounding up sleepy kids and older adults making their way slowly back to the cabins. "Ollie's going to come to our cabin after the kids are settled. You in?"

"You wanting more of my money?" I forced an easy tone. This might be a solution to my dilemma, even if I wasn't entirely in the mood for another beer and more battle-bragging story swapping.

"You know it." Calder grinned at me, undoubtedly giddy at the memory of all he'd won off me over the years. He was an absolute shark at cards, and it was only because he was otherwise so damn likable that any of us continued to play with him. "Figured you might need the break from Arthur anyway."

"Eh. He's not so bad." Unbidden, one of the songs we'd sung on the drive crept into my head, soundtrack to a music video montage of the surprising amount of fun we'd had together. But for some reason, I was reluctant to confess to the playlist he'd made just for us and to the way we'd sung and laughed. "Nah. It was...okay."

"Well, at least you're not miserable." Calder collected the empty bottles from where we'd been sitting on a low log bench. "That's good. So, gonna let me rack up some winnings?"

On the other side of the now-extinguished fire circle, Arthur gave his mom a tight hug before starting on the path toward the cabins. *I don't like being ignored in plain sight, that invisible feeling.* Why didn't Calder and Ollie and the rest of them ever invite Arthur to hang out? The last of my beer soured in my stomach. It might all be pretend, but I still didn't need to be a heel, add to Arthur's invisible feeling.

I could be a better boyfriend than that.

"Actually, I'm tired." I did an exaggerated yawn and stretch. "All this rest and time off is catching up with me."

"Okay. Get your beauty sleep." Laughing, he stooped low

to check for more trash before waving as his group headed toward one of the larger bunkhouses.

"Don't let Arthur's chatter keep you awake," our mutual friend Max tossed back over his shoulder. Calder and I were the only ones who knew the relationship was fake, and Max added a suggestive wink that made my skin heat. Lord but I wanted to wear Arthur out.

"Will do." Talking. We should talk. Long speeches would be good because it would mean we weren't kissing. *Fuck*. I was so screwed, and yet I still let my legs carry me back to the cabin where I let myself in to find Arthur lounging on the bed, phone in hand. A low fire flickered in the stone fireplace, giving a cozy glow to the whole room.

"You're way earlier than I expected." He glanced up from the phone and didn't sound particularly thrilled about this development.

"Sorry." I kicked off my shoes near the door.

"No, I'm not complaining." His smile was way more tentative than usual and made my stomach do this weird flippy thing like right before we started a descent in the sub. "I figured that you'd end up playing cards with Calder's crew late into the night."

"Nah." Trying to figure out where I should put my body was hard. The bed still seemed like shark-infested waters, but continuing to stand was awkward too. I settled for leaning against one of the two high-back chairs. "I was bushed. Thought we could watch TV or something."

Arthur laughed and made an expansive gesture. "No TV."

"What?" Hotels and rental houses always had televisions.

"It's a historic camp," Arthur explained patiently. "Part of the appeal to my mom and other organizers is the 'digital detox' aspect."

"Well, hell." I sank into the chair, which was overly stiff

in that old-fashioned furniture way and not at all suitable for sleeping. *Double hell.*

"Not too late to go join the card game." Still smiling, Arthur pointed to the door.

"No, it's okay, we can just…" I glanced around like an answer might pop out of the gleaming woodwork.

"I'm not gonna jump you, Derrick. Chill." Bounding off the bed, Arthur knelt in front of his bag. "And you're talking to the guy who can't hold still. I don't *do* bored well, and I'm not joining the dawn meditation crew anytime soon. I packed accordingly."

"Oh?" Stretching my neck, I tried to see inside his bag.

"Yeah. Always travel with a geek. I can use my phone as a mobile hotspot so we can watch something on my tablet." He tossed a small tablet on the bed. "And because streaming can be iffy out here, I've got a digital chess set for either solo or two-player action. And this Spanish dice game. Two card games that admittedly are nerdier than poker, but Calder isn't the only one who can play to win."

More boxes joined the tablet on the bed, and I could see a notable assortment of snacks peeking out of his bag as well.

"I'm impressed." Pushing up out of the chair, I came over to the bed and picked up the largest of the boxes. "I get sick of poker and its variations, honestly. Let's see the chess set."

"Cool." Arthur beamed like I'd admired a new puppy. "You play?"

"Yeah." Chess felt safer than huddling together to watch something on the little screen and definitely safer than anything else we could get up to on the bed. To that end, I carried the box back to the table between the two chairs. "I used to play with my grandmother. She was a fierce competitor. Always played white and didn't have patience for non-standard sets."

"No superhero chess for her? Or *Lord of the Rings*? I have one with all the characters instead of the usual pieces." Arthur took the other chair. The table was narrow enough that the chairs almost touched. Leaning forward so that his hair nearly grazed my skin, he spun the board around. "And here, you can be white this time. My treat."

"Thanks." I slid open the compartment under the board that held magnetic pieces that worked with the digital board. "And yeah, Grandma liked to play by the rules. But we had a good time."

"That's nice. I learned chess initially from my grandpa— Dad's dad who learned chess back when he was in the navy. None of my brothers really took to the game, though, and the way Calder talks, you'd think sailors were only capable of poker."

"Ha. Not hardly. Plenty of chess players in the military. I've had any number of good games with crewmates, but few rival my grandmother for sheer mettle." The memory of those Sunday afternoons with her, learning the rules, hearing her stories, and eating ginger cookies made my chest ache and my voice wistful.

"She sounds great. Where did you grow up?" Arthur asked as he set up his side of the board.

"Northern Illinois, Great Lakes Region, not too far from a big naval training center. Grandma was a civilian contractor for years there, then retired to this fifty-five-and-up community on one of the smaller lakes nearby. Wasn't supposed to have had me there, but the manager made an exception when I landed on her doorstep." I wasn't going to get into that whole tale right then, so I brightened my tone as I summed up my childhood. "It was…interesting growing up without many other kids around."

"Wow. I can't imagine. There were always other kids

around for us. My brothers. Cousins. All the kids on base housing and nearby neighborhoods. Always someone to play with, especially if you made friends easily like Calder, Oliver, and Roger did."

"Yeah." I nodded. His tone and the things he'd left unsaid underscored that there was more than one way to feel lonely. The way the Euler boys were spaced, Roger was the oldest with Oliver his ready sidekick, then Calder close enough to hang with the older two, but Arthur was enough younger that he'd probably been frequently left behind. "I'm sorry you didn't have it as easy."

"Eh. It's okay. I got really good at entertaining myself, hence coming prepared for this trip." He set his last piece down with a flourish.

"Well, I appreciate your planning ahead." Neither of us seemed inclined to linger too much in the past, so I turned my attention to the game at hand. Arthur was a stylish player with a number of bold, flashy moves, some of which seemed more designed to get a laugh than to advance his cause.

"Damn." He shook his head as I collected one of his rooks to add to my growing pile of his pieces. "You're good."

"So are you." Our hands brushed as he quickly countered my move with one of his own, nabbing one of my few remaining pawns. His unpredictability coupled with his skill made him fun to play against, and I wasn't sure whether it was the fast-paced game or his nearness that had my body humming. Likely both, and holding my own against the resident genius was a rush that had me whooping like a new recruit when I finally pulled out the win.

"Nicely done." Still smiling, Arthur seemed almost as pleased about my win as I was. "Should we play next for who is sleeping in the tub?"

"No one is getting the tub." I groaned and stretched. Somehow over the course of the game, I'd stopped fighting so hard against the inevitable. And no way could I go from a friendly game filled with stories of other matches we'd played over the years to banishing the guy to the tub or the floor. "You were right."

"I was?" Arthur's eyes went wide.

"We're adults and we can share a bed. Platonically." Swallowing hard, I glanced over at it. It seemed smaller by the second.

"Excellent." Arthur fist-pumped like he'd scored some major prize, and I had to laugh at his unbridled enthusiasm.

"I love how easy to please you are."

"Yeah?" Voice going softer, Arthur tilted his head like he couldn't quite figure me out. That was okay. I couldn't figure me out either.

"Yeah. I wish everyone could be as optimistic as you." I was so used to all-business sailors who got their jobs done on automatic and who kept their heads down, but people who found joy in small moments were more of a rarity in my life. "The way you let little things make you happy…it's a great quality."

"Thanks." He licked his lips. His very full lips. Every contour of his mouth was burned on my soul, and I watched his mouth with a new hunger as he continued, "I think that's the nicest compliment someone has given me."

"You deserve it." My voice was too husky. What the heck was happening here? I wasn't sure, and what was worse, I didn't want to stop it either. "I'm not one for empty praise."

"I know." Arthur held my gaze until the air in the room thickened, electricity crackling between us like dry lightning on a humid day. "Derrick?"

"Yeah?"

"Are you still buzzed from earlier?" he asked softly, not the question I'd been expecting.

I blinked. "Did I not just kick your ass at chess? My tolerance is for shit after being on the boat so long, but it would still take more than two beers to get me tipsy."

"Good." Nodding firmly, he shifted in his chair, bringing his hair close enough to sniff again.

"Why?" I whispered, more than a little afraid I knew the answer already.

"I want you sober when I do this." And with that, he leaned the rest of the way in, the scant few inches separating us closing as he brushed his mouth across mine.

Chapter Twelve

Arthur

The first time I kissed Derrick had been for show. Memorable though the kiss was, I'd spent days convincing myself that the audience had heightened my responses. Nothing could live up to that kind of playacting for real.

Or so I'd thought.

Then I kissed him because I wanted to, without a damn soul around, both of us sober and not caught up in anything other than firelight and good conversation, the sort where I felt truly seen and appreciated. I kissed him out of gratitude, but also because I couldn't resist. All the temptation had built up to the point that the kiss seemed almost predestined.

And I discovered how very wrong I'd been. Kissing Derrick behind closed doors was *better*. After I gave him a soft, chaste first kiss, I paused, lips millimeters apart. No audience whooping. No cameras. No friends shouting encouragement. If Derrick wanted to keep the kiss going, he'd have to make the move on his own.

He moaned low, a sound of surrender, then kissed me in earnest. And lord, the man could kiss. On a dock in full sunlight or in the world's most uncomfortable chairs, he could *kiss*. He kissed like he ate—slow and deliberate, like he wanted to taste each individual ingredient and like I was the feast he'd been waiting months for. Or rather, he kissed the same way I made music, like nuance mattered and no amount of time was too much to invest if it meant getting it right.

More pressure. Less. Soft. Hard. Teasing. He'd try something, then me, then him again, as easy as if we'd negotiated turns weeks in advance. He tangled his hand in my hair, pulling me closer, and I braced a hand against the table to keep it from toppling, and still we kissed. Derrick tasted like beer, which I'd never liked, but on him, the malty flavor mellowed to something sweeter I couldn't get enough of.

"Damn. I could do that all night." Breathing hard, Derrick groaned against my lips.

"Let's." I didn't even finish my laugh before he was on me again, another kiss, hungrier now, more insistent, his tongue delving deeply as his grip on my head tightened. "For real, though, how about moving to the bed before we either roast valuable parts or become one with these awful chairs?"

"The *bed*." Derrick sounded stricken and he slumped back in his chair, releasing his hold on me and taking the moment with him. "We shouldn't."

"Why not?" I wasn't giving up so easily. We'd been on the verge of something transcendent, and every neuron in my body still vibrated with awareness. "Everyone already thinks we're doing it. Why not have sex for real?"

"Because it would complicate everything." Derrick scrubbed at his short hair. "Make a messier ending."

"We already have our breakup plan." Leaning forward, I stopped short of touching him again, hand hovering then returning to my lap, my body as indecisive as Derrick's brain. "This doesn't have to change that. Whether we hook up or not, we're still toast next week."

"That's just it. I like you too much as it is." Derrick's pained expression canceled out any bump to my ego. He might like me, but he wasn't happy about it. "You're too nice for a casual one-off."

Too nice. Fuck my life. I'd heard that a time or twelve before. I flopped back in my chair, head hitting the high back. "So I'm too likable to fuck? Sabrina's right. I'm gonna die a virgin."

Derrick's eyes went wide and his face faded to several shades paler. "You're a virgin?"

Hell. Me and my big mouth. He couldn't have sounded more horrified than the way his voice tilted up on the word *virgin.*

"Oops. Hadn't meant to say that part aloud."

"Well, you did. And now we absolutely can't have sex." Pushing up out of his chair, Derrick paced away from me. "You can't wait until twenty-five then lose your virginity as part of a fake-boyfriend scheme. That's just wrong. You wait that long and it should be...special."

"First off, the twenty-five part was not intentional." I held up a hand. My stomach churned, not liking how easily Derrick had ruled out sex. "Waiting just kind of happened. I have a tendency to get distracted and caught up in work. And as you've noted, I'm geeky even by music geek standards. It turns out that rambling about ancient instruments doesn't count as foreplay to most dudes. And being the RA in charge of enforcing dorm rules didn't do my social life any favors either."

"You're not that geeky." Derrick offered a half smile that didn't make me feel any better.

"High praise."

"I mean, you're hot. Very hot. And likable. You could pull on any hookup app, but you chose not to go that route. Wait for someone who counts. Please."

Oh God. The only thing worse than Derrick's weak-sauce argument that I was too nice was him being patronizing with the advice.

"You could count." My voice was surly, but I was fast running out of fucks to give about my tone.

"I can't—"

"I don't mean romantically." Neither of us wanted to go catching feelings, but I strongly believed we could screw around without forming a lifetime attachment. "I meant that I need practice before it's the real deal. Because guys tend to react exactly like you did with pearl-clutching horror when they hear the word *virgin*."

Derrick made a sour face but didn't deny his reaction. "Looking to get it over with is a shitty reason to have sex."

"That's not what I'm saying. I didn't go the anonymous route because I didn't want my first time to suck. But we've got mad chemistry." Surely he couldn't deny that. The sizzle when our lips met was *real*. "And you're nice. You're not going to be a jerk about it. It's not going to suck, at least not the bad kind. The other kind of suck—"

He cut me off with a frustrated noise. "Arthur."

"See what I mean? I ramble. Guess it's not that surprising that I've scared off more than one potential hookup." I grinned at him as he sat on the edge of the bed. "Can we get back to the kissing? In bed maybe. I think we're both better at that than talking. We could just do things I've done before if you really hate the idea of being my first."

"I don't hate…" Raking a hand through his hair again, Derrick scrunched up his face. "Jesus, Calder would waterboard me if he knew I was even considering being your practice sex."

"Calder never has to know." Fucking brothers. Ruining my love life even when they weren't in the room. "And fuck that noise even if he did find out. I'm twenty-five as you just pointed out. I'm not some innocent who needs protecting."

"No, but you *are* a good guy who deserves a good first time.

Not everyone gets that. Mine wasn't terrible, but it wasn't particularly memorable either."

"So make mine memorable." Leaving my chair, I went to stand in front of him by the bed.

"Arthur." Derrick gave me a hard stare.

"Okay, okay, I'm not going to keep begging. I'd rather you were enthusiastically on board than having to talk you into this. All I'm saying is that it could be *good*."

"It could." He groaned again. "And for the record, I'm not saying never. Because you are tempting as hell. But I need to think before we go further. I don't want regrets—from either of us."

"Damn. Way to make sure I can't argue with that. All mature and reasonable."

"Not feeling particularly reasonable right now." Falling backward onto the bed, Derrick gave the pillow a hard punch.

"So what? We're supposed to simply go to sleep now?" With nothing better to do, I went around to the other side of the bed.

"No. Yes. Fuck if I know." Voice muffled by the pillow, he rolled away from me.

"You're cute when you're flustered." Careful to not touch him, I stretched out next to him. We were both fully clothed. This promised to be a long, uncomfortable night.

"Good night, Arthur." Derrick reached up to flick off the light, leaving us with only the faint glow of the gas fireplace. It was almost romantic, if one could ignore the acres of tension between us.

The only way I knew how to make that tension recede was with a joke. So I pretended I wasn't wide awake and being strangled by my jeans and laughed lightly. "Bet we'd both sleep better with a goodnight kiss…"

That got a growl from Derrick. "If I kiss you, we're not stopping till morning."

"That's hardly a deterrent." I talked to the ceiling and resisted any urge to reach for him. I'd said I wasn't going to beg, and I needed to stick to that.

"Go to sleep," he demanded in a pained whisper. "Please."

"Trying," I lied, knowing full well that it would be hours before I slept and that I'd spend the whole damn night hoping that his thinking led him to the same conclusion as me. Time was wasting and there was a lot of fun we could be having if he'd simply stop being so stubbornly noble and kiss me again.

Chapter Thirteen

Derrick

I was used to confined places. In fact, I was probably the most prepared person on the planet for sharing a small space with another human.

And the absolute worst choice to try to do it with Arthur. Arthur, who smelled amazing, who kissed like I was the key to the last life raft on a sinking ship, and who was a *virgin*. And my best friend's *virgin* little brother to boot. Who wanted to practice boyfriend skills and sex with me.

Lord help me, I was not going to survive this night, let alone this week.

Eventually, lying there in the dark like the idiot I was who had flounced off to bed fully clothed grew intolerable. Arthur was motionless and quiet but quite possibly still awake when I crept from the bed. Operating in the dark, I shucked my pants, retrieved a pair of pajama bottoms from my bag, brushed my teeth, used the facilities, and dallied in the bathroom until I ran out of reasons to avoid the bed.

As I reentered the main room of the cabin, I exhaled softly at how appealing the Arthur-shaped lump under the covers was. Leaving the bed had done absolutely nothing to help my willpower. Fine. Maybe the universe was going to have to win this round because I wasn't strong enough on my own.

"Arthur?" I whispered, already mentally laying out the terms of my surrender.

"Zzzz," a soft snore replied.

Oh. I refused to acknowledge the way my shoulders slumped or the bitter taste of disappointment in my mouth. *Pull it together.* The crisis had been averted. I slid into bed, hugged the edge, and willed my body toward sleep, like I'd learned to do when I was on duty with precisely four hours of shut-eye available. Eventually, it must have worked, because I slept and slept deeply at that, a deep, dreamless coma.

But not, as it turned out, motionless. I might not have dreamed, but I also hadn't remained on the edge of the bed either.

I'd figured that Arthur would be the cuddly one and that I'd have to gently pry him off me in the night more than once. And I'd maybe been subconsciously craving that, but in the end, it was me who'd done the migrating in the night.

"Huh." I blinked awake in the early morning light after way more than four hours of sleep, more than a little horrified at my armful of Arthur.

I'd wrapped myself around him like a barnacle, holding him close, one leg over his, and an arm snaked across his chest. He too must have left bed at some point in the night because his jeans were gone, replaced by soft boxer briefs. Even through the layers of cotton between us, his ass was warm and inviting and nestled right against my groin. My lips were pressed against the back of his neck, as if my sleepy self had already been busy staking a claim on him.

Maybe this wasn't *so* bad. Trying not to wake him, I attempted to move my arm, but he hauled me closer with a surprisingly strong grip on my forearm.

"Please tell me you're done thinking," he whispered. "Or... do you need us to both pretend to stay asleep so you can keep going? I'm good with giving you plausible deniability if you wanna claim sleepiness made you cuddly. Either way, *please* don't stop."

"I should." I groaned low. "I'm not good at pretending."

And that right there was my whole problem. I wasn't good at this whole fake relationship thing, at reminding myself that this wasn't real, that it didn't matter how good he felt in my arms, he wasn't meant to stay there. Also, my moral code wasn't going to let me blame sleep for taking advantage of him.

"I am." Arthur laughed, and his chest moved under my hand. And that difference between us, the ease with which he could playact, was maddening. And tempting. It would be so damn easy to go along with him.

"We should…" I made a frustrated noise, and my breath ruffled his hair. His skin was right there next to my lips, and I couldn't stop myself from kissing his neck instead of finishing my decree.

"Do that again. Yes, we should." Stretching like a cat against me, Arthur made a satisfied little grunt that went straight to my aching cock.

"Yeah." I huffed out a breath, the fight leaving me in a rush so intense I swore I could hear the universe laughing at how weak my willpower truly was. Experimentally, I rocked against him and had to moan with how good it felt. His ass was warm and firm but also soft and welcoming.

"How about we try the thinking thing later and this right now?" Arthur pitched his voice low and seductive as he pushed back against me.

"Mmm." That sounded like the best suggestion ever, and I held him even tighter, dropping another neck kiss. He moaned, clearly as into this as I was. Logic aside, I wanted him, wanted this, had spent all night craving this on some deep, primal level.

Parting my lips, I licked and teased, more purposeful now,

nibbling simply to luxuriate in how it made him shiver in my arms. Each wriggle from him was an electric surge to my cock. Simply the taste of his skin and his little noises and movements were enough to get me close to the edge. It had been so long that I wasn't even sure I could last long enough to shed my pants, get skin to skin.

Far from playing the shy virgin, Arthur knew exactly how to ramp me up, moving deliberately against me, finding an urgent rhythm together before dragging my hand lower down his torso.

"Please."

"I've got y—"

"Breakfast!" A gong sounded in the distance, but voices were closer, what sounded like a group of people passing by, someone yelling, others laughing.

"Please ignore that." Arthur continued to wriggle against me, but the happy bubble surrounding us had burst.

My muscles went stiff and tense, and I groaned. "Fuck."

"Yes. That." Arthur kissed my hand. "Right now—"

"Pancake time!"

"We need to get out of bed," I whispered to Arthur. "Now."

"Nuh-uh." He pulled me tighter against him. "We can be fast. And super quiet."

"If you're that quiet, I'm doing something wrong," I couldn't resist teasing, resuming my slow grind against him.

"Up and at 'em!" A louder, more masculine yell this time.

"Okay. That's a clear signal from the universe that this shouldn't be happening." Groaning, I rolled away from Arthur.

"Nope. Not accepting that fate." He easily followed me, draping himself over my back as I sat up.

"We are not doing it with a pack of your relatives outside and the call for chow every three minutes," I said sternly. "You deserve—"

"So noble." Arthur kissed the back of my neck, exactly like I'd done to him, and I shivered, feeling the brush of his lips all the way down to my cock. "Bet we can't hear them in the shower."

"Tempting." Even as I said it, logic was rushing back in, replacing my lust-addled thoughts. I stood before I could give in to the urge to topple him backward on the bed. "But I mean it. You deserve more than some one-off hookup squeezed in before breakfast."

"Luckily we have all week." His laugh was deep and musical and made my stomach quiver with want. His wide grin said he knew damn well that he had me.

"I—"

"Morning kayaking after breakfast! No lazing in bed!" another voice yelled right before the gong sounded again.

"Coming!" I yelled back, loud as I could.

"Not hardly," Arthur grumbled even as he too scrambled out of bed and started rooting around for clean clothes. "You're killing me here, Derrick."

"You'll live." My fate, on the other hand, was still hanging in the balance. I wasn't coming out of this week unscathed, that much was for sure. And there was only so much resisting a guy could do. "If we're gonna—"

"Oh, we're going to." He gave me a look so pointed that my skin heated, and I had to glance away before I launched myself at him, right there on the rug beside the bed.

"Then we need to do it right," I said firmly. "Later."

"That better be a promise and not a way of putting me off again."

My groan that time was the sound of surrender, soft and low and full of want that I could no longer hold back. "It's a promise."

Chapter Fourteen

Arthur

My pornographic thoughts were probably not suitable for a family pancake breakfast, but I couldn't seem to manage to banish them either. Derrick and I had been so *close*, on so many levels. Close to having sex, close to getting off right there, and close to each other, bodies pressed together, even our breathing in sync. It wasn't an exaggeration to say that I'd never had such a good wakeup, the way Derrick's lips on the back of my neck had coaxed me awake.

That he probably wouldn't have made a move had he been fully awake was a minor concern. I'd heard him say my name the night before. He'd been tempted to give in right then, but he'd sounded so pained, and I hadn't liked the idea of him hating himself in the morning, so I'd feigned sleep. In the morning, though, Derrick had sounded more horny and less wounded, and it was impossible to not press my case, so to speak, with him wrapped around me. He wasn't the only one struggling to be noble.

Later. He'd said it was a promise, and I hoped to God it was because he wanted it as badly as I did and not because I'd finally worn him down. And now, all I could think about was later, what we might do and how and when and to whom and—

"Please pass the syrup." Taylor, the oldest and more well-mannered of Ollie's rambunctious kids, interrupted my decidedly R-rated thoughts.

"Here you go." I passed Taylor the syrup and managed a smile as well. Derrick and I had ended up at a mixed table of breakfast stragglers—Ingrid, some of the nephews, and a few bleary-eyed male cousins who looked like they'd had a few more beers than prudent after the campfire.

"Mom says you're in charge of the talent show this year." Taylor wrinkled his nose.

"Yep." I nodded. He'd evaded my sign-up sheet the night before with a similar expression, but I wasn't giving up. "Are you going to do it? You didn't sign up last night."

"I don't have any talent." He shrugged his bony shoulders and sounded so down that my chest panged.

"Sure you do."

"Nothing that can win me a prize." His lower lip jutted out, the sort of stubborn misery I knew only too well. Screw this family's obsession with winning. I'd do the show, but we were doing this my way.

"Winning isn't everything." I didn't expect my lecture to work, but I also couldn't stay silent. "Sometimes it's enough to have fun or make people laugh. No matter what you do, everyone will clap."

"Because they have to. We're *related*."

Derrick, who had been preoccupied with his pancakes, laughed at that. "Well, I'm going to clap and I'm not a relative."

"Yet." Taylor made his voice all ominous, which made me both chuckle and wonder what the current gossip was about me and Derrick. "Mom said—"

"Let's focus on finding your talent." No way did I need to scare Derrick off our plan for *later* by someone mentioning a future that absolutely wasn't happening. I leaned toward Taylor. "Do you play an instrument? Sing? Dance classes?"

"Nope, nope, nope. I play games, but Mom said no electronics this week. She's all 'Fresh air is healthy for your brain' and stuff." He sighed like outdoors was torture, a sentiment I agreed with, but my laughter was more for how spot-on his imitation was.

"Hey, that was a pretty good impression of your mom."

"Oh, yeah." Taylor sat up straighter and his voice shifted to sound prouder. "I'm good at that. I can even fool teachers, but I'm not supposed to try that again. Rules."

"I hear you. Who else can you do?"

"Grandpa. 'Back in my day in the navy, that's not how we did things.' Or my dad. 'Any job worth doing is worth doing right, Taylor.' And I can do you too."

"This I have to hear." Derrick was way too eager, but I was laughing too hard at Taylor's antics to object.

"So Arthur is all 'I have a playlist for that' and 'Oops. Didn't mean to crash into that.' But if I'm going all-in on the impression, I need messed-up hair and earphones to really pull it off."

"I think we found your talent." Chuckling, Derrick shook his head.

"I have to say I agree." I'd live with Taylor making fun of me if it gave him more confidence. "Let's put you down for some impressions. Rehearsal before dinner?"

Taylor shrugged. "Okay. Nothing better to do."

I did have something—or rather *someone*—to do, but I supposed I could wait that much longer to be alone with Derrick. *Later.*

"Nothing to do?" Oliver's wife, Stacey, came over and rested her arms on the back of Taylor's chair. "There's kayaking, Taylor. It's a beautiful day to expand your mind."

Both Derrick and I burst out laughing because Taylor's impression of her truly had been perfect, right down to her earnest inflection and the way she held her head.

"You okay?" Stacey turned my direction.

"Oh, yeah. Your kid is talented. That's all. He's going to do impressions for the talent show."

She groaned. "Don't encourage that."

"But, Mom." Taylor did an impressive job of drawing her name out to six syllables.

"Fine. But no imitations of me. And none in poor taste." She wagged a finger at all three of us.

"I'll rein him in," I promised even though I had no such intention.

"I know you will." She gave me a beatific smile. "And I'm so happy you have a guy this year, but man, I miss your help with the older boys. They were up until two last night and up again at dawn."

"Not sad to have missed that. I need my sleep."

"Uh-huh. That's exactly what you need." Stacey's smile shifted to more knowing. The back of my neck heated because she wasn't wrong, but knowing everyone was talking about my love life was getting less funny by the minute.

"Time to head down to the docks!" My dad's booming voice echoed through the dining hall. He didn't talk a lot at these things, but he could still get plenty commanding when he wanted to. "The kayak instructors are waiting."

"Can I have Derrick as my kayak buddy?" Taylor wheedled with big eyes.

"I think Arthur needs him more." Stacey shook her head at him before glancing my way. "I bet Ollie you'd be eating lake water before ten. Don't let me down."

"I'm not that hopeless." I kind of was, but I hated how everyone simply assumed I couldn't cope in nature.

Apparently overhearing part of our conversation, Oliver

headed our way. "Yeah, you are. I'm not even sure what the topic is, but yeah, you are."

"Arthur and kayaking." Stacey's eyes sparkled. She and Oliver had done a destination wedding centered on ecotourism with a ropes course featuring prominently. "I was just about to tell Derrick good luck with that."

"Yep." Oliver clapped Derrick on the shoulder. "You're going to wish you were single by noon. I bet—"

"No more betting I'll fail." I cut him off before he could make yet another bet with either Stacey or Derrick.

"Come on. Have a little fun. You've won me all sorts of favors over the years." Oliver's fond look for Stacey bordered on TMI.

"I'm sure we'll be fine." After standing, Derrick stretched his arms. "I haven't done a kayak in a while myself, so we can figure it out together."

"Yep, they're eating the lake." Oliver nodded decisively.

It was nice how Derrick had stuck up for me, but privately I was inclined to agree with Oliver and Stacey. If Derrick didn't have mad skills, we were doomed. But there was no avoiding trying. Everyone was already heading to the lakefront, and coming up with an excuse to avoid the outing would have been more trouble than actually attempting it. However, I didn't have a lot of faith in our ability to stay upright and dry.

"Ah. It's a beautiful morning." My dad came up alongside us as we walked on a path toward the row of canoes and kayaks waiting for us along with two camp employees. "The smell of pine and the rare sighting of an Arthur in the wild."

"Dad."

"What? I'm happy you're here. Err…both of you." He darted his gaze toward Derrick. "And I was just betting your mother—"

"Not you too. I'm not going to capsize. You people can

put your stopwatches away." Now I was fucking determined. I was tired of being the butt of jokes. And if it took being awesome at kayaking to make the laughter stop, then so be it.

For once, I listened intently to the guide's tips and tricks.

"Now you want the more powerful, experienced person in the stern because they can tell the direction of the boat and make any correction." The young guide had an earnest voice and an uneven tan, pale feet poking out of water sandals but darker calves.

"I can do that," I whispered to Derrick. "I've probably paddled more recently than you. Don't listen to them. I'm not that bad."

"I'm sure you're competent." He gave me a patient smile that did nothing to pacify me. "But I'm heavier by a fair bit. I know from past outings that you have to balance the weight or you run into problems."

I made a frustrated noise because he wasn't wrong.

"If you really want to steer, you could probably go with Taylor and I could—"

"You can ride in back," I said quickly. No way was he foisting me off on one of the kids.

Up front, the guide had moved on to explaining how it was important to pick paddles with similar blades and shafts, which made some of the teen nephews and cousins snicker.

"Oh, to be fifteen and find everything phallic." Derrick chuckled softly next to me. "And we'll do fine. I'm not going to let us capsize."

"Maybe I'll be the one to rescue *you*," I snapped back.

"Maybe." Voice thoughtful, Derrick rubbed his chin. And I wanted that, wanted to surprise him and everyone else, wanted to be the hero for once. My stomach cramped with the urge to be what Derrick needed, and not simply on the lake, but in all things, including the sex we were absolutely having later. My determination grew. I was going to impress Derrick at some point this week and that was that.

Chapter Fifteen

Derrick

"Are you sure you've done this before?" I finally had to ask Arthur after our kayak spun in a circle. Again. The lake was gorgeous, pristine blue waters rimmed by gently sloping mountains, but I'd enjoy it more if I was less worried about us tipping.

"Yes." Arthur's voice was tight. I couldn't see his face, but his shoulders were tense too, and I wished I could rub them. It wasn't his fault that outdoor activities weren't his thing and that his sporty family kept giving him shit about it.

"Hey, it's not an insult. I'm only trying to match your pattern." We kept zigzagging our way across the lake because we couldn't match our forward strokes. Arthur's movements were highly erratic—fast one moment, leisurely the next, like he was trying to give paddling his best effort, but his attention kept wandering.

"Sorry. It's not you." Arthur looked back over his shoulder with a pained expression. "I'm tired of being hopeless. I have rhythm and coordination, I swear."

"I know you do." I gave a strong forward stroke in the opposite direction to correct our course before we could spin again. "Maybe you just need a beat or music."

"Do not suggest singing where the others can hear you

unless you want to be subjected to camp songs for the next four hours."

"Consider me warned." I laughed because even cranky Arthur was still fun, and indeed, some chatter and chanting that could be singing filtered back from the kayaks farther ahead of us. "Perhaps it's just a matter of practice."

"I've got a long list of things I'd rather be practicing." His voice was suggestive enough to do devious things to my insides. The summer sun beat down on us, and his relatives were scattered all around us on the lake, and still I wanted to drag him behind the nearest rocky outcropping and kiss him senseless.

"Like?"

"What?" Arthur made a surprised noise that made me chuckle. I'd laughed more in the last twenty-four hours than I had in months. It made my chest expand, like suddenly I was getting fifty percent more oxygen, and I grinned at the back of Arthur's head.

"Tell me what you want to practice." I pitched my voice low, but the others were far enough away that I figured it was safe to tease. If I was going to have a secret fling with my pretend boyfriend, at least I was going to enjoy myself.

"You're not going to tell me to behave?" His shock was totally worth whatever level of hell was reserved for guys like me who messed around with their best friend's brother.

"Well, the middle of a lake is probably not the *best* place to flirt, but I'm way more curious than I should be about your personal wish list and how I can help you fulfill it."

"I want to kiss you again for starters." Voice all dreamy, Arthur actually settled into a paddling rhythm I could follow, enabling us some decent momentum to match my revving pulse.

"I think that can be arranged."

"Like a couple of hours of that would be nice. And—"

"Come on, slowpokes!" A canoe filled with the family of one of the cousins shot past us. There were so many of the various cousins and in-laws that I'd completely given up trying to keep track of names. This group all wore matching blue T-shirts and impish grins.

"Fuck my life." Arthur groaned and stretched, paddle almost getting away from him before he yanked it back.

"Kissing sounds like a better plan," I said mildly.

"Yeah, it does." Arthur sighed, losing the rhythm again and making me need to work hard to avoid tangling our paddles. "Tell me your absolute favorite thing," he demanded after I straightened the boat back out. "Maybe kayaking isn't my strong suit but I want to be stupendously awesome at sex."

"You get any better at kissing and I'm going to need a cardiac team on standby."

"I'm serious." Ahead of us, the mountains undulated, and we were far enough away from the camp that the shoreline was all green and lush, tempting me again to find a hidden spot amid all the trees and rocks where he could practice kissing to his heart's content.

"Me too." I groaned because the next item on the agenda was a picnic lunch, and chances were high that there would be a Euler lurking behind every bush. "And honestly, I'm super easy to please in that department and, as Steve said, achingly vanilla, sorry to say."

"Steve can fuck off. I happen to love vanilla things." Arthur didn't sound one bit deterred by my admission, and indeed was downright enthusiastic as he finally settled back into a paddling pattern I could follow. "And add some whipped cream, a cherry, maybe some hot fudge, and I've got all the excitement I need."

"I think whipped cream is for the advanced classes." Bantering with Arthur was better than an actual hot fudge sundae.

"Damn it, why do we have to be on a lake right now?" He gave a dramatic huff, which only had me smiling wider.

"Hey, it's not that bad. At least the scenery is gorgeous." The sky was the sort of blue one seldom saw in more urban areas, a startlingly bright shade competing with the turquoise water for beauty. The shadows of the mountains reflecting on the surface of the lake added to the tranquil yet expansive vibe of the place.

"I'd take the four walls of the cabin if it meant—"

"Look at you guys going straight now!" Oliver and Taylor zoomed close enough to yell at us. "Way to go!"

Splash. Of course, their attention made Arthur lose focus and our paddles clanged together. "Oops. Sorry."

"Nah. I think that was me that time," I lied.

"I'd offer to race you to the picnic spot, but I wouldn't want to make you feel bad." Oliver made no attempt to hide his amusement over our difficulties.

"You're on." Voice all angry, Arthur didn't glance back at me for confirmation before starting to paddle harder.

Well, okay, then. I didn't fully understand sibling rivalry, but I'd been pushed by ill-advised bets enough in training to know where he was coming from. It was hard to back down from a challenge, and I got caught up in the race right along with Arthur.

Apparently being pissed off improved Arthur's focus because he kept a steady paddling pace for once, and I could more easily match his speed. Ollie was counting out strokes for Taylor in a quick rhythm that kept them even with us, something that I should have thought of doing and undoubtedly would have had my brain not been so sex-addled.

Later. I still wasn't sure why I'd relented, other than that I was human and there was only so much temptation I could take. Bottom line, even if ill-advised, I *needed* this thing with

Arthur, and the anticipation had me far less sharp than usual. What should have been an easy victory against Oliver and the kid turned into a neck-and-neck race.

Ahead of us, a row of kayaks and canoes were already lined up on a rocky patch of shore, and some of the older kids watched our approach, waving and cheering. At the last second, we inched ahead of the other kayak, and our boat was first to touch the rocks.

"We did it!" Arthur whooped.

"It was a tie," Oliver grumbled.

"Close enough." Undeterred, Arthur helped me moor the boat while gloating at Oliver.

"You're cute when you win," I said before I remembered we had an audience.

"Damn. You truly are perfect for each other if you find that smug mug cute." Oliver rolled his eyes at us.

"You're almost too good at the boyfriend act," Arthur whispered when they were out of earshot.

"Maybe I meant it." I hung back as we approached where one of the guides was distributing sack lunches.

"Yeah, right." Arthur's eye roll was near identical to Oliver's, and I didn't get a chance to press my case before one of the aunts was asking for our sandwich preferences.

"Over here." Calder waved us to the log where his crew was sitting. As I'd suspected, there were zero opportunities to drag Arthur off into the woods for more kissing practice during the lunch break. Calder and our military buddy friends dominated the conversation, and ordinarily I'd enjoy listening to stories about their past adventures, but right then I would have traded all three of them without a second thought for a cabana with a locking door.

And while the kayaking went much smoother on the return trip, my distraction level only increased. Arthur was extra bouncy, celebrating little victories like us sticking with the main group without zigzagging, and the happier he got, the more desperate I became to get him alone and get some of that sunshine for myself.

"See? Kayaking wasn't so bad, was it?" I asked as we approached the camp's docks. I spied our cabin among the trees and that made me paddle faster.

"No, it really wasn't." Turning his head, Arthur grinned at me. "Not a bad day at all."

We worked together to return the kayak to the guides waiting on the shore. Wiping my forehead, I whistled low. "At least we had sun for it."

"Says the guy who doesn't require SPF 100 to be out in this weather," Arthur teased as we headed for the path back to the cabins. "And after all that work, I'm desperate for a shower."

"Me too." Our cabin still seemed too far away for my tastes. I sped up my steps. "Race you? First one back gets all the hot water."

Arthur easily matched my pace even as he snorted. "A competition? You really do fit in almost too well with this family. And I'd rather tie you."

"Oh?"

"Then we'd have no choice but to share."

"True." Laughing, we both trotted faster, more in sync than we'd been while kayaking, and by the time we reached our little porch, I was filled with an unfamiliar giddy energy, feeling young and alive and even more craving the taste of Arthur's mouth.

I could have either let him win or beaten him handily, but instead, I made a show of reaching for the door lock at the exact same instant as him. Fate sealed, we crashed into the cabin together, door thumping shut seconds before I pushed him against the wall.

"Okay, now that was fun." Arthur's grin was downright edible and he was a most adorable captive as I trapped his hands over his head.

"Yeah, it was." I leaned in and claimed his mouth. He tasted like sunshine and laughter and mint, and I was done holding back. Inhaling deeply, I let myself get drunk on his coconut scent. I was going to get horny every time I smelled sunscreen after this, and it was going to be worth it. Kissing Arthur was like eating cotton candy, sweet and light, and not nearly enough to fill me up.

Even as I kept the kiss going, I tugged his shirt loose from his shorts and snaked my hand underneath to rest on his side. That first hint of bare skin was absolutely electric and I growled softly.

"I want you so badly I can't decide between right here and the shower."

"Both. I vote both," he panted as I nipped at his neck.

I laughed darkly because we were totally on the same page. "Doubt we have time for both before dinner. But we can make the most of—"

"Fuck." Arthur cut me off with a pained groan. "Before dinner. I agreed to a rehearsal for the talent show, didn't I?"

"You did." Exhaling hard, I released his hands from the wall and stepped back. "It's okay. A quickie probably wasn't the smartest thing."

"It was a fucking brilliant idea. I want all the quickies." Shaking his head, he made a noise that was half chuckle and half groan.

"Later. We'll do it right. Promise." I pressed a fast kiss to his mouth, trying to erase his disappointed expression. "But you probably shouldn't keep the kids waiting too long."

"Yeah." He raked a hand through his hair.

"Do you need my help with the show?"

"Nah. I can put you to work, but it seems like one of us should get a shower. Why don't you shower fast then join us when you're done?"

"Okay," I reluctantly agreed, my body still not happy with the abrupt end to the kissing.

"But you're going to owe me shower fun before the week is done." He wagged a finger at me before straightening his clothes.

"Count on it. Later."

"I'm starting to hate that word. Later better come sooner."

"Tonight. Promise." Even as I said the words, my cock stirred, already eager to get back to what we'd started. I had no business making Arthur any kind of promises, but no way could I pass this up either. Tonight. Him. Me. And no more interruptions. I'd make it happen.

Chapter Sixteen

Arthur

Derrick needed to hurry. And not simply because I was dying to be alone with him and running out of patience for *later*, but because I was currently under a pile of kids who had way too much energy after being confined to boats all day.

"Whoa. I thought you were going to practice a musical number, not wrestle." Derrick's voice was warm and oh-so-welcome as he pried Roger's twins off my back. They'd dive-tackled me to the grass and some of the other cousins had joined them in piling on me.

"Thank God you're here." I sat up before accepting his hand up. We were nominally holding the practice in the grassy clearing behind the dining hall, and all their parents seemed to have conveniently disappeared, leaving me with a horde of overhyped, hungry kids. "That's what I thought too, but this is turning out to be like herding wet cats."

"Otherwise known as training new recruits." Derrick gave a sharp nod, then whistled loud enough to scare whatever wildlife was lurking in the nearby woods. "Listen up, tiny terrors. Time to practice. Arthur's going to tell us about the music. Arthur?"

"Wow. You're better than my dad at getting their attention." I had to shake my head because Derrick in navy chief mode was damn imposing. And more than a little sexy.

He shrugged modestly. "I know how to run a tight ship. My training better be good for something."

"I'm still impressed."

"Better be. And better start talking." He made a sweeping gesture at the kids, who had all come to sit obediently in front of me. Working fast, I explained what I was thinking for the format of the show with an opening number, several talent acts, midway number, more acts, and then a closing number, with each of the numbers being short snippets of songs I had picked. Nothing too long or complicated and lots of high-energy, upbeat music.

"Do we have to dance?" Taylor made a face that was echoed by the expression of several of the others.

"Yep." I smiled encouragingly. "It'll be easy. And fun."

One of the twins groaned. "Boys don't—"

"None of that." Derrick shut him up with a single stare before turning to me. "Show us the steps."

I'd brought a portable speaker for my phone, and I used it to demonstrate the first selection, showing some simple chore-ography I'd come up with on the fly. Tons of big arm movements that could cover a lot of missteps.

"You weren't lying." Giving me a smile, Derrick stretched on the grass as I turned the kids loose for some practice. "You do have rhythm."

"Told you. It's nature I'm allergic to." Right on schedule, I sneezed from the combination of grass and pine needles still clinging to my skin as I settled down next to him.

Chuckling, he brushed off my shoulders. "You've certainly earned your shower later."

"Yeah? How was yours?" I asked in a low voice as I clicked Repeat on the song.

"Lonely." He matched my whisper, but the word still made me shiver with want. Stopping our make-out session had been near impossible. He'd finally been all kinds of eager and insistent, and I couldn't get enough of that side of him.

"You could— Hey, no kicking!" I had to abruptly abandon my flirt to stop one of the twins from kicking his brother in the stomach.

"But that's my talent! I'm going to break a board with my karate kick!" Vince demonstrated by kicking at the air.

"Excellent. Your brother, however, is not a board."

"Darn." Vince didn't look the least bit sorry, but he at least quieted down enough that I could lead the group through another practice. After we went over the steps, the other twin, Seth, came over to where Derrick and I were sitting on the ground.

"Thanks for stopping Vince. His kicks hurt. And I still don't know what to do for my talent. I hate karate class."

"I hear that." I was still scarred from years of organized sports I would have liked to avoid. "What do you like to do?"

"Games. I'm gonna be a streamer when I grow up. But Dad says no one's going to pay to hear me talk nonstop."

"Sure they will. I know lots of professional gamers." I smiled at him because Roger could stuff it with that attitude. The world was changing. Vlogging and streaming were making several of my friends good money. "It's a fun career choice. But since the moms want this week to be electronics-free, let's think. Know any magic tricks?"

"Talking fast doesn't count?" Seth grinned back at me.

I tilted my head, considering. "How fast?"

"Like lightning! I can do all the words to 'Take Me Out to the Ball Game' in under twenty seconds." Seth proceeded to demonstrate, doing the fastest rendition I'd ever heard, managing to keep the tune even as he rushed through the song.

"Sold." I gave him a high five. "We'll call it Seth's Super-Fast Songs and you can do a couple like that. People will love it."

"Awesome." He raced back to the other kids. Some of them were turning cartwheels instead of practicing the steps, but we were minutes from the dinner gong, so I didn't rein them back in.

"You're good with them," Derrick observed as the music moved on to the next song, which inspired one of the kids to show off a backflip.

"Not particularly good at keeping them in line." I laughed because even with the high-energy antics, this had still been fun.

"Eh. That's what you've got me for, right?" Derrick bumped my shoulder. "I meant more that you're good at relating to them. That's like the fourth kid I've watched you find a talent for."

"They've all got something. It's just a matter of finding it."

"Yup." He met my gaze, and the appreciation in his eyes was almost better than another kiss. "That's why they're lucky to have you in charge of this thing—Hey! No climbing!"

The moment abruptly shattered as the twins and Taylor scampered up one of the trees. Taylor swung back and forth on one of the branches before dropping to the ground.

"And that right there is why I'm glad I'm not in the kids' cabin this year. Love them being someone else's responsibility."

Derrick nudged me again. "Better as the cool uncle than the dad?"

"Trust me, no one wants me to parent," I said automatically, but a weird pang went off in my chest. Derrick and I made an excellent team. Having someone like him around was enough to make me reconsider my long-held stance against kids. A glimmer of a vision of a future that wouldn't be flickered through my brain, Derrick and me and a pack of rowdy kids.

Not privy to my inner yearnings, Derrick laughed lightly. "Same."

But I remained ambivalent even as the parents arrived back to collect their kids for dinner. Derrick would make an awesome dad. Probably not with me, but someone. Being jealous of an imaginary future that Derrick didn't even seem to want was not the most productive use of my time, yet I still stewed over it as we lined up for dinner.

"Come on, man. At least make it best two out of three." Calder had the same pleading look for Oliver that he'd had whenever Oliver and Roger had gone off to do something together, leaving Calder stuck at home to watch me.

"What's that?" I asked as Derrick and I found seats at the table. Maybe it was petty, but I was happy to see Calder put out about something. "Did you actually lose at something?"

"Ollie won a hand of cards last night." Calder made a dismissive gesture. "No big deal, but I have to watch the kids tomorrow night so he and Stacey can have a date night." Calder shuddered dramatically at the word *kids*, which got a laugh from the whole table. Derrick might have solid dad potential, but Calder had no such aptitude or inclination. "I need another chance to redeem myself."

"No way, man. I won fair and square." Sitting back in his chair, Oliver folded his arms. "You might not be my first choice as babysitter, but I'm not turning down some alone time with my wife."

"Arthur!" Calder made a show of pretending to only just now notice my presence. "Maybe you want kid duty?"

His dramatics got a predictable laugh from the rest of the table, but I shook my head.

"No way." I hated how he always assumed people would

be willing to bail him out simply because he was so charming. "You can handle a couple of hours of kids."

"I'd play you for it. You could come play tonight." Leaning forward, he turned all that charisma my way. Luckily, I had a lifetime of learning not to take bets with him, and I was already shaking my head.

"Nope. You only invite me when you want something. I'm turning in early." I risked a glance at Derrick. He'd promised me *later*, and I was damn sure planning to cash in on that. I had zero patience for Calder and his friends, especially when I had something way better on offer.

But I wasn't the only one looking Derrick's way. Calder clapped him on the shoulder. "Guess that means you're all ours. You got out of cards last night, but you owe us a game."

"Yeah, man. Someone needs to put Calder in his place again," Calder's friend Max chimed in. Great. A team effort to tear Derrick away from me. My muscles tightened, but I worked to keep my face neutral. If Calder got wind that our pretend relationship might include some very real kisses, we'd never hear the end of it, and I didn't want to risk Calder's reaction being enough to put Derrick off his promise to me. Besides, it was kind of nice having a secret from Chief Know-it-all.

"I don't know…" Derrick pursed his mouth even as Calder and Max both leaned in. We were outnumbered. Damn it.

"You're not getting out of this." Calder had the same self-assured grin that usually got him exactly what he wanted.

Opening and shutting his mouth without saying anything, Derrick shot me a helpless look. And I supposed I owed him after he'd helped me with the kids. I didn't like it, but I could be the bigger person than my stupid brothers.

"It's okay." I shrugged like I hadn't been counting down

the seconds until we could get horizontal. "I need to work on some more choreography for the kids."

"Thanks. And good luck." He nodded at me like that was that, and I supposed it was.

Nothing left to do but eat and then head back to the cabin on my own. I took a long, lonely shower then collapsed on the bed with my tablet. Unable to concentrate on my music, I stared hard at the locked door. Derrick better hurry indeed.

Chapter Seventeen

Derrick

"I've got you right where I want you." Calder laughed wickedly as he set his beer aside.

"So you think," I said mildly, not grabbing the bait. We'd been friends so many years that he undoubtedly thought he had all my tells memorized. Thus, I'd extra worked hard the whole evening to not reveal a damn thing about where I'd rather be.

Because Calder might be having the time of his life, playing cards and shooting the breeze with his friends and brothers, but I was most decidedly not where I wanted to be. Where I wanted to be was back in the cabin with Arthur, finally putting an end to all this teasing between us. And every time my mind wandered back to him and my endless fantasies, I lost another hand and ended up suckered into another game.

"Raise?" Calder pushed more chips into the pot.

"Yep." I matched his call.

"I'm out." Predictably, Max folded. He was the type of rock who only ever stayed in when his winning was almost assured. I'd played enough with Calder over the years to know that playing it safe seldom paid off, and sure enough, I won on a backdoor flush, turning my two hearts into a flush with a lucky deal.

"Damn it. How'd you do that?" Calder grimaced before taking another swig of beer. The tension in his shoulders and jaw said that he was about to ask for a rematch so I made a big show of yawning.

"Talent. Guess I'm just better." I yawned and laughed more. "And I'm out now too."

"Leaving? We're just getting started!" Calder's wheedling tone and determined grin made him look younger. And he was fun, as always, but I still pushed away from the table before he could talk me into staying.

"I'm tired and lord only knows what your family has planned for the morning."

"Hiking. Five bucks says Arthur fakes an injury to get out of it." Calder rolled his eyes. "But it's a nice view. You should come."

I was planning to come, very soon, but in a whole different context. And right then, faking something to get to sleep in with Arthur sounded amazing, not that I was telling the guys that.

"I'll see you in the morning. Probably in better shape than you." I gestured at the beer bottles and card table.

"F-off." Motioning me toward the door, Calder gave a good-natured chuckle. "I don't do hangovers."

"Uh-huh. Night." Free at last, I headed back to my cabin with Arthur at a fast clip. I hoped like hell he was still awake so I could make up the wait to him. But I pulled up short as I reached the porch. The front window was dark, no light peeking around the drawn curtains. Damn it. I let myself in, trying to be as quiet as possible in case he really was asleep. I toed off my shoes and crept into the room.

"Arthur? You awake?" I whispered at the lump in the bed.

"Yeah. Barely." Rolling over, he held up his glowing tablet before flipping on the low light of the bedside lamp. "I'm almost out of battery power."

I knelt by his side of the bed and brushed his floppy hair out of his eyes. "I'm sorry that took so long."

"It's okay." Sighing softly, he stretched into my touch. "We're getting enough teasing without adding Calder into the mix. I get not wanting him to know that we had...plans."

"Trust me, I've still got plans." I ghosted a kiss across his mouth, relieved at how he rolled toward me, not shutting me out despite me maybe deserving the cold shoulder. "I could barely focus on cards. All I could think about was earlier, how good you tasted."

"Yeah?" Eyes warm, he leered at me.

"Yeah. And now you smell nice too." Burying my face in his silky soft hair, I inhaled deeply. The sunscreen scent had been replaced by more of his usual mint and tea clean scent. He hadn't totally shaved, but his scruff looked newly trimmed and his hair was still slightly damp. "Enjoy your shower?"

"Would have enjoyed it more with company." He waggled his eyebrows at me.

"We'll see what can be arranged for later in the week." Kissing him again, I made this one longer, more of a promise that I could do better by him.

"Good. Get up here." Tugging at my shoulders, he didn't stop until I was wedged in next to him. "Tell me you're going to do more than sniff my hair."

"So bossy." I nuzzled from his neck up to his temple simply for the joy of making him laugh.

"Hey, I've been waiting. Night's a-wasting." He yanked me more on top of him.

"Definitely don't want to waste this." The covers were tangled between us, but the luxury of having his firm, warm body underneath me was not something to squander. I kissed him more firmly now, thrilling to how eager he was, how he didn't wait for me to deepen the kiss. It was rare to meet someone as enthusiastic as me about kissing, someone who could give as good as they got rather than a battle for control or the equally frustrating experience of a totally passive partner.

With Arthur, his happy noises in between kisses were enough to have me painfully hard. The need to touch him kept building with every pass of our lips until my whole body trembled.

"This okay?" I pushed the covers down to reveal his faded T-shirt and thin cotton pajama pants.

"More than." He wriggled like a puppy as I swept my hand down his torso before claiming his mouth again. As I plundered his mouth, I wedged a hand under his shirt to explore all the warm skin waiting there for me.

Making a frustrated noise, Arthur plucked at my own tee. "You have on too many clothes."

"You too." I shoved his shirt farther up so I could trace the line of red fuzz heading from his navel to the waistband of his pants. "I had this fantasy of you waiting in nothing but a towel."

"Mmm. Next time." Pulling my shirt free from my jeans, he worked a hand under the fabric to stroke my bare back, and I had to inhale sharply from how good his touch felt.

"Good. I wanna unwrap you." Sitting up, I tried to do exactly that. There was so much I wanted to do that my brain swam with all the possibilities, making my movements clumsy. My bumbling efforts ended up with us both tangled in fabric and chortling.

Finally, we untangled enough to both undress next to the bed. And damn, even in dim light, Arthur was spectacular. Lean, but wiry, with a smattering of freckles and chest fuzz as red as his hair. More ginger fuzz on that treasure trail I'd been playing with earlier and lower too, surrounding a tasty-looking cock. For a skinny guy, he was hung, long shaft and oval uncut tip that I couldn't wait to have in my mouth.

But first I wanted another kiss and I pulled him back onto the bed, into my lap. The move put him at the perfect height for more making out, and one kiss turned into ten turned into both of us breathing hard and clutching at each other.

"Fuck. I like this," he groaned as I moved to kiss his scruffy jaw.

"Good. Me too." I trailed my tongue down his neck to nip at his well-defined collarbones. "So much."

I kept reminding myself that Arthur was new to this and to not go too fast, but slowing down was near impossible with the sounds he made when I kissed and licked at his neck. I bit a little harder than I probably should have, and he shuddered in my arms.

"Oh, do that again." Eyes closing, he tipped his head back, exposing even more creamy, freckled neck for me to feast on.

"This?" Trying to make sure I was below where his shirt collar hit, I sucked hard at the tender triangle where his neck and shoulder met, nibbling my way across those collarbones I couldn't get enough of.

"More." He arched his back, hard cock nudging my abs, making me be the one to shudder next. And I couldn't ignore the unspoken invitation either. Keeping one hand on his back, I moved the other one between us.

"Okay to touch you here?"

"God, yes, please." Canting his hips, he bumped my palm with his cock until I took it in my grip. "Fuck. That feels amazing."

"Yeah, you do." Still dropping random kisses on his neck, I stroked him slow, keeping my grasp loose, discovering what he liked. Judging by his steady stream of moans and curses, he liked it all, but it was fun teasing him, sweeping my thumb across his slick tip, dancing my fingers down the shaft before stroking again, a little firmer now.

"Can I play too?" He wormed his hand underneath mine to find my cock.

"Uh-huh." Like I was going to deny him that. I was dying for his touch, and a sound like I'd taken a fist to the gut escaped my lungs as he explored and touched. He had calluses in different places than mine, a musician's long elegant fingers, and each stroke made me groan anew.

I kept my grip on his cock, but we kept bumping wrists and laughing in between moans and more kissing and touching.

"Here, let me show you something…" Gently, I moved his hand aside so I could take both our cocks in my grasp.

"Fuck." His back bowed against my other hand, the tension in his muscles as sexy as the feel of his cock against mine. "That. *Oh.*"

The note of wonder in his voice thrilled something primal in me. "Something new?"

"Yeah." A shudder rippled through his torso before he rocked up into my grip. "So much better than my imagination."

"Mine too. Kiss me again." Using my free hand, I hauled him in for another kiss, delving deeply as I stroked us both. He braced his hands against my shoulders, keeping me close, like there was any chance of me escaping. Kissing me back, he made needy little noises that went straight to my cock.

"Wait." Breaking free, he panted against my cheek.

"What?" I stilled my hand as he made a pained grunt.

"Too close." A tremor raced up his back, right under my palm. Seeing him right on the edge like that had my own muscles trembling.

"It's okay." Kissing his cheek softly, I made a soothing noise.

Honestly, I was surprised we'd both lasted this long considering all the build-up we'd had. "I wanna make you come."

"Not yet. Not ready for it to be over." Even as he shook his head, his body kept surging up to meet my fist. "There's so much more I want to try."

Lord, he was going to kill me. Or get me off first, simply from thinking about his wish list.

"We've got time," I promised. "Trust me that I'm way too worked up to do anything else justice right now."

He felt too damn good in my arms to think about letting go. It was self-indulgent of me, but I desperately wanted to get him off like this where I could watch his face when he came. Also, simply touching him was so intense that I was a little worried that anything more might ruin me for all future sex. Hell, this might be enough to do the job on its own. No other kisses could live up to these.

"Want you to go too. This does it for you?" Eyes drifting shut again, he tensed as I sped up my hand.

"You do it for me." This time when I tried to kiss him, he let me, meeting me eagerly.

"Fuck. That feels…"

"So good." I wanted to watch him, but my own eyes kept closing from how damn good this felt.

"Think I'm gonna…" That awe was back in his voice and it was almost enough to push me over first, but I clenched my back muscles, holding it off even as I urged him on.

"Do it."

"Want you to come too. Please."

"I will. Promise." So many promises, both silent and spoken, ones I couldn't seem to help from offering up. Each promise added up, pulled me further down the path to a dangerous entanglement, but hell if I could stop. Not right then especially, as my hand had stopped listening to my brain, moving faster and faster.

"Oh. That." His moan was part surprise, part surrender, and utterly intoxicating as he came all over my fist. The first spurt hit my stomach, the warmth all it took to shred the last of my control.

"Fuck." My hips bucked as all that tension I'd been holding back released, the wave of relief so intense I forgot to watch his face, so caught up in my own pleasure. And his. I reveled in the way he clung to me, the way he panted and laughed softly as we both drifted back down. I kissed him over and over because I couldn't not, because sharing this felt so good.

"How do you do that?" He shook his head when I finally slowed the kissing. "You practically came on command. Damn. That's impressive."

"Practice." I chuckled.

"Well, duh." A blush spread across his cheeks.

"I didn't mean with another person. More like I've spent so much time with my right hand that I'm pretty good at timing it."

"You are good at waiting." Groaning, he grabbed his discarded shirt to wipe both our hands and stomachs.

"But it was worth it?" Tilting my head, I considered him carefully. I didn't only mean how I'd kept him waiting the last two days. If that was his first time coming with someone else, I hoped it was at least as memorable for him as it was for me.

"Yeah, it was." Cleanup done, he graced me with a gentle kiss on the mouth. "Now, tell me we get to do that again."

"Hell yes we do." And there it was, that entanglement that came with continuing to make promises to Arthur, the risks in keeping this thing going. A smarter guy would put an end to this, but not me. All I could do was hope that the next time came quickly, before common sense caught up with me.

Chapter Eighteen

Arthur

"I can fake it." Making my voice as seductive as possible, I nuzzled against Derrick's chest. Like the prior night, he'd wrapped me up in a full-body embrace sometime in the night, but this time, we were both naked. Consequently, I was in even less of a mood to rouse myself from the bed simply because the breakfast gong had sounded.

"I know." Derrick groaned and kissed the top of my head. "But we're already lying about so much."

"I don't see how adding a pretend sprained ankle or something else that conveniently disappears later is another black mark on our souls." I didn't mean to come off as super cranky, so I kept my voice light. All I wanted was to maximize what little time I'd get with Derrick this week. "And it means we can stay right here."

"Mmm." He held me tighter, hard cock pressing against my side. "Right here is pretty great."

"It is." The sex had been so good that my insides were still all warm and trembly at the memory. I'd had make-out sessions before, but nothing had prepared me for the all-consuming need I felt with Derrick, the way he swamped all my senses, and how much more connected and alive I felt than with solo orgasms. And there was so, so much more I wanted to try with him. We'd ended up kissing and rubbing off again before sleep, but there was still vast uncharted territory I wanted to explore while I had the chance.

That in mind, I rolled, pushing Derrick more to his back, so I could—

Bong. The stupid gong rang again followed by loud voices. "French toast!"

"Oh. Haven't had that in a while." Derrick's stomach let out a growl as he started to sit up. "Sorry. Guess you made me work up an appetite."

"Not gonna apologize for that." I grinned at him and moved out of the way so he could sit the rest of the way up, even as I wanted to shove him back down and show him what hungry really was.

"Bus to the trailhead leaves soon!" A booming voice sounded as people passed by our cabin.

"We're going to be on it, aren't we?" I moaned as Derrick stood up, leaving the bed that much colder and emptier.

"Might as well." He shrugged like hiking held equal appeal to a sex-filled morning spent sleeping in. "Maybe it'll be fun?"

"Not as fun as last night," I grumbled as I too left the cozy bed behind.

"Few things are." Derrick gave me a wink as he rummaged in his bag for clothes.

"I can think of about a dozen more things I want to try." Reluctantly giving up on convincing Derrick to go back to bed, I found fresh clothes of my own.

"Only a dozen?" Wrapping me up in a hug from behind, he kissed the back of my neck. Him cuddly was a gift that I didn't want to waste, yet he released me before I could tumble us both onto the bed.

"Not too late to fake a hangover or headache yourself," I called as he headed toward the bathroom.

"Calder knows I was sober when I left the card game." Smiling, he pointed at the bathroom door. "Come on, it's a double sink. We can share brushing our teeth and then let's get you fed."

Getting ready together felt all cozy and domestic even if I failed to talk Derrick into shower fun. Damn being a responsible adult. At least the French toast was tasty and the coffee strong. We'd ended up at a table with Taylor and the twins again, and the kids finished their food in record time.

"Watch this, Uncle Arthur!" Taylor called as I came back from getting a food refill. Beaming at me, he did a pretty good approximation of the footwork I'd shown them the night before.

"Huh. Guess they actually were paying attention," I said to Derrick as I sat back down. Taylor and the twins kept practicing, humming the song. They were a little off-key and bungled some of the lyrics, but it was still adorable to see them trying.

"Of course they listened." Derrick nodded with the authority of a guy who could command a room anytime he chose. Still, his praise made me even warmer than the coffee. "You picked a good song too. All kids need a self-esteem boost."

"It's the parents I'm trying to get through to." I cast a glance over to where Oliver and Roger were eating with some of the cousins and their wives.

"I know." Derrick squeezed my upper arm. "And I think you will."

My gaze returned to Derrick, and he met my eyes, an unexpected seriousness there, as if he actually understood what I was trying to accomplish here. Having someone in my corner made my chest tight. Wanting to convey how much the support meant to me, I leaned in so I could—

"Load up, hikers!"

Poof. The moment evaporated in a flurry of activity, the soft kiss I'd intended another casualty of Euler family enthusiasm.

"This waterfall better be worth it," I grumbled as I followed Derrick and the others to the ancient camp bus. At least I got to sit next to Derrick. Maybe this wouldn't be terrible.

"Who wants a song?" my mom chirped once the bus was underway. On second thought, maybe it would be exactly as interminable as I feared. Sure enough, Mom's attention landed on me. "Arthur! Maybe you could teach the kids the words to that bear song we used to do when you kids were little."

"I don't know—"

"Go on." Derrick nudged me. "I wanna see this."

"Okay." I did it because Derrick was watching, and he was possibly the only person here who laughed with me, not at me. Making him smile at the antics of the kids and me was worth any temporary humiliation on my part. I was good at all the old camp songs, even if they weren't to my musical taste at all, and I taught the kids a couple more before we arrived at the trailhead.

The trail took us deep into the rain forest on a soft, boggy trail lined with lots of moss-covered evergreen trees and assorted ferns and other greenery. It was another sunny day, but the forest was dense enough to be dark and cool. Wooden guardrails rimmed the more difficult sections of trail and also gave the kids ample opportunity to attempt to climb to their doom. Eventually, though, we reached the first waterfall with everyone in the hiking party still intact.

"Wow." Derrick's low whistle at the narrow but towering waterfall made heat unfurl in my gut. Of course, everything the guy did that morning reminded me of sex, whether it was breathing hard on a steeper section of trail or making happy noises at some pretty sight. "Now, that's worth the trip."

He gestured at the waterfall as the rest of the family snapped pictures.

"It's pretty, but I'd still rather be working on my wish list of things to try," I whispered.

"If we were alone, I'd drag you behind that waterfall and—"

"Whee!" Some of the kids raced between us, taking advantage of the lull in action to play tag.

"Better be careful." Derrick stopped one of the smaller girls before she could duck under the guardrail. "Don't want to slip off the trail. You'll end up all muddy."

"I don't mind!" She squished her feet in the soft earth on the side of the trail, and I had to laugh as all the nearby kids did the same thing.

"Better watch it. You're giving them big ideas."

"Probably." There was a softness around Derrick's smile that I'd never seen before. And then he went and grabbed my hand while I was still trying to figure him out.

"Hey, what's that?" I glanced down at our linked hands.

He shrugged, but a faint pink stain spread across his chiseled cheekbones. "It's called being an attentive boyfriend."

"Ah." I didn't pull my hand away, but I also didn't like the weird flippy sensation in my stomach. I was no longer sure what was real and what was an act. When we were alone, every look and touch felt important, as real as life could be, but then we'd end up around the others again, and I'd lose my ability to judge. And what was worse was that I'd asked for this, begged for it. If Derrick was an amazing fake boyfriend, it was all my doing.

I couldn't change the rules on him now, so there was nothing to do but squeeze his hand, try to enjoy the sweetness of the gesture.

He was still looking at me a little funny, that softness around his eyes lingering along with his blush. "Arthur—"

"Group picture time!"

I groaned because chances were high that I'd never find out what he'd been about to say. Another missed moment in the name of family togetherness. But if he could be a good sport, so could I. Following him over to the tree where my mom stood, I squashed in alongside Calder and Oliver.

"Everyone squish!" Aunt Sandy demanded as she waved her professional-grade camera at us. "Closer!"

"Arthur, dude, you're on my foot," Calder complained as I dutifully shuffled inward.

"Quit whining."

"Boys!" Turning her head, my mom gave a sharp bark in our direction before returning to smile sweetly for Sandy.

"He started it!" Calder and I said at the same moment, like we were little again. We both laughed, but it was absurd how a few days together peeled back the years and exposed old rivalries.

"Everyone say cheese!" Aunt Sandy clicked away.

"Cheese!" We suffered through a few more pictures before disbanding to continue on the trail.

"Bet I can beat you to the top of that ridge." Calder eyed me speculatively, exactly like we were kids again and he was daring me to do something with the bigger kids. Like most of the family, he'd been excellent at using his own competitive nature as a motivator.

"Are you capable of enjoying nature without a competition?"

"Nope." He grinned, and several people close by laughed. "And it's okay if you're chicken—"

The laughter sealed my fate. "You're on."

The thing about Calder was that he was big like a tank that had two speeds, whereas I was smaller and had agility on my side. Also, I'd put in some serious treadmill hours since the last time we raced. Accordingly, I darted out in front of him, quickly establishing a lead, knowing full well that he'd finish strong. Scampering up the hill, I let out a triumphant noise as I neared the ridge. I was going to win. *About damn time.*

"Arthur!"

I didn't turn at the sound of my name from a female voice I couldn't readily place. I wasn't going to listen to a lecture about not racing or being a good example for the kids, not when I was so close to finally beating Calder at one of these stupid challenges.

The angle was increasingly steep and slick, but I kept moving quickly. Too quickly. My left leg lost its footing, and then I was sliding back down the hill, crushing ferns and causing deadwood and rocks to tumble after me. My bare arms and shins scraped against the uneven terrain until I landed in a deep boggy, muddy puddle that smelled like dead things, like ancient dinosaurs had chosen this exact pit to decompose and now I was disturbing their eternal slumber.

"Oh f—"

"Language!" my mom scolded me from the top of the hill. "Little ears!"

"Sometimes no other word will work, Mom."

"You okay?" Derrick had apparently raced after me, and now he reached a hand down to haul me out of the muck.

I rolled my neck and wiggled my limbs before accepting his help up. "Yeah, I'm good. Just wounded my pride. Again."

"You could have been hurt!" Derrick's eyes were hard, a greater level of concern than I would have expected. "Why'd you do that?"

"You know Calder. Always a bet. I just wanted to win and figured this was my chance to prove I'm faster now."

"You are." Derrick's face softened. "But you need to stop letting the others get your goat."

"Why? It's so much fun for them." I tried to brush myself off and ended up only smearing more mud around and encountering several shallow scrapes on my legs and arms. "Ouch. God, this mud is extra sticky."

"You've earned a bath in that big tub when we get back." Keeping a hold of my hand, he helped me slowly make my way back up the incline.

"And an iced coffee, but this far from civilization I'm going to be lucky to get leftover drip coffee from breakfast, let alone anything fancy."

"I will personally track you down something cold and sweet while you're in the tub." He smiled warmly at me. He was the sweet one. So sweet I almost couldn't stand it. And far nicer than I deserved, considering I'd brought this latest disaster entirely on myself.

"You could—" I couldn't finish my invite for him to join me because we'd reached the others and were quickly surrounded by a horde of kids.

"Eww. Uncle Arthur, you smell!"

"Stinky!"

"Yep." All I could do was laugh with them. "See? Mud isn't as fun as it looks."

"Like I said, you've earned that bath." Derrick shook his head.

"And a treat." I was holding him to that.

"Yup. I'm going to find you something even if I have to go into town. And while I'm at it, I'll find you something for those scrapes. None look that deep, but it's got to hurt."

What was truly going to hurt was never having a fake boyfriend this nice again. But I wasn't going to let myself dwell on that, and instead I started dreaming up ways to get him in that tub with me. Muddy might not be the worst thing if it led to dirty fun.

Chapter Nineteen

Derrick

I should have stayed in bed with Arthur. But no, I'd had to have a fit of conscience and drag him hiking instead of letting him fake a minor ailment. And now he had an actual injury, which was in part my fault, because I'd talked him into going, but also I hadn't talked him *out* of the bet with Calder. Or told Calder to stop acting like he was fourteen and Arthur some pesky nine-year-old. They were both adults, and neither had had any business racing up that muddy slope.

But it wasn't Calder who had made me gasp.

Wasn't Calder who had me call out.

Wasn't Calder who had me racing down the hill to make sure he was okay.

I didn't do panic. Like, seriously, any tendency to panic had been trained out of me in sub school, and the fact that I didn't panic in tense moments was in large part why I had been chosen. But then I'd seen Arthur tumble and I'd...

Panicked. And even now, a few hours later, I still couldn't decide who I was most upset with—Calder, Arthur, or myself.

"You take as long as you want in the tub. Use all the hot water," I commanded Arthur as we disembarked from the bus back at the camp.

"Okay." That he readily agreed only underscored how miserable and hurting he likely was. He looked a wreck—mud caked in his hair and smeared across his face and limbs along with multiple minor scrapes and bruises. He was so messy that it was a wonder they'd let him back on the bus. And a wonder he hadn't been more seriously injured.

"I'm going to find you an iced coffee if it means making it myself," I promised him as I steered him in the direction of our cabin. "You go relax. I'll handle this."

"On a mission for coffee?" the bus driver asked after Arthur had lurched off down the path.

"Yup." My attention was still largely on Arthur's retreating form.

"There's a place back off the highway, closer to Port Angeles. That's probably your closest option. The kitchen just closed after lunch and won't reopen until dinner unless you want me to hunt down the dregs of what we have in the staff room."

"No, no dregs." I'd likely had way worse over my years in the military and also before then, with plenty of bad retirement center coffee too, but Arthur was worth way more than some leftovers. "I'll go into town for the coffee."

"You're going for coffee?" Stacey, Oliver's wife, eyed me with an intent that made me shuffle my feet. "Could you bring me back something?"

"Oh, hey, me too." Looking more like his father every year, Roger had a twin under each of his beefy arms. As the oldest, he'd probably been born with a chief's bearing.

Before I could reply, Taylor stepped in front of his mother. "Can I ride with you? I can hold the drinks."

"Well…"

"Dad showed me your car in the parking area. It's *sweet*."

"It is," I had to agree.

"We're coming too." The twins escaped their father to flank

Taylor, three identical pleading expressions. "We've never rid-den in a real hot rod."

"Do you have seat belts?" Stacey eyed me more critically.

"Yes, ma'am," I assured her, realizing too late that a lack of seat belts would have saved me the three eager copilots.

"His driving record is even cleaner than his room," Calder chipped in.

"Good." Roger nodded like everything was all settled, and maybe it was because somehow I ended up in short order with a fist full of cash, a ripped notebook page with coffee orders, and my pint-sized passengers racing ahead to my car.

"Hey, can I add something to your list?" Calder jogged up next to me as I headed after the kids.

"How about a reminder that you're thirty and not nine-teen?" I shot back. "Quit antagonizing your brother."

"Whoa. Way to stand up for your man, but the audience is gone now. You can't tell me you're actually enjoying this boyfriend gig?"

"I don't hate it," I said evenly as I stalked toward the car. "He's a good guy."

"He is. Big heart, like Mom always says." Calder chuckled fondly. "But it sure was funny, him covered in mud."

"For you, maybe."

"Wow. You really can be such a—"

"Little ears," I took great delight in reminding him as we reached the car, where the boys were running in circles around it.

"There's volleyball later. You better not be too busy with nursemaid duties to play."

"We'll see." Honestly, the chance to serve a ball into my friend's thick skull sounded pretty darn amazing. But I didn't want to keep the fight going either. I'd said what I wanted to say. "Add your order to my list quickly while I load up the boys."

After I unlocked the car, I double-checked the backseat seat belts. "Everyone gets buckled up and no one messes with the windows or doors."

"I've never seen windows with a crank before," Taylor marveled.

"Look at you, the honorary cool uncle," Calder teased as he finished scrawling his order on the piece of paper.

"Thought that was your role."

"Nah. Arthur's got cool uncle on lockdown. Me, I've got no clue what to do with kids."

"Better watch it or the universe will send you ten." After I took the paper back from him, I pocketed it and the cash.

"Shut your trap. You know damn well that I'm married to the navy, same as you. No one's thinking of either of us as daddy material."

"True," I agreed, waving Calder on his way before starting the car. However, my brain wandered back to my conversation with Arthur the night before. Now there was someone with serious fatherhood potential. Neither Calder nor I were cut out to be family men, not in the same way that Arthur was, no matter how he grumbled about his big family. He was a natural with kids and had the sort of life where I could absolutely see him and some future husband with a house full of musically inclined kids. I hated the future husband dude already.

And undoubtedly Arthur would have done a better job than me at answering all the kid questions they peppered me with as we got underway.

"How fast does this thing go?" Taylor asked, but before I could answer, the other questions started piling on from the twins.

"Will you show us?"

"We won't tell Mom if you burn rubber." Vince, the wilder twin, motioned toward my odometer like I might actually take him up on it. "Pinky promise."

"What's it like being on a submarine?" Seth asked as I achieved a nice, sedate highway speed. No way was I risking a ticket with a back seat full of kids.

"Yeah, what happens when someone farts on a sub?" Taylor added.

"And how do you know whether it's night when you're underwater?" Vince threw in his questions before I could answer the first two. "Is it true they put you in a dunk tank in school?"

"Slow down," I ordered after about ten minutes of the question artillery. "First, I'm not going to speed, so you can stop asking that. And I'll tell you all about life on a sub if you let me talk."

"Talk," Taylor parroted like I was the one holding up the conversation.

"I wanna know everything." Seth stretched like he was settling in for a story, so I gave them one, talking about air filtration systems on the sub, clocks and shifts, lighting and more.

"Why'd you want to be on a sub anyway?" Taylor asked as I finished explaining sleeping arrangements. "My dad says you couldn't pay him to be on a sub."

"That's 'cause your dad is *army*. My dad says your dad is a crap swimmer." Vince was rather gleeful in delivering this insult.

"Is not."

"Is—"

"Enough." I silenced the backseat battle with the same tone our chief of the boat used with unruly new recruits. "I like being on a sub because we're all a team and everyone plays a key part. It's not like the big ships where you can get lost in the crowd. I know the name of every single person on my sub.

I like that. And I like what we do in the sonar department as well—finding patterns, looking for discrepancies."

"Nerd work," Vince scoffed.

"Hey," Taylor protested. "Derrick's not a nerd."

"Thanks—"

"That's Arthur. Now he's a nerd."

"Hold up. There's nothing wrong with being a nerd. Or liking data and science. Being smart is a good thing." I smiled as I thought about Arthur and his impressive brain with its library of musical knowledge and trivia.

"Yeah, Vince, you should try it sometime." In the rearview mirror, Seth was glaring at Vince. Gamer kid had clearly taken the nerd crack personally, not that I blamed him.

"I'd rather be fast," Vince shot back.

"Or blow something up." Taylor sounded way too eager to create damage.

"Oh! Or kick it down!"

"I'm gonna make more money than both of you," Seth said firmly. And he probably wasn't wrong there either.

"Stay in school, all of you. You might change your minds about your career choices." I slowed as we neared the outskirts of Port Angeles.

"You sound like my mom." Taylor wrinkled his nose when I glanced back.

"Maybe she knows a thing or two." I laughed then pointed at my dashboard. "Now let the GPS tell us which way to go."

The first place we tried was closed already, but the second had a cheerful open sign in the window.

"Do we get drinks too?" Vince asked.

"No coffee." The last thing these kids needed was caffeine, but when they all made sad noises and puppy-dog faces, I quickly added, "How about smoothies?"

"Thanks, Uncle Derrick." Taylor followed the twins out of the car.

"He's not our uncle," Vince reminded him.

"Might as well be." Taylor shrugged.

I wasn't about to touch that comment, so I herded them into the little coffeehouse. To my surprise, I liked having them along. There was something reassuring about their chatter, kind of like being around my crew on the boat. Perhaps a family was simply a different sort of team.

Maybe...

No. I shut that line of thinking down. Luckily, I had the mile-long drink list to worry about. Three drink carriers later and we were back on the road, where they peppered me with even more questions, but I didn't mind.

Much.

"That was so cool," Taylor raved as we arrived back at the camp. "Thanks."

"Yeah, thanks." All three of them gave me big grins, and yeah, as it turned out, I didn't mind having them along nearly as much as I'd feared.

I nabbed the drink and platter-sized brownie I'd bought for Arthur before letting my helper crew distribute the rest of the drinks. Heading back to the cabin, my brain shifted gears from the endless kid questions to thoughts about whether Arthur would be waiting in a towel. Or maybe still be in the tub, all slippery and soapy.

Even better.

Chapter Twenty

"You still soaking?" Derrick called from the other room right as I was about to turn into a waterlogged sponge if I stayed in this tub any longer.

"Yup. You can bring me my drink," I yelled back, fully expecting him to tell me to come fetch it myself. But the warm water felt so damn good on my sore muscles. My mom had pressed a bag of Epsom salts on me, and Stacey some bubble bath that smelled like pricey herbs.

I felt like a well-seasoned, salt-basted turkey after my long, fragrant soak, but I was in a far better mood than earlier and could grin way more easily when Derrick appeared in the doorway to the bathroom, giant iced coffee in hand.

"Hey, merman. I got you the largest size they had." He smiled indulgently at me, warming me even more than the water.

"Excellent." Not about to turn down tub-side service, I wriggled under the water as Derrick brought the drink over. He even held it for me to take a long sip.

"You truly are the best pretend boyfriend ever. Like undercover FBI agent-level good at the ruse." Beaming at him, I took another drink before he set the cup aside.

"You watch too many bad movies." Derrick knelt down next to the tub.

"More like I read too much of Sabrina's alternate universe fan fic." I laughed as he shifted around, apparently settling in for a chat with me still all bubbly. "Speaking of, are you here to play valet? Going to scrub my back?"

"Does Sabrina write period pieces too?" Picking up the soap from the little tray on the side of the tub, he also reached for a washcloth from the nearby rack.

"Wait." I held up a hand before he could proceed. "I wasn't serious."

"I was. Lean forward." He pushed on my shoulder.

"Why do you have to be so perfect?" Sighing, I complied and sat forward. I wasn't stupid enough to turn down a chance to have his hands on me.

"I'm not." His face was far too serious to be joking with me.

"What? You could have fooled me." I stretched as he rubbed my back, his firm touch even better than the warm water at relaxing me.

"Ask your brother. I'm known for being a hard-ass on duty and a cranky loner off."

"I get the loner rep, but you're *nice*," I insisted. He used his thumbs to massage my neck, and I had to bite back a groan. "I'm the one who's been cranky this week. I don't know why I can't seem to enjoy family trips."

"Maybe it's because I don't have the same baggage as you. To me, this is a fun escape. Like visiting a movie set. I'm not the one who had to grow up in the family, though, so I've got the luxury of being nice."

Huh. He wasn't wrong. There was a whole history here, one that made it hard to simply let go and enjoy the present.

"That's really astute of you." Bending more forward, I made

it easier for him to rub more of my back. "Now you're nice *and* smart."

"Well, I try on both fronts. Even if the kids think being a smart nerd is overrated."

"You? A nerd? Never." I flicked a bubble in his direction.

"Ha. Tell that to Taylor and the twins. And let's see. I like data and organization, would rather play chess than poker, know all sorts of random trivia thanks to my grandmother's love of game shows, and I generally play by the rules. I think that makes me a nerd."

"I think that makes you pretty perfect," I countered. "All that and you're hot as fuck too? Damn. It's a wonder you didn't have volunteers lined up outside the barracks to be your rebound."

"Hot, huh?" He leaned in for a soft kiss on my mouth.

"You own a mirror. You know you're all that." Even now, Derrick was so damn appealing, the way his brown hair was as rumpled as his T-shirt from the hiking, the gentleness around his eyes and mouth, and the strength in his hands on my shoulders and back.

"You're full of it." Eyes twinkling, he gave me another kiss. "And you're not so bad yourself. You look damn sexy with all those bubbles playing peekaboo with your skin."

I preened. "You could join me."

"I could." He kissed the side of my neck, making me shiver before he snaked a hand down my chest. "Got anywhere else I should rub?"

"Well, if you're going for full service…" I stretched suggestively, letting my hard cock bob above the water, getting a laugh from us both.

"Maybe I am." His next kiss was more aggressive, the way he growled and nipped before delving deeply.

"Get in here with me."

"Some other time. Promise." He slid his hand lower, palming my cock, making me groan because I had such a love-hate relationship with his promises. "Right now, I wanna get you off like this."

"But I can't reach you." My complaint wasn't all that convincing because the way he was touching me made me feel like some sort of pampered emperor, and I sure as hell didn't want him to stop.

"Yup. You're all mine." Laughing darkly, he gave me another kiss, this one possessive and commanding. "Last night I really wanted to watch your face when you came, but my eyes shut at the last second and I missed my chance."

"Hey." My skin heated, and I ducked my head. "Now you're making me self-conscious."

"Don't be." He tilted my head up so he could claim my mouth again, before adding, "I think you're so fucking gorgeous."

"I'd think *you* were hotter if you let me get you off too," I countered.

"Shush. I'll keep until later." Nibbling my neck, he coaxed loose another moan from me as his grip on my cock tightened.

"You are the king of delayed gratification." I'd let him win this round, but later he was going to be all mine, and merely the thought of all I wanted to do to him made me shiver. "I'm going to make it more than worth the wait."

"Good." He sped up his hand, water sluicing over my aching cock. "Let me have my fun now, though. Kiss me."

I did, finding his lips for a clumsy kiss interrupted by more moaning as he added a twist at the top of each stroke that was going to get me there fast.

"Oh. That."

"Good?"

"So good." Arching my back, I tried to spur him on. Already my body was far too ramped up for any impulses to draw this out. "Not sure how your hand can feel so much better than mine."

"Maybe I'm just magic." Chuckling, he kissed me again, deeper this time, one hand on the back of my neck while the other continued to drive me out of my mind. He was magic all right, and I forgot to be self-conscious about him watching me and instead gave myself over to his touch and his kiss.

"Fuck. Derrick." My breath came in harsh pants as he jerked me harder. The now-tepid water splashed, some hitting my face, but I was singularly focused on my impending orgasm.

"Yeah, baby," he urged, voice low and sexy. "Let it happen."

Didn't have to ask me twice. I was that close that he didn't have to change his grip or speed, simply keep kissing and touching me and climax was right there. "Gonna…"

"Do it," he growled, but I was already coming, crying out and shaking so hard it was a wonder the tub didn't rattle apart from the force of it. "Damn. I knew it. That was the hottest thing I've ever seen. You're sexy as fuck when you come."

"Thanks." Not sure what to do with the compliment, I leaned forward so I could drain the tub in advance of rinsing off with the sprayer. I still couldn't get over how different climaxing with another person was. If I'd known about this intensity, I would have made sex more of a priority years ago. But then I wouldn't be here with Derrick, experiencing all this for the first time.

I managed to avoid drenching him as I quickly washed off any lingering traces of bubble bath and the orgasm. I had some scrapes and bruises, but now that the dirt was gone, nothing needed a bandage, and it was mainly my pride that had taken the brunt of the fall.

"Don't blush." Derrick handed me a towel as I flipped off

the water. "I mean it. You're so fucking sexy. I'm gonna watch you come again later tonight as well."

"How about right now?" I pitched my voice low and seductive, not that it ever seemed to work on Derrick. But he said I was sexy, and I certainly felt more attractive in the light of his warm gaze. "Bet I could go for doubles if you let me get you off too."

"I will." Predictably, he held up a hand when I would have advanced on him. "After volleyball and dinner."

"Volleyball?" Stopping to rescue my coffee from the floor, I followed him back into the main room. "I'm supposed to play sports after you reduced my nerve endings to the equivalent of old piano wires?"

"Yup. You are."

"There are other balls I'd rather play with." If seduction wasn't going to work, at least I could bring the jokes.

"Don't tempt me." His eyes flared dark before he too laughed and pointed at my coffee cup, which was damp with condensation. "Darn it. We took so long your coffee melted."

"Trust me, your hands are more than worth slushy coffee. And it's still good. Exactly what I was craving." I took a watered-down sip. I'd drink three-day-old swill if it meant more kissing with Derrick. "Thank you."

"Don't thank me. Taking care of you is fun."

Fun. There were a lot of things I wanted to be for Derrick, but fun wasn't a bad start. Like he'd said, maybe he didn't have enough fun in his life, and if he found doing nice things for me that enjoyable, I wasn't going to stop him. "Maybe I should let you do it more."

"Maybe you should." Voice light and teasing, he winked at me, but something far more serious unfurled in my chest as I pulled on some fresh clothes. With every encounter, this felt less and less like a game, but no way was I pulling back now. Instead, I matched his laugh. "To volleyball and beyond!"

Derrick wasn't the only one who could make promises for later, and I was damn sure going to make his wait memorable.

Chapter Twenty-One

Derrick

"I can't believe I let you talk me into this." Arthur broke off another piece of brownie and handed it to me as we walked to the sand volleyball court beyond some of the larger cabins. "The last time I played, I'm pretty sure I narrowly avoided a concussion."

"I'm sure you're not that bad." I smiled at him, both to be encouraging and because something about sharing the treat was so sweet that I wanted to savor the moment. I hadn't been kidding about enjoying taking care of him. Watching him enjoy his coffee and brownie was deeply satisfying in a way that made my muscles warm and loose and my smiles that much easier.

"I'm hopeless at all sports involving balls." After eating the last bite, Arthur licked a stray chocolate crumb off his thumb, and I nearly groaned with wanting his mouth on me instead.

"Not all." Watching his tongue swipe at his fingers, I seriously regretted turning down an orgasm earlier. I hadn't wanted him to feel obligated, but my body was still protesting my noble impulse and was ready to haul Arthur back to the cabin, prove what exactly we were both good at.

"Point." He met my gaze, faint blush saying we were on

the same page there. "But whatever the game, I do my best work solo and one-on-one. I suck at team sports."

Right as I was about to make a joke about sucking, a pack of kids greeted us, and I stowed away the flirting for later.

"Uncle Arthur!" Taylor grinned at both of us. "How was your coffee?"

"Good." Arthur's blush deepened. I hid my own grin behind my hand. That little interlude had absolutely been hot enough to melt ice, and I didn't feel the least bit guilty about distracting him from his drink.

"We got to help," Vince announced as he bounced up next to Taylor.

"I heard. Thanks. You did great jobs." Arthur's tone was always so kind and patient for the kids.

"It was fun," Taylor added. "Even if Uncle Derrick wouldn't speed."

"Uncle Derrick, huh?" Arthur teased as the kids sped away. "You must have made a big impression during your outing."

"They just like me for my car."

"Don't we all."

We were both still laughing as we reached the volleyball area right as Oliver whistled.

"Hey, volleyball players!" He hopped on top of a nearby picnic table to address the group. "To make this fair, we're going to count off for teams."

As we all lined up, Calder and his friends were near the front, and I did some fast math as soon as they were counted off. I deftly swapped places with Vince and motioned to Arthur.

"Quick. Move one back."

"What?" Arthur frowned.

"Just do it," I insisted, pointing again. "You can help me teach Calder a lesson."

"Now you're speaking my language." Arthur ducked behind his cousin Ingrid, right as the count reached me. And sure enough, my machinations resulted in Arthur and me being on the opposite team from Calder.

"What the—" Calder strode up after everyone was assigned to a team. "How did you end up on the other team?"

I shrugged. "Luck of the draw."

"And you got most of the kids." He pointed at our side of the court where Taylor and Seth were having some sort of dance-off with two of the girl cousins. Some of the other kids were happily digging in the sand. "Good luck with that."

"I think we've still got a good chance." Yeah, Calder's side had more height, but Taylor was tall for his age and we had some older cousins who would make decent blockers.

"You want to bet?" Calder bumped my shoulder. "Post-camp laundry?"

"You're on." I didn't have to think twice.

Next to me, Arthur groaned. "Can't you both play for enjoyment?"

"No fun in that." Calder grinned, his usual good-spiritedness replacing our tension from the parking lot. There was no activity that he wasn't willing to make more fun with a friendly bet, and having been stuck doing monotonous tasks with him more than once, I had to say it wasn't the worst quality to have.

"And do try to avoid injury this time, Arthur." Oliver jogged over, volleyball under one arm.

"Oh, they're going down," I muttered as Arthur and I headed to join our team.

"You're cute all competitive on my behalf." Arthur sounded somewhere between amused and exasperated. I didn't entirely get his irritation.

"Why play unless you're in it to win it?" I motioned the rest of our team over.

"Why indeed." Arthur rolled his eyes at me, but he didn't say anything else as the kids and assorted other players surrounded us. Somehow I ended up the default captain, organizing who stood where and working out a rotation for those who wanted a turn serving.

"Once a chief, always a chief," Arthur teased, voice lighter now. The game got underway with Calder's team scoring a fast point off a strong serve that cut right between Seth and Taylor.

"Come on, gang! Heads up!" I encouraged before passing the ball to Taylor, who promptly served it straight into the net. Family rules said kids got a second chance, but that try also bounced off the top edge of the net.

"Sorry." His chin drooped as he passed me, and I patted his head.

"It's okay. We'll get the next one."

But we didn't. Max got another fast point on us for Calder's side. At least Seth got the ball over the net with his turn, but Calder stuffed the return in short order. Then Ingrid served for the other side, and Taylor showed some serious gumption diving to prevent another fast point.

"Great job! Nice dig!" I called to him right before Max set up Calder to slam the return right past Arthur.

"You sure you don't want to renegotiate that bet?" Calder yelled, all jacked on adrenaline. He was fun when he was winning, but I wasn't on his team.

"No way."

"Excellent." He gave me a thumbs-up. "Can't wait for sparkling clothes."

I took the next serve myself and drove the ball between Calder and the baseline for our first call. "Finally."

"You and Calder are taking this way too seriously." Arthur shook his head.

"You don't want to beat him?" I was surprised. I would have thought he'd be all fired up by my point and ready to crush Calder's team, but Arthur simply rolled his shoulders and stretched.

"I so rarely win against any of them. Honestly, I stopped caring years ago."

"Well, I still think we've got a good shot." Somehow his statement made me want this for him more, want to provide him that satisfaction against his brothers. I drew my shoulder blades together, posture tensing, like my will alone could lead us to victory.

"Good job, Ethan!" Taylor yelled as one of the older cousins managed to angle the ball past Oliver for another point for our side. We were coming back. Stoked, I doubled down on coaching.

"Get it!" I directed to Taylor. "Come on, Seth, pop it high!"

"Wahoo!" The boys celebrated as the game continued to heat up.

"You can do it. A little higher this time." Arthur tossed the ball to Taylor when it was his turn to serve. I stifled a groan because we didn't need to eat more net. But this time Taylor got it over, and our whole team cheered. However, the closer we came to winning, the more detached Arthur seemed, talking less to me, and more to the kids, and I wasn't sure what I'd done wrong.

"We've got this!" I tried to embody team spirit as we rallied to tie Calder's team. But Arthur barely cracked a smile even as I managed to coach Seth through setting up a floater for a cousin to poke down for an easy point. "Way to go!"

"Yes! We win!" Seth and Taylor broke out a victory dance as we squeaked out a two-point victory.

"Lucky break," Calder scoffed. He wasn't terribly put out, though. It had been a great battle, and he bounced on his feet. "Bet you can't do it twice. Best two out of three?"

"You're on," I agreed before I glanced over at Arthur. That had been a rush. But apparently he didn't feel the same way because he shook his head.

"You guys play but I'm out. Gonna try to get some practice in before dinner with the kids who didn't want to do volleyball." He headed away from the sand court, carefully stepping over two kids digging at the edge of it.

"Hey!" I jogged after him. "Are you okay? Not injured or sore from your fall?"

"I'm not injured." Arthur had a sad little smile for me as he patted my upper arm. "I'm fine. Enjoy your game."

I felt like I was missing some important point as he walked away. He didn't seem as fine as he claimed, but before I could chase him down, Calder called me back to the game. I continued coaching Taylor and Seth and the rest of the team who had stuck around, and the boys whooped and hollered with each point. I missed Arthur, though. Missed having a reason to spur the team on to victory. Missed showing off for him.

A lot of my fight had left with Arthur, and it wasn't surprising when we lost two fast sets to Calder's team. The kids didn't seem all that disappointed, still hopping around and turning cartwheels, but I felt guilty because I knew my distraction had played a role in our demise.

After the game I wandered over to the dining hall where people were milling around, waiting for the gong to ring. Arthur was surrounded by a different group of kids, and he was smiling far wider than he had playing volleyball. Tinny music echoed from the phone he was holding up as he showed dance steps to a pair of little girls, one of whom promptly tripped mid-spin.

"Oops. I messed up again." The girl's chin wobbled, dark eyes welling up. I prepared for waterworks, but Arthur simply laughed and tipped her head back up with his finger.

"That wasn't a mistake! You invented a new move. Here, let me try." He did a much more graceful version of her trip, managing to make spin-trip-spin look intentional. "Wow. That's fun!"

"You're silly, Uncle Arthur." The girl grinned at him, no more tears, crisis averted. Damn, Arthur was impressive. I couldn't help smiling too.

"And you're brilliant," Arthur said as he knelt down to the girl's level. "Keep doing you, okay? Keep it fun."

"I will." Grabbing his hand, she swung herself back and forth.

Keep doing you. Keep it fun. Hell. Was that where I had gone wrong? By focusing so hard on winning, had I taken away the thing that made Arthur who he was?

He headed into the dining hall with his fan club of kids at his heels, leaving me kicking at the dirt and wondering how in the hell I was supposed to make this right. My neck hurt. Now I needed a real apology for my fake boyfriend and fast unless I wanted to be the one sleeping in the tub that night.

Chapter Twenty-Two

Arthur

"Are you and Derrick going to make up?" Ingrid asked after breaking up a kid battle over who got which stick for roasting marshmallows. We were in charge of s'mores distribution again, and after such a long day, the kids were even more rambunctious than usual.

"What?" I played dumb and handed out another pair of graham crackers. "We're not fighting."

"Yes, you are. You didn't sit together at dinner, and he keeps giving you these long puppy-dog looks." Ingrid deftly intervened before Seth and Vince could spear each other.

She had a point. I'd seen Derrick coming my direction and quickly slid into the last seat at Aunt Sandy's table rather than wait to sit together. I was perfectly aware I was acting petty, and I still didn't entirely understand why I was so upset. And weirdly, knowing Derrick had noticed and might care buoyed my mood. "He does?"

"Definitely." Grinning at me, she flipped her braid over one shoulder. "You should put him out of his misery and forgive him for whatever tiff you guys had."

"It's stupid anyway," I admitted. Even trying to rationalize in my head, it seemed ridiculous. My fake boyfriend was too good at defending my honor, and I took issue with his enthusiasm. Yeah. Anyone would laugh at that beef.

"Even more reason to let it go." Ingrid apparently didn't need the full explanation to dispense advice as we handed out food to the last of the line. "Okay, I think that's all the kids."

"And hey, now we're out of chocolate." I held up the empty box. "Guess there's none for us."

"Yes, there's some for you." Derrick appeared in front of us almost as if I'd summoned him. And he held out a small paper plate. "I made you one."

"You did?" I didn't move to take the plate even as Ingrid made an *awww* noise. "Why?"

"Because you were so busy with the kids, I figured you might miss your chance."

That got another *awww* from Ingrid, who made a show of cleaning up the picnic table and leaving Derrick and me to stare awkwardly at each other.

"Oh." I went ahead and accepted the plate even if I didn't fully understand what he was after here. I ate the s'more, mostly because it felt rude to not, but I was more interested in figuring out what Derrick was up to than the treat.

"And I didn't want to miss *my* chance to apologize."

"Oh," I said again. A peace offering. I was the one who had stalked off and given him the cold shoulder, and he was still the one to say sorry first. I should be the one lamenting missed chances, not him. He truly was perfect. And maybe it was all for show or to practice being a decent boyfriend, but warmth spread across my chest nonetheless. "You don't have to apologize."

"Yeah, I think I do." His mouth twisted as he exhaled hard. "I let Calder and the match get in my head, and sucked all the fun out of playing for you."

"It's okay. It's just a game." I could say that now, even

though it wasn't. It was never simply a game with this family, and that was most of my issue. I stepped away from the table to avoid the kids zooming around.

"Yeah, but that's what I forgot." Derrick followed me into the shadows. A short distance in front of us, the fire glowed bright, and one of my uncles strummed a guitar. Derrick pitched his voice low, giving us the illusion of privacy even surrounded by others. "I'm so used to Calder taking every bet so seriously that I forgot that there are plenty of other ways to have fun."

"Not everything has to be a competition." I might as well tattoo that on my chest for all the good it seemed to do around here, but Derrick nodded sympathetically.

"I know." Moving slowly, he put an arm around my shoulders. I had plenty of time to move away, but I didn't. His warmth and nearness felt almost as good as his understanding. "I'm sorry."

"Me too. I'm sorry I ignored you. I'm not even sure why I got so miffed." I leaned into his embrace, feeling my tension drain away by the second. Ingrid was right. Fighting was dumb. And she didn't even know the half of it like how little time we had left together. Derrick didn't want to miss his chance and neither did I. "You're a good coach. The kids loved you. It's more that I hate letting my brothers pull me back into old patterns where winning is the only thing that matters."

"*You* matter." Tone solemn, he tipped my face toward his with gentle fingers.

"Thanks." My voice was all husky now, anticipation gathering low in my belly. Forget winning. What mattered was maximizing my time with Derrick, cramming as much kissing and good feelings in as I could. His words, though, did underscore how good he was at saying exactly what I needed to hear at the perfect moment. Not for the first time, I worried that perhaps he was ruining me for all other guys.

"You have some chocolate on your cheek…" He swiped at my cheek with his broad thumb. "Right here."

"Thanks." I shivered way more from his touch than from the rapidly cooling night air. I wanted to kiss him in the worst way, but there were a few too many people close by for more than a quick peck. "You want to see something cool I found?"

"Absolutely."

"Grab a flashlight." I gestured at the box full of assorted lights on the picnic table. We each scooped up one and crept away from the fire circle, the strains of an old folk ballad following us into the shadows of the forest. Rather than heading toward our cabin, I ventured the opposite direction, toward the lakeshore, bypassing the rocky beach near the main camp in favor of taking Derrick to a narrow inlet.

We weren't that far from camp, but it felt like our own private cove, and above us the moon hung low, casting a magical glow over the spot.

"See how pretty this is in the moonlight?" I'd discovered it earlier, wandering around aimlessly after dinner, and sharing it with him made me bouncy, all my earlier weighty thoughts gone.

"Yeah. It really is," Derrick agreed, but he was looking right at me, not the water. The back of my neck prickled.

"And it's private." I looped my arms around him, trying to anchor the buoyant feeling inside me to something concrete and real. Being around him made me New Year's champagne levels of giddy, but he was also so grounding that I wanted to squeeze him tight and never let go.

"Private enough for this at least." Kissing me softly, he took all the magic of this spot and magnified it, made me more than a little tipsy on him and the moment.

"Private enough we could skinny-dip," I teased as we broke apart before I kicked my hiking sandals off.

"Hell no." Derrick shook his head as I dipped a toe in the water. "I'm all about letting you have fun, but that lake is cold!"

"Says the sailor."

"We're generally warm and dry, thank you very much." His laugh was far warmer than either the water or the night air, so I flicked some water his direction simply to make him laugh more. "I did so well in basic training that I had a chance to try for SEAL training or sub school after that, but the SEALs had way too much frigid swimming for my tastes."

"So you're saying you're chicken…" Trying to bait him further, I shrugged out of my shirt, tossed it to him. "Bet I could dare you into trying it."

"Thought we were going to leave competitiveness behind, have more fun."

"Exactly." I waded back over to him, pulling him close. "Have some fun. Live a little."

"Oh, I'm living." Eyes full of a wonder I wasn't sure I'd ever seen before, he kissed me so tenderly that a shudder raced through me. If I'd been composing a soundtrack for us, this would be the moment where the music swelled to something epic and rich, a melody to return to over and over. This was the sort of kiss that a lot people probably lived their whole lives without, and the composer in me ached to capture the moment. And the human part of me simply ached period. It wasn't even a contest any longer. I was ruined for anything less than Derrick, and I kissed him back with a desperation I hadn't known I possessed.

"Damn." He was breathing as hard as I was when I finally let him up for air.

"See? No way can I be cold with kisses like that, even in

the water. Come play." I tugged him toward the water, but he resisted.

"Let me take you back to the cabin, warm you up even more. We can play there," he coaxed, pulling me farther away from the shore.

"Tempting."

Reeling me in, he kissed me before waving a finger at me. "Sound carries out here, and we don't need an audience when I make you scream."

"Promises, promises." Sighing, I put my sandals and shirt back on because the water really was too cold for the fun he was offering. Warm cabin was starting to sound pretty good, even if I still wanted to bottle the moonlight up.

"Race you—*wait*." Derrick stopped mid-tease, sucked in a breath. "Sorry. Not a bet. Walk with me back?"

He held out a hand, and that was it, the last piece of my resistance gone. I melted like a chocolate bar in the presence of a perfectly toasted marshmallow. I was a goner for this man, and I didn't even care anymore. Anyone would melt in the face of such sweetness and be happy with their fate.

Smiling up at him, I grabbed his outstretched hand and started to run, dragging him along with me until he started to run too, and then we were dashing through the night. Laughing, we skirted behind the cabins to avoid people walking back from the fire circle, then sped up again to bound up our porch and stumble into the cabin.

"Wasn't that more fun?" I asked him as I locked the door behind us. "Not racing?"

"Yeah, it really was." Still holding my hand, he leaned in for a soft kiss. After flipping on the fireplace, he tried to steer me toward the bed. "Now to warm you up."

"No, you don't." I mimicked both his stern tone and finger wag from earlier.

"No?" He raised his eyebrows.

"You keep focusing on me, which is awesome—"

"I agree." Smiling seductively, he again tried to topple me onto the bed, but I hadn't grown up with three brothers for nothing. I knew how to use his forward momentum to reverse our positions, so that I was the one pushing him down.

"But I want a turn too." As soon as he hit the bed, I straddled his thighs, claiming him as my prize. "I think we've both waited more than long enough for that."

Holding his face in my hands, I kissed him soundly until he made the most gorgeous sound of surrender, kissing me back but letting me control the contact. Still drunk on him, I kissed him over and over, exploring his lips and mouth until we were both groaning.

"Okay, you win," he said breathlessly as I nipped at his stubbly jaw. Him clean-shaven and in a dress uniform was quite spectacular, but I also loved him all rumpled in vacation wear and too busy having fun to shave.

I poked him right in the center of his chest. "No, we both win."

"Absolutely." His eyes were glassy as he tried to pull me in for another kiss. "Damn, you're hot when you get all bossy."

"Yeah? If you like that…" Sitting back slightly, I yanked at his shirt. Chuckling, he made a show of being extra-docile and helping me undress him until that magnificent chest and all his golden skin and acres of muscles were all mine.

"You too." He didn't stay compliant long once naked, pushing my T-shirt up, eager grin erasing my exasperation.

"I'm focusing on you." I batted his hands away.

"Yeah, well, more of you to look at *is* for me." Winking, he tried again for my shirt, and this time I let him because flattery would get him everywhere. But as soon as we were both naked, I pushed him back on the bed and sank to my knees in front of him. My scrapes and bruises from the earlier fall protested a little, but I carefully kept from wincing. I wasn't going to let Derrick or a few bumps distract me out of this, not this time, but hurrying up did seem prudent.

Leaning in, I stroked my hands down his chest and dropped a kiss on his firm abs, right next to his straining cock. And all of a sudden, my stomach wobbled, unexpected nerves making my voice as unsteady as my touch. "I want all of your tips on how to do this right."

I'd fantasized about this so much that I dug my toes into the rug, trying to ensure that this wasn't a dream. Also, fantasy me was *good* at this, but real me was feeling every opportunity I'd missed to gain experience. But Derrick simply laughed and trailed a finger down my face.

"At this point, you could literally blow air on it, and it might be enough." His eyes were dark and glittery as he gazed down at me. And he got major bonus points for not suggesting that I didn't have to do this. I did. Even as I laughed along with him, my need only grew.

"Ha. Like this?" Puckering my mouth, I exhaled like I was trying to extinguish a candle, feathering my breath over the length of his cock. The first few times we'd fooled around, he hadn't let me have nearly enough time to explore how good his thick length felt in my hand. I rectified that now, stroking him as I continued to blow lightly, using air to caress him along with my fingers until he was breathing hard and fisted a hand in my hair.

"Enough teasing," he growled.

"But it's fun," I said right before I licked a long stripe from root to tip. His sharp inhale told me I was on the right track, and I licked more, discovering what spots made him moan. He kept his hand in my hair, not pushing but subtly guiding me in a way that made my own cock pulse. Experimenting, I went from licking to openmouthed kisses to sucking.

"Fuck. Yes. More," he urged as I took more of the shaft in my mouth. The heavy weight of him on my tongue was even more arousing than those fantasies of mine, and I hummed happily as I started a slow slide back and forth.

"Mmm." Gripping his base firmly, I kept myself from going too far down, setting a shallow rhythm that earned another low groan from him.

"Okay, I think you're a ringer. No way are you—" He cut himself off with a pained noise as I tried adding some tongue action to my sucking. "Fuck. Do that again."

I pulled back enough to grin at him. "Maybe I'm just a quick study."

"Knew you were a genius." He leaned back on his elbows. His enjoyment probably had more to do with a lengthy dry spell than any skill on my part, but the praise still emboldened me, made it easier to go faster, take more.

"Yeah. That. So…"

Reducing the big bad chief to babbling nonsense was an endorphin rush on par with a ten-mile run. "Good?"

"God, yes." He kept rocking his hips toward me, and his thigh was tense as a boulder under my other hand. But then he shuddered and used his hand on my head to still me. "Wait. Too close."

Oh fuck yes. No way was I backing off now. "Gimme."

"Damn. You want… Yeah. Okay. I've tested twice since… *fuck.*"

Laughing softly at his inability to finish a sentence, I redoubled my efforts, and simply knowing he was close was arousing enough that I had to move my hand from his thigh to my cock. Not stroking precisely, but the pressure of my grip was exactly what I needed to reach a place I usually only found in making music, a zone where time ceased to have meaning and where my actions seemed driven by something larger than myself. It was a place where I could give myself over to my instincts, trust that they'd be enough to get us both there.

Every moan and curse from Derrick pushed me higher and higher until I was moaning too, sounds muffled by his cock and somehow sexier for it.

"There. Right there." Some invisible thread of control snapped for Derrick, and his body bucked, chasing my mouth as everything got frantic and sloppy until he was climaxing and so was I. Coming with oxygen at a premium was a new one for me, made the peak that much sharper and the edges of my vision blur as I shot all over my fist. Those same instincts of mine that got us to this place made me reflexively swallow as Derrick too shuddered and shook. The salty, slightly bitter flavor was enough to coax one last spurt from my cock before I released his cock.

"Fuck." He flopped back against the bed. "Can't feel my legs."

"Good." Too spent to even laugh, I rested my head against his thigh.

"You're awfully smug. Damn. That was something else. Come up here so I can return the favor."

"Too late," I groaned as I wiped my hand off on my T-shirt before collapsing next to him on the bed.

"You came from that?" Rolling to his side, he peered down at me. "Wow."

"Yeah, well, it's your fault." My face was hot, more self-conscious than I would have thought. Trying to cover that, I made my voice flirtier. "You turn me on too much. But give me a few and I'll take you up on the offer."

"You're incorrigible." He gently tickled my side, but he

didn't say no. Win. With a repeat on the horizon, I felt less embarrassed about coming so fast.

"Lots of lost time to make up for." I winked at him even as my back tightened. It wasn't so much about making up for what I hadn't gotten around to in the past as wanting to squeeze every drop out of today, get my fill of Derrick fantasies before it was too late. But focusing on our agreement to keep things light was far preferable to admitting how much I was dreading parting.

"Hey, it's raining." Derrick motioned over at the closed window. The curtains meant we couldn't see the rain, but the soft *plink* of raindrops on the windowpanes and the roof echoed through the room.

"Maybe this means we'll actually get to sleep in." I stretched, trying to outrun my more melancholy thoughts, get back to the happy, sexy place Derrick seemed to be in.

"Always look on the bright side." It was the same advice I'd often given, including to him. Tomorrow's problems would be here soon enough. Choosing to live for tonight was only smart. Might as well ensure as many magical moonlit memories as possible.

Chapter Twenty-Three

Derrick

"I want to wake up like that every morning." Arthur's grin was enough to light up the rainy, dreary morning. I'd made the executive decision that we could be late to breakfast and instead proceeded to show Arthur that I could give as well as I got.

And holy hell, I'd gotten it good last night. My thighs trembled simply from the memory of his mouth. First-timer's luck? I wasn't sure I bought that, but whatever it was, Arthur had given me an all-time orgasm, and it was only fair—and fun—that I reciprocate. And apparently, I'd done well because he was still lying there all dreamy. His hair was all sleep and sex messed up and his dopey grin did excellent things for my ego.

"Coffee's probably getting cold," I teased.

"I like it better that way anyway." He nudged me with his foot, not seeming in any hurry to leave our cozy bed nest. "And hand-delivered. Thanks again for yesterday. You're going to make someone an awesome boyfriend when you're ready to date again."

His wistful tone made my chest hurt. "Don't be so sure."

I had no plans in that area and simply the idea of doing all these things with someone not Arthur made my jaw clench.

I didn't want someone new. I wanted him and that was becoming a problem.

"Derrick…" There was a question in his eyes, one I wasn't ready for. Not meeting his gaze, I hopped out of the bed and scrambled for some clothes.

"We should get you fed before they close the kitchen." My words came out too fast, but maybe Arthur was also looking for an escape because he didn't press me on the matter.

"Okay."

Of course, as soon as he started getting dressed, the urge to drag him back to bed returned. However, the change in topic and location would do us both good. We didn't need to dwell on the future, not when the present was so damn good and not when there wasn't a thing either of us could do to change that future either. He'd go his way and I'd go mine and that would be that. It was the only sensible course of action but one I was less and less sure I wanted.

After getting dressed, we headed out into the rain to the dining hall to join the rest of the stragglers in eating the last of the waffles while other folks enjoyed their second cup of coffee and milled around discussing the weather.

"Please tell me it's a board game and hot chocolate kind of day," Arthur said to his mom as she slid into a chair opposite us, coffee cup in hand.

"Better. We're taking advantage of the rain to do crafts. It'll be fun!"

"At least it's not hiking in the mud." Arthur gave her half a smile in return, which made her laugh.

"You had enough mud yesterday." She was almost always cheerful, a trait I admired, even if I had no clue how someone could be so bubbly twenty-four-seven. Even Arthur with his boundless good humor and patience got moody, which weirdly reassured me. Him being cranky about family stuff made my own broody tendencies feel more normal and also made him more human.

"True. Today I'm staying dry." He wagged his fork at her.

"Good plan. If you help with crafts, you can be in charge of board games this afternoon if the rain keeps up."

"Excellent. I've got a new dice one I'm dying to play. Does being in charge mean I can say no betting?"

"Your brothers just like having fun." She made a dismissive gesture. "You know that. It's not serious."

"Winning is always serious business in this family." Frowning, he leaned forward.

"Nothing wrong with that." Her smile never wavered.

"I don't know. Tying can be awfully fun." I shot Arthur a pointed look, memory of last night still fresh. Holding hands and dashing through the moonlight had been far sweeter than any victory.

"You two truly are perfect for each other." Her voice was light, but the words hit me like a dart because she was right. We were perfect, and that sucked because perfection was so damn rare.

"Yep," Arthur agreed and again my chest pinched hard. "Bring on the crafts. At least those aren't competitive."

He was wrong, though. The twins and Taylor staged a game of building Popsicle stick towers, with frequent shouts of "Winner!" and "Loser! You suck at stacking."

"Language," Stacey said mildly, not looking up from the collage she was making with her younger kid.

I, being the least artsy person in the world, put myself on cleanup duty, mopping up spilled glue and collecting paper trash. Meanwhile, Arthur was rolling modeling clay with the same girls he'd been teaching dance steps to the night before.

"What are you making?" I asked, resting my arms on the

back of his chair. The girls were constructing some sort of colorful blobs, but Arthur's efforts seemed a bit more deliberate.

"We're doing our dream homes." Tilting back, he smiled up at me, making me want to kiss him. I settled for ruffling his hair.

"Tell me about yours," I urged, surprised at how much I wanted to know.

"This is the main part of the house." He gestured at a square he'd built in cheerful blue clay. A vision of a little blue house floated through my brain. Somewhere quiet, with rooms that smelled like mint and tea, not the strange odors that seemed to permeate ships and barracks.

"I like it," I said softly.

"And this is the bathroom with a big tub." He winked at me and my cheeks heated.

"And there?" I pointed at a yellow rectangle, which rivaled the blue one for size.

"That's the music studio." His fond smile did something to my insides. Made them warm and gushy when I wasn't a warm and gushy guy.

"It's bigger than the rest of the house," I teased even as I could picture it, a large, sunny space with good acoustics.

"Yeah, well, I need room for all my ancient instruments." He stretched, arms hitting me. I captured them, more to have him near for a second than to protect myself. Laughing, he quickly freed himself. "God, an actual office would be so nice. Dedicated composing space, no roommate drama."

"Yeah," I agreed. *I could give him that.* The thought was fanciful, as out of place as a doily on a submarine, but I couldn't shake it. As a chief, I didn't have to live in the barracks at all. I had plenty of options, but no real incentive to explore any of them.

You could. I didn't like that thought either. I didn't want to want these things, didn't want to feel their absence on such a visceral level. I was happy with my life how it was. I didn't need a house. But then I looked down at Arthur's sculpture again, and oh, how I wanted.

"It's not happening any time soon." He whacked the clay, and just like that the dream collapsed, smushed by his hand until the pretty blue house was now a bird, one that he used to make the girls and me laugh by flying it around. "What should I make next?"

"Do a boat," one of the girls requested.

"Here, I'll do Derrick's boat." A few turns of his long fingers later and he had a reasonable approximation of a sub. "Glug. Glug. See it sail?"

"Subs don't sail." The older girl had an arch look for him.

"Okay." Cheerful as ever, he kept moving his creation around. "It's swimming the ocean blue. Seeing sea creatures and exploring."

"Ha. If only that was our mission." I laughed, but something twanged deep in my chest, a memory maybe of my younger self, of what I'd thought this life might be like, and the reality of what it was. And it wasn't a bad reality at all, but it also wasn't the stuff of Arthur's daydreams either. And that made me sad for reasons I couldn't afford to think about right then.

"The sun's out!" The other girl cheered, quickly joined by the voices of other excited kids.

"Darn." Arthur started cleaning up the clay. "Way to foil my plans."

"I'll play your dice game later," I promised. "We don't need rain for that."

"Best boyfriend ever." He gave a happy wriggle, and in that moment, I truly hoped I was, hoped I was exactly what he wanted and needed.

Chapter Twenty-Four

Arthur

"I think we're lost," I announced to Derrick as we passed a stump I swore we'd seen twenty minutes prior.

"We're not lost." That he could keep his patience with me even when I was being extra dramatic was one of the things I liked most about him. That and how he was holding my hand, even with no one around to see his perfect-boyfriend act except me.

"I haven't heard the others in at least ten minutes." Turning my head, I glanced behind us, but yep, only trees, not a Euler in sight.

"Five of those don't count." He gave me an arch look before copping another feel of my ass. It was true that we'd lost track of the others around the time he'd dragged me behind a particularly dense thicket of trees and kissed me until my toes curled in my hiking boots.

"True." My skin heated and the temptation to repeat the interlude made my pulse thrum. "Still, I think we're going in circles, and we haven't added anything new to our list."

I held up the list for the annual scavenger hunt. It was filled with things that might be found in or around the camp like four-leaf clovers and bird feathers and playing cards. So far we'd found a blue shirt and a flip-flop, but only because I'd had both those things back at our cabin. However, another kissing break there had put us further behind the rest of the teams.

Not that Derrick seemed to care.

"So? We're having fun, right?" After shrugging, he grabbed my hand again. "Isn't that your whole message? Have fun, don't worry about winning?"

"Yeah, but that doesn't mean I *like* coming in last either." I might rail against the family competitive gene, but I could also admit to being plagued by dreams of winning, same as my brothers.

"Hey, maybe they'll have an award for the team who got the least number of items. Then we can still be winners. Er… losers. Winners at losing?" Derrick gave me a lopsided grin.

Winners at losing. The notes to a song I'd been trying to write all week slid into place. This. This was the big idea I'd been waiting for. "You're brilliant."

"I am?" Derrick tilted his head, nose wrinkling like I'd stopped making sense, which was a strong possibility. "I was more trying for goofy and kissable there. I'll take brilliant though."

"You're definitely kissable." Stopping at a clearing, I leaned in to give him a quick kiss. "And you gave me the best idea."

"Oh? Tell me." The way he demanded, all eager and happy for me, made my chest so light that his hand was the only reason I didn't float away.

"Okay, so you know how I've been pissed about the idea of certain kids winning and certain kids losing at talent night?" I'd made him listen to several rants on this topic in the last few days.

"Yeah. I like how your choreography makes sure they each have a moment to shine." The pride in his voice sounded genuine, not like part of the good-boyfriend act. He'd paid attention to those rants too, always listening and not telling me to just deal with my bad attitude. In fact, his concern always managed to take the edge off my anger, made it so that I could continue finding ways to enjoy myself outside of the family drive to succeed. Like kissing him senseless every chance I got. People who listened as well as Derrick were rare as fuck and needed to be rewarded.

"Thanks for your help, too. But what if they were all winners?"

"What? They can't all win." Looking every inch the by-the-rules military man, he pursed his mouth.

"Sure they can." It was my turn to be the patient one. "We make the rules. If I say everyone wins, then everyone wins. No more first-place and runner-up bullshit. I'm going to have Best Smile and Loudest Laugh and Highest Kick. Everyone wins something and no more ranking the results."

He nodded thoughtfully. "Like superlatives in school, but they're all good ones?"

"Yup. A whole stack of winners." I bounced on my feet. I fucking loved my brain sometimes. It was all I could do not to dash back to camp right then.

"Your mom may hate this change. I think she liked the idea of handing out trophies."

"She can deal. And we can use her prizes. I'll just need a few more." I finally caught sight of one of the taller camp buildings, a two-story lodge, and I started heading that direction.

"Hey, where are you going?"

Oops. I'd totally forgotten to tell Derrick the rest of my plan.

"Sorry. I get like this composing, too. I get a big idea and I want to do it right away. I'm so pumped that I want to start making certificates and prizes. Screw the rest of the scavenger hunt that we weren't going to win anyway."

"Yep." Derrick took my hand and led me several steps out of the forest, right to…

"The path? You knew where we were the whole time?"

"Maybe." Derrick didn't look all that contrite. "Maybe I like being lost with you."

"You are *so* getting lucky later," I promised because it was that or collapse in a giant puddle of goo over his ability to say the absolute perfect thing.

"Counting on it." Derrick sped up his steps toward main camp. "We can probably raid the art supplies from yesterday."

"Seriously?" I stopped in the middle of the path to whirl on him. I hadn't expected him to drop the scavenger hunt. Or want to help. "You're simply going to follow along with my idea?"

"Why not? It's a good idea. And you're cute all fired up. Who wouldn't want to help you?"

"Who indeed. Damn, Derrick, I—"

Derrick cut off my big sappy declaration with another kiss, which was probably for the better. Telling him how much he meant to me, how very much I liked him, wasn't going to change reality. But like him I did, everything from how he kissed me to the bounce in his step as we hurried to the dining hall building. I was the one with the big idea, but he was right there, handing me colorful construction paper and locating a tub of markers.

"Okay, put me to work." He grabbed a blank piece of paper and attached it to a clipboard. "I can start a list for you of who's getting what."

"Organization. I love it. Knew you were good for something." I made stacks of the various colors of paper, trying to visualize how I wanted the certificates to look.

"Hey, I'm good for lots." Already he had a neat list of names in blocky handwriting, the sort of initiative I found super attractive. I was used to pulling off projects like this without assistance, and having him help was a much-appreciated novelty.

"Yeah, you are." Leaning in, I gave him a fast kiss.

"Don't tempt me into forgetting your big plan." He turned me back toward the table. "Work first, then play."

"I'm going to hold you to that."

"Gladly." He gave me a look with enough heat to melt a box of crayons. Damn the way he fired me up. He distracted me from work in a way that nothing else ever had.

"Oops." Too busy cataloging all the shades of amber in his eyes, I accidentally smeared the glitter pen I was outlining a name with. "Hopefully Lila doesn't mind a little extra glitter on her sign."

"Never too much glitter. One year I made ornaments with my grandma. I was in middle school, much too cool for crafts, but she insisted. I found glitter in my hair for weeks, but it was worth it for how much her friends raved over the ornaments we gave them." Derrick's nostalgic tone made me wish yet again I could have met his grandmother, if only to thank her for raising such an amazing human.

"That's awesome." Handing him Lila's sign to put with the other finished ones, I started the next. "I love your stories about her and her friends."

"They were quite the group. A few of them are still kicking."

"Really? We—err, *you* should totally road trip to see them." I stopped just short of volunteering myself for another vacation with Derrick.

"Maybe. I send cards as I can when I'm stateside."

Derrick's thoughtful tone made me weirdly hopeful he might take my suggestion. And if he did, then maybe I could renew my bid to join him and...

And what? I could already hear the playlist, but I had to

drop my fantasy even if I loved the idea of Derrick and me and the open road and not a relative in sight. A vacation just for the hell of it, just the two of us, no fake relationship, simply because we liked hanging out.

"Bet they appreciate the contact," I said instead of pressing my idea.

"I think they do. It was fun to send a picture of my car to Flora, the lady who taught me how to change oil. She sent a reply saying I overpaid, but also Grandma would have been proud at me saving up for it."

"I'm sure she'd be proud of you for all sorts of reasons." Reaching over to his chair, I gave him a fast one-armed hug.

"Thanks. I think that's why I like being around your family so much." Derrick added my next sign to the pile, straightening them into a precise stack he was cross-referencing with his list. "It reminds me of the best days hanging with Grandma and her friends, the friendly bickering with an added benefit of seeing what cousins and siblings would have been like."

"I'm sorry you didn't get that when you were little." I had a tendency to dwell on my own childhood inadequacies and disappointments, but Derrick's stories were a good reminder that plenty of people had had it far worse than me. A little teasing was hardly on par with being an orphan. "But I'm glad you had her in your life when you needed her."

"Yeah. My early years were kind of…hectic. Lots of loud arguments and moving around a lot." Derrick's eyes took on a far-off cast, but I didn't dare interrupt him because this was the most he'd shared about his biological parents. "I don't remember a ton, to be honest. My parents had a very dysfunctional off-and-on-again relationship before they died in a car accident. The social workers placed me with Grandma. Upended her retirement, but she never complained."

"Why would she? You're pretty awesome." I gave him another hug, this one tighter. I couldn't take his loss away, but I could let him know he wasn't alone now. I wanted to tell him he could borrow my family whenever he wanted, wished that was something I could offer him for more than a week. Derrick deserved a family.

"Thanks." He leaned into my hug. "And thanks for listening. I don't talk about the past a ton."

I could sense from the tension in his shoulders that he didn't want the conversation to turn too heavy, so I made my voice teasing as I nudged him. "You? The silent type? Never."

"Ha. But I mean it. You make me want to talk and talk."

"I like that." Our gazes linked, and it was all I could do to not swoon in the face of that compliment and the warmth in his eyes. Something was happening here, something big, something I couldn't name, and I was powerless to look away.

However, right as I leaned in farther, the door to the dining hall swung open and Aunt Sandy burst in. Apparently, there was no moment too sweet for familial interruption around here.

"What are you guys doing?" she asked. "You can't hide out here all day."

"Sure we can." I laughed, but I felt my words in my soul, another powerful brainstorm hitting me. We didn't have to do the scavenger hunt. Or anything else we didn't want to do. *We make the rules,* I'd told Derrick. And maybe that applied to more than simply awards or activities. Perhaps there was a deeper lesson there if I was brave enough to listen.

Chapter Twenty-Five

Derrick

"Training circus seals might be easier than this." Arthur clutched a clipboard in one hand as he gestured with the other at the throng of kids milling around the back of the dining hall in the makeshift backstage area for talent night.

"More of our recruits might listen to us in real SEAL training." Laughing, I clapped him on the shoulder. "You've done amazing. The last run-through sounded great and no one fell."

"Thanks. I want things to go perfectly." His nerves were kind of cute. And also, something I could help with.

"They will. And luckily for you, I'd make a decent ringmaster for that circus." I gave a piercing warning whistle, breaking through the kid chaos. "Okay, team, huddle up!"

"I never thought I'd find whistling such a turn-on." Arthur used a low whisper as the kids made their way back to us.

"What can I say? I'm a guy of many talents," I joked right before I whistled again to hurry the kids up. "Everyone listen up. We need to form a line from youngest to oldest."

"That's going to be our show order," Arthur added, glancing down at his clipboard. "That way the little kids have to wait the least."

"I wanted to be first!" Vince was predictably the loudest dissenter.

"No, I should be first," Taylor countered, shoving his cousin.

"I'm older." Seth had a self-important air, but Vince made a scoffing noise.

"By thirty seconds, doofus."

"Still older." Seth crossed his arms over his bony chest.

"Whatever. If you're older, I'm going first." Fist pumping, Vince did a move that was somewhere between martial arts and victory dance.

"Hey, I'm younger than both of you. That makes me first." Taylor's triumphant wiggle served to make both twins groan.

"Enough." I whistled again and added a handclap for good measure. "There will plenty of applause for everyone. And going last is great too. Then you're like the closing pitcher in baseball."

"Ha. Dudes, I'm the closer." Seth seized the opportunity to glare at the other two.

"No, I'm—"

"You stand here. And you here." I directed them into order for the line. "If you can stay quiet long enough for Arthur's announcements, I'll let you look at my car's engine tomorrow."

Vince got a speculative look. "Before we leave?"

"Yeah, before then." Damn it. I didn't like the reminder of how few hours we had left. I didn't want to think about tomorrow, driving back with Arthur, planning for our breakup and returning to a real world where Arthur wasn't in my bed each night. How had we run out of time? My stomach churned.

But there was no time for brooding. We had a show to put on. After we got the kids in a line, I wrote down the order for Arthur so that he'd know who to introduce when, while I handled the music for him.

"I need a better costume," Seth lamented when I returned to his part of the line. "And Taylor has props."

"Yeah, but he can't sing as fast as you. If you do your best, it won't matter what you're wearing. Be the best Seth you can be." I channeled a hefty dose of Arthur in my advice. *Be the best you.* That was exactly what I'd done all week. It felt like I'd been the best version of myself in a way that maybe I hadn't been since my early days on the sub. I liked who I was around Arthur and the Euler family. This was who I'd wanted to be with Steve. Maybe Arthur had been right about both of us needing boyfriend practice. Or maybe Steve hadn't been Arthur.

Across the grass, Arthur straightened Lila's tutu before showing a different girl how to bow with a flourish. Yup. That was the answer. It wasn't me. Wasn't getting boyfriend practice or even this place. It was Arthur. He was magic.

And for his sake, I wanted the show to go as well as he hoped. His family damn well better appreciate all his hard work.

"Everyone ready?" he asked as he retrieved the box of prizes from a nearby stump. "It's showtime. Don't forget to smile. And have fun! This is all about having fun."

"And winning," Vince added darkly.

"I'm gonna slay you." Seth bared his teeth at his brother, but Arthur simply gave a patient nod.

"Just by showing up and trying, you're all winners." His voice was as reassuring as his demeanor, but the boys rolled their eyes.

"Life's no fun without a winner," Vince insisted. He sounded exactly like Calder. How much of my life had I wasted thinking like them? Even now, counting down to my next advancement in rank, my next award or ribbon. My drive to achieve had brought me this far, but had it brought me happiness? I was no longer so sure.

"It's more fun when you tie." Arthur shot me a small, secret smile. Hell, I'd lose every bet for the next two years if it meant more smiles like those.

"And when others around you win too," I added.

"Like your crew." Taylor nodded sagely, but actually I'd been thinking less of my shipmates and more about how proud I was of Arthur and these kids. In fact, as I helped him lead them into the dining hall, I wasn't sure I'd ever been this proud or nervous for another person.

"Good luck," I said as he passed by me on his way to the front of the room, where all the older family members were already waiting.

"Thanks. Tell me I get a reward later that doesn't involve auto repair."

"What? I can't bribe you with a look under my hood?" I joked before touching his hand, voice more serious now. "You get whatever you want."

I meant it. There wasn't much I wouldn't try with him if it made him happy. Him happy meant everything to me.

Thus, it shouldn't have been that surprising that my stomach kept wobbling and my pulse racing, weirdly nervous for him wanting the event to go off without a hitch.

"Welcome to talent night!" Arthur was cheerful and commanding as he took center stage at the front of the room. He didn't even need my whistle to get people's attention. He probably could have wrangled all the kids without me too, but he'd let me help and made me feel necessary. Maybe like me, he simply liked spending time and working together.

That thought made me so warm that I almost missed the cue to start the music for the opening number. It was an upbeat pop number that came from a family movie I'd never seen, but the song was an ode to being oneself. Arthur had ensured that the kids sang loud and clear and his choreography was super cute.

Be yourself. With him I could do exactly that, and watching him be Arthur, dancing and singing with the kids, made my chest expand so far I worried for my ribs. He was exactly who he needed to be, and I wanted him to never change.

He continued to be effervescent as he introduced the little kids who went first. A number of dancers and nervous singers along with some comical animal impressions rounded out the first part of the show.

"Now we have Taylor, who is going to share some impersonations of humans you may recognize."

Taylor kept to his promise and didn't do one of his mother, but his ability to mimic Oliver and his grandfather got big laughs. And he slapped on headphones for his "Do you" and "Just have fun" Arthur impression that showed that maybe he'd been listening through all the dance rehearsals.

"And I can do Derrick too." He grinned big as he replaced the headphones with sunglasses of a similar style to ones I'd worn that week. Giving a stern look, he did a whistle that wasn't a bad imitation of mine. "Listen to Arthur! Arthur's the best."

He finished with a dopey lovesick look that made the audience laugh loud. And made me think. Hard. That wasn't me, was it? Hanging on Arthur's every word, following him around, looking at him like he personally had stapled the sun into place. Except maybe that was me, and I wasn't even sure it was a bad thing. Who wouldn't be a little lovesick over Arthur?

As the audience applauded for Taylor, I chewed on my lip, brain still churning. Vince was next and took three tries before kicking apart a flimsy board.

"Next, Seth is bringing us his special super-fast singing."

An extremely twitchy Seth shot me a nervous look as he stepped forward. I gave him a big thumbs-up and mouthed, "You got this."

My chest pinched hard. All week I'd considered this project as something I was doing for Arthur, a way to help him. But maybe it had been for me too. And I wasn't sure I was ready for all these deep realizations about myself and life, but at the same time, I wouldn't trade the small smile Seth gave me. This show had meant something to all of us.

Seth's fast renditions of several classic songs earned him lots of applause, and he exited with a far bigger grin than he'd started with.

"Way to go," I called to him as Arthur assembled everyone for the next musical number. This song was all about the importance of trying, with lots of big arm movements and earnest singing. Like with that look from Seth, it felt like the universe was trying to tell me something via the song, a message that maybe I didn't want to hear right then.

Trying and failing is better than never trying at all. I wasn't sure where I'd learned that. Possibly Grandma. As Arthur led the kids through their steps, I stopped fighting my own emotions, let the song wash over me, let myself wallow in the pride and admiration I was feeling. In that moment, he was my guy, and it was wonderful, and I couldn't wait to get him alone, let our bodies do the talking.

Maybe it was time for me to try too.

"Now for our winners!" At the end, Arthur handed out the prizes. Every single kid got an award and a round of applause. Watching their faces light up, I finally understood why Arthur had fought so hard for this. It wasn't that he didn't like winning, but rather that he wanted everyone to have that thrill of victory. And he'd done it, given each of the kids a moment to shine. At the end, I applauded harder than anyone else.

"That was so fun! Thank you for all your hard work." Arthur's mom came up to him after the show, when the kids had all rushed back to their parents, who were busy taking pictures and admiring costumes. She had a tight hug for Arthur before adding, "I'm not sure we needed quite so many winners, but the kids seem happy."

"They're all winners." Arthur disentangled himself from the hug.

"Yeah, they are. Nice job, bro." Oliver came over right then, unexpectedly agreeing with Arthur. He had a hearty slap on the back for Arthur and more words of praise for the show before turning to me. "Are we going to see you for cards tonight?"

"Nah. I think... I have plans." I glanced over at Arthur. We hadn't said as much, but he had to be all jazzed on adrenaline from the performance, much like a successful mission, and I wanted to be there for him.

"Oh, I see how it is." Oliver gave a knowing eyebrow waggle.

"How what is?" Calder came loping over, friends following behind him.

"Romeo here is ditching cards again." Oliver was rather gleeful in delivering that bit of news even as Calder frowned.

"Is he?" Calder had a speculative look for me, one that matched his deceptively casual tone and promised a lengthy inquisition later, but I had run out of fucks to give for bets and card playing. I had better things to do. Also, it was the last night here, and there was nowhere I'd rather be than with Arthur. No way was I ditching Arthur to play cards even if it earned me a lecture from Calder.

"Sorry. Already made plans."

"I see." Calder's mouth pursed. He'd have questions for me

later, undoubtedly ones I'd rather not answer, but I'd rather brave that gauntlet than lose my chance with Arthur.

"You didn't have to do that," Arthur said a few moments later when we were packing up his speaker and other supplies. "You can go play cards."

"I don't want to. I'd rather celebrate your big night."

"It did go well, didn't it?" His little smile was more than worth whatever retribution Calder wanted to dish out. I'd do his laundry for a month or sit through a dozen card games if it meant getting to see Arthur like this. Arthur's pink cheeks and glowing eyes made me feel as light and bouncy as he always managed to be, like I too might sing and dance at a moment's notice.

"It really did. You did good." Not caring who might still be milling around, I gave him a tight hug from behind. "And I believe I promised you a reward. I'm not going back on that."

"Good. I know exactly what I want."

"I can't wait." Whatever he wanted, I was going to try my damnedest to give to him.

Chapter Twenty-Six

Arthur

Derrick was in the mood to indulge me, and luckily for both of us, I still had a hefty chunk of my sexy wish list left to request, all things we would hopefully both enjoy. I couldn't wait.

"Everyone wins," I said more or less to myself as we headed toward our cabin.

"They do." Plucking the box with my speaker and other supplies out of my arm, he gave me a fancy spin, like an orchestra was lurking in the forest, and this path was our own personal dance floor.

"I thought being goofy was my schtick, not yours." I kept my voice light to cover how damn charmed I was.

"Hey, you don't have a monopoly on silliness. Or romance." He kept up our little impromptu starlight waltz with another spin.

"Is that what this is? Romance?"

I'd still been teasing, but Derrick's face went surprisingly solemn. "I think so. Yeah."

"Not sure I can handle you all romantic." Dropping the joking, I went for honest. Him charming and attentive, being the best fake boyfriend ever, was devastating enough. But adding actual romance to our little fling would be a bad, bad idea.

"What do you think we've been doing all week?" Frowning, he stopped the dance, making me instantly regret my comment.

And making me stop and think. What *had* we done all week? All the sneaky kisses and little gestures. He'd been being romantic for days now, and I'd been purposely obtuse, chalking it all up to the ruse. But I needed to admit if only to myself that I too hadn't acted in quite some time.

"Good point. But—"

"No *buts*." He set a finger over my lips. "Not tonight, okay?"

As usual he was right. This wasn't the moment to have a deep conversation about the state of our fling. We were supposed to be celebrating. "Tonight was pretty darn magical."

"You are pretty darn magical all on your own." Grabbing my hand again, he peered so intently into my eyes that I had to look away, terrified of what he might find written on my soul.

"Maybe you make me that way," I countered, more truth there than I'd like to admit.

"Nah. You didn't really need my help."

"Didn't mean the show." I stretched to brush a kiss across his lips, trying to bring back the playful mood.

"Me either." He kissed me back, soft and sweet, before spinning me again, this time in the direction of our cabin. "Come on, Cinderfella, let's get you your reward before the clock strikes midnight."

"Worried I might turn into a pumpkin?" Midnight did loom far closer than I wanted it to. *Last night.* I'd tried all day not to think about it, but thoughts of how much goodbye was going to suck kept wiggling past my defenses. And judging by the return of Derrick's serious face, he too wasn't happy about time slipping away from us.

"Something like that." Unlocking the door, he ushered me into the cabin. "You're all mine now."

"I am." After he turned the fireplace on, I looped my arms

around his neck, pulling him close. Midnight could wait. Right now this was everything, and I kissed him like time had no meaning, like we could be right here when the sun came back up, and I'd be totally happy to be still kissing.

But eventually the need for oxygen did win out, and he pulled away, breathing hard as he darted his gaze toward the bed. "Tell me what you want."

"I want to try fucking." All week we'd been sort of dancing around the subject, inching closer but not yet crossing that line. I'd sensed him holding back, and I hadn't pressed the subject because everything else we'd tried had been so damn good. But now time was running out and I was at least going to ask. "And I know you're going to say—"

"Yes. I'm going to say yes." His voice was as serious as his eyes, but his mouth was soft as he gave me another fast kiss.

"Damn it, Derrick, I had a whole speech planned." Laughing, I broke apart enough to push at his shirt. "I know you're good with what we've been doing and that you probably think I should wait, but I want this. I want it to be you."

"I want it to be me too," he whispered as he let me remove his shirt. "And maybe that's selfish and—"

"Be selfish." I ran my hands over his strong shoulders. "Please."

"Well, if you're asking…" Chuckling, he caught me for another soft kiss. "Which way were you craving?"

"There's a choice?" Much as I appreciated him offering, I'd always assumed Derrick was all about topping.

"Dork." He gently smacked me with his discarded shirt. "Of course there's a choice. Plenty of them. Maybe not all in one night—"

"I want you to fuck me." All my remaining breath gusted out. If I let myself be honest, I'd wanted that for years, and no way was I missing my chance. However, the other option would likely lead to even more heated fantasies later. Derrick turning out to be happily vers? Yes, please. Sign me up.

Derrick must have liked the request because he smiled slowly, a wide, sexy grin that made his dark eyes sparkle.

"Tell me you brought supplies." Still in his jeans, he turned toward the dresser. "I've maybe got a condom in my shaving kit, but not sure I'm trusting the expiration date."

"I've got us covered. Not that I was planning. Or hoping." My rambling was coming out much too fast, but I couldn't seem to slow it down as I lunged for my bag. "Somehow lube and these condoms Sabrina gave me as a joke gift hopped in my bag when I was packing."

"Well, I'm grateful." Laughing as I tossed the stuff on the bed, he suddenly sobered as he picked up the box. "Wait. These were a gag gift? Do they work?"

"Standard condoms. Fun mystery colors." I plucked the box back out of his fingers and returned it to the bed. "Trust me that I want this so bad, I can handle whatever shade it turns out to be."

"Me too." Derrick pushed my shirt off so that I matched him, and then we both slid our pants off, leaving us bare and kissing by the side of the bed. "Damn, you're so hot."

"Flatterer. I'm already a sure thing." I made a giddy sound as he pulled me to straddle his lap, with him sitting on the bed. All week, this had been one of my favorite ways to make out because it made me feel so close to him and also negated our height difference nicely.

"I mean it." When he peered up at me, the warmth in his eyes was unmistakable.

"Well, I certainly feel hot when you look at me like that." Arching my back, I deliberately made my cock brush his stomach, loving how that made him inhale sharply.

"Oh, I'm looking at you. And you look damn tasty." His

gaze intensified to something primal, and then I was the one gasping as he claimed my mouth in a blistering kiss. We kissed and kissed, so thoroughly that I was rocking against him and he was groaning softly when we finally came up for air.

"You can...*fuck*." Whatever tease I'd been about to make died as Derrick slid a hand between us, stroking my cock with a firm grip. After all that kissing, I was way too ramped up for that kind of teasing. "Unless you're trying to make this over with in a hurry, please."

"Please what?" He looked up, all satisfied grin and fake innocent eyes. I fumbled around, finally finding the lube and shaking it at him. Still didn't move off his lap because the position was too delicious to waste.

"Please fuck me. Now."

"So very bossy." Palming my ass, he squeezed and rubbed, heating me up there too.

"Believe it was you who said you like me bossy." My cock painted a wet stripe across his abs, and I made a needy noise.

"I like you all sorts of ways," he said archly. After taking the lube from me, he used slick fingertips to rob me of the ability to do much more than softly moan as he rubbed circles right where I most wanted his touch. "Especially like you like this. Man, your eyes..."

"Oh." I managed a single syllable as he pushed a finger in. His fingers were surprisingly so different from my own that the sensations were overwhelming, the newness more disconcerting than any physical discomfort.

"Doing okay?" he asked, slowing his explorations.

"Yeah. Ready." *So ready.* I found his mouth for another kiss while he continued to touch me. I'd waited so long for this, and that urgency came out in the kiss that fast turned sloppy and desperate. "Please."

"Don't want to rush this." He nipped at my jaw. "Want to get it right."

"You are." I groaned as his devious fingers found a particularly good spot inside me. "You so are. Come on. Please. Want it."

"Now who's the flatterer?" Withdrawing his fingers, he grabbed a condom. "You want it like this? Might be easier on you."

"You letting me drive?" I laughed even as my stomach did this little flip, anticipation rising. "Not gonna turn that down."

"Good. I like this." Then he was the one to laugh as he opened the condom and revealed a green so neon it might be visible from space. "Damn. That's some mystery color."

"Yep. Still want it. Get it on," I demanded, moving back on his thighs so he had room to roll the condom on. Yep. Very neon. And I was very much not caring.

"Slow," he ordered as he held the base of his cock and urged me into position with his other hand. Like his fingers, the blunt pressure was different from playing around on my own. Not painful, but something to get used to. "That's it. Breathe."

"Easier...said...than...done."

"I know." Keeping his voice low and soothing, he ran a hand down my back. "Go as slow as you need."

Easing down, I willed my body to relax, making small movements with my hips. My brain kept trying to catalog all the new sensations, but then I lowered a little farther and that spot inside me lit up. I wanted more. Right that second. "Oh. That."

"Like that?" Derrick rocked up into me then, guiding my motions with his hands, and I finally got out of my head enough to simply move with him. My body seemed to know the rhythm on its own, and the more I let go, the better it felt.

"More."

"Fuck. Yes." Our movements became more frantic, like Derrick had been waiting for that signal from me that he too could let go.

"Kiss me," I demanded, needing even more contact, more connection. Kissing him like this felt different, a new level of intensity, and I couldn't get enough. Energy arced from the top of my head, past our linked mouths, intensifying around my ass and cock, and spreading out all the way to my toes. He held me so close that the tenderness was almost too much while also being the compass guiding me through the waves of sensations.

"Fuck. You're going to get me off." Groaning, Derrick tipped his head back, eyes falling shut, neck and shoulder muscles straining. "Too good."

"Oh yes." I hadn't realized how much I wanted that until he said it. He always had such a tight lid on his control that watching it snap was mesmerizing. "Do it, please."

He worked a hand between us, stroking my cock in concert with our motions. His other hand was warm and present against my back, the tension in his grip so arousing, knowing I had him that worked up. His touch felt good, but coming myself felt far less urgent than watching him give in to the pleasure.

"Come on, Derrick." My grip on his shoulders tightened, anticipation thrumming through me. I wanted him to shatter, wanted to know that I'd inspired that. Trying to spur him on, I moved faster. Harder. Met each of his thrusts until we were both moaning.

"That's it." He kissed me with a new desperation right before shuddering. "Oh. Fuck. Coming."

I could *feel* it, the pulse deep inside me, the way he groaned and shook, and it was almost enough to take me along for the ride. Giddy and more than a little buzzed on power, I felt skyscraper high. "Fuck. That was so hot."

"Yeah, it was." His voice was sleepy, but he sped up his hand on my cock. "Your turn now."

"Not sure..." I shifted around, body searching for something that seemed to be just out of reach.

"I got you." Gently, he withdrew his cock before he dropped his hand from my back to my ass, squeezing.

"Oh." There it was, the edge, rushing up toward me, each sensation magnified now. The tightness of his grip. The subtle ache in my ass. His lips on my neck. "Fuck. Yes. Right...."

Then I was coming, and he was holding me and murmuring nonsense as I shot over and over, so hard my whole body curved inward until I couldn't stay upright and collapsed against him. Tumbling backward, we ended up in a messy heap, him softly kissing my temple while I made involuntary happy noises.

"Was that worth the wait?" he asked, tone a little too careful to be completely casual.

"Hell, yes." On so many levels the wait had been more than worth it. That had been gorgeous and special and everything I ever wanted in a first time.

"Good." He kissed my mouth then, but I didn't miss the flash of relief in his eyes. This meaning something to him only jazzed me up further, made me move restlessly against him.

"Damn. I'm still all ramped up from the show. And I don't want to fall asleep." I didn't want to waste a minute of this closeness, didn't want morning to come, wanted to lie right there forever.

"I know. Me either." He pressed another kiss into my hair.

"We could always play chess." Laughing, I nudged him with my elbow.

"Ha. I know exactly what you need."

"Excellent." Didn't matter what it was, I was game, especially if it kept me from thinking.

Chapter Twenty-Seven

Derrick

"I knew this tub was good for something." Arthur stretched like a happy puppy, his damp head falling back against my shoulder. We were wedged in the tub, him sitting in front of me, sudsy water surrounding us. I'd found a candle under the sink, and we'd lit it, keeping the room lights low so we could admire the moon over the lake through the window. "This was an excellent idea. Thanks."

"You sure hinted enough all week." I trailed my fingers down his ribs. The water smelled like the herbal bubble bath Arthur had dumped in. Years from now, I'd likely smell rosemary and be overcome with nostalgia, and I was okay with that as I wanted to do whatever I could to preserve this moment.

"I did, didn't I?"

"You did." I laughed because despite having fooled around in the shower earlier in the week, he had continued to remark how we'd both fit in the tub. He wasn't exactly subtle about what he wanted, but I loved that about him. Giving him what he wanted was easy and made me feel like a lotto winner.

"And look at us. We made it the whole week and no one needed to sleep in the tub."

"We did good." I hugged him tighter against me. He wasn't

the only one who didn't want to sleep. I wasn't ready for morning at all.

"We did." Arthur gave a contented sigh. "Never thought I'd say this, but I wish the week didn't have to end."

"Me either." I took a deep breath. I wasn't getting a better opening than that for all the thoughts that had been plaguing me all day. "Maybe it doesn't..."

"*Derrick.*" Twisting in my arms, Arthur glared at me. I was violating the rules of this fling, but ever since that song about trying, I kept coming back to the idea that we owed it to ourselves to give this thing between us a real chance.

"Hear me out. There's no real deadline for us to break up, right?"

He exhaled hard. "Other than the fact that my brother is probably chomping at the bit for that to happen."

"I'll handle him," I promised, saying the words I should have said sooner. Calder was amazing and I wouldn't trade our friendship for anything, but Arthur was *Arthur*, and I wasn't going to let loyalty to Calder be the stumbling block to one of the best things I'd ever found.

"*Handling* sounds ominous." He barked out a laugh.

"I decided to stop caring so much about his reaction." Had I reached that conclusion sooner, we might have had one more night, and right then, every hour felt precious. "You and I already slept together. And like you pointed out numerous times, you're a fully consenting adult. If he wants to deck me over us hooking up, that's on him."

"Yup. It is. But I also don't want to tank your decade-plus of friendship." Arthur rubbed my knee. "If we end it now, you can both pretend whatever happened was simply part of the ruse, maybe avoid a fight over this."

"Perhaps it would be worth the fight." Voice solemn, I put my hand over his on my leg. I didn't say that lightly, but I also couldn't shake the feeling that for the rest of my life I'd regret not fighting for more time with Arthur.

"What do you mean?"

"I mean I don't want to end it now," I said firmly.

"Thought you were dead set against a rebound relationship—or any relationship for that matter?"

It was true that I really didn't want another messy breakup like Steve, but a week of pretending to be Arthur's boyfriend had left me convinced that what I did want was an Arthur. "But here I am having one anyway."

"Here we are." Arthur sounded so sad that I wasn't sure what I could do other than try to gather him closer.

"You don't have to sound so miserable."

"I'm not." He flicked a stray bubble off his chest. "More like I'm pouting because I don't want to end it either, but I know it has to."

"Does it though? Is there some rule that says we can't simply keep it going? I'm likely to be stateside for a while. We can—"

"Keep hooking up?" He was a little too fast at answering for me. Frowning, I brushed the soap off his neck.

"I was going to say *date*, but sure." Hooking up or friends with benefits was way more casual than I felt about Arthur, but I'd take him however he wanted it to be. "Whichever you'd be most comfortable with. I'm not looking for a label. I just want more time with you, whatever you want to call it."

Arthur groaned at that, making me wince.

"Sorry. Not the most romantic answer, I know."

"No, you're all kinds of romantic and that's the problem. Sex by itself makes it hard enough to remember I'm not supposed to be falling for you." Stretching a leg out, he kicked at the faucet with his toe. "Dating would be like signing up for the heartache express."

"Would it? I don't want to break your heart, but I also

don't buy that that's inevitable." I didn't even try to say that I disagreed that the sex was that good because it was. Every time we had sex, I fell a little more for him. Earlier had been among the best, most profound sex of my life, and I wanted more, precisely because it wasn't simply getting our rocks off. This was the kind of connection people fought wars over, and I was going to fight for him. "And for what it's worth, you're not the only one with feelings in the game."

"Damn it, Derrick. You make it so hard to do the right thing."

"Maybe there's not one right thing," I countered. "I'm going to miss you like heck whether tomorrow is the final goodbye or six weeks from now or six months. Guess I'd rather stockpile some more good memories if it's going to hurt when we part no matter what."

"Look at you arguing for living in the moment and worrying about consequences later." He laughed and rubbed his foot against mine. "You sure we didn't accidentally swap brains?"

"Maybe you've rubbed off on me."

"I definitely did that." He snorted. "More than once."

"See? You make me laugh. I think I need more of your goofiness in my life."

"You do." His tone had shifted from playful back to wistful, but I continued to hold out hope that he'd see things my way.

"I'm not arguing that I'm your forever guy."

"No? I thought you were the romantic here."

"I meant more that I know you don't date military personnel, but I was hoping that maybe you could make an exception this once, keep me around until Mr. Forever comes along." I did an admirable job of keeping my voice even, not revealing how much I'd like to remove Mr. Forever's spine. Or how much I wanted to be him. That part wasn't happening, but maybe, just maybe, I could have this for a while longer.

"It's not some random rule."

"I know. It's dangerous work and then there's the distance aspect. I get that it's not easy to be in a long-term relationship with someone in the military. But I still see some room for middle ground here."

"It's not the risk or the distance as much, although that's part of it. God knows I get wrapped up enough in my work that I forget about even my in-town friends. It's not so much about being lonely. It's more that I watched my mom take a back seat to Dad's career, over and over. He'd forget anniversaries and birthdays, and she'd always cover for him. Bottom line is that the navy let him get away with being a crap husband."

This wasn't the time to point out that his parents were still together and that perhaps they saw things differently than Arthur. He had real pain and a real point here. "Hence your thing about not wanting to be ignored."

"Yeah."

"I'm not going to lie. My career's important to me. But I also don't think it's possible for me to ignore you, not like that. Not the important stuff. What happened to giving me a chance to practice being a good boyfriend?"

"You are a good boyfriend. The best." Leaning back, he brushed a kiss along my jaw before shifting sexily against me. "I want to say yes, if only because my wish list still has a lot of items left on it."

I met him partway in a lengthy kiss, and I wasn't too proud to use sex to push my case. We were good together, too good to pass up a chance for more time together.

"Then say we can try. Dating. Or casual if that's your preference. We can figure it out as we go. All I ask is that you talk to me. When you are ready to say goodbye, say it." My voice got thick there at the end because there would be a goodbye, no matter what. That much was inevitable. Mr. Forever would arrive, and I would gracefully take a step back. And try not to remove the guy's spine.

"I'm not going to ghost you. I'll talk to you. I'm not your idiot ex."

"That you most certainly are not." I kissed him again, softer this time, before whispering, "You make me happy."

"Yeah?"

"Yeah." Admitting it felt like giving the universe the power to rip this away right now, but I also couldn't not tell him how happy he made me. Even now, my pulse still hummed with the memory of him with the kids, singing and dancing, and the pride he'd inspired in me.

"Do I get tub fun if I say we can date?"

"You get whatever you want." Dating sounded marvelous, way better than any more casual option. That earned him another kiss right there. And the tub water was cooling rapidly, but I'd brave even the Arctic if it meant more time with him.

Chapter Twenty-Eight

Arthur

"It's too early." I blinked against the strong morning sun. Not even the prospect of the annual last morning donuts and cinnamon rolls was enough to make me want to leave this bed.

"This is what you get for talking me into round two last night." Derrick cuddled against my back, and no way was I rolling away from his delicious presence.

"Oh yes, I had to do a lot of convincing." I nudged his chest with my shoulder. He'd been damn enthusiastic about finishing what we'd started in the tub. We'd quickly discovered that the tub was better for teasing than actually getting off, and had ended up racing back to the warm bed where we'd made out until it was way late.

"Maybe I wasn't that reluctant." He chuckled against my neck. "We did forgo a fair bit of sleep, though. I'm too old for all-nighters."

"And yet somehow you're all perky this morning, oh ancient one."

"Years of five hours of sleep and needing to be up and at 'em quickly. No one wants a tech who's dragging ass."

"But I want your ass, dragging or otherwise." I bumped my own butt into his groin to make my case. "How about you skip the getting-up part and sleep in with me?"

But before he could answer, a whistle sounded. "Donut time! Everyone come say goodbye."

"I don't wanna say goodbye." I huffed out a breath, not caring if I sounded pouty.

"We don't have to. Remember?" Kissing the back of my neck, he gathered me closer.

I remembered. Even in his tender embrace, my muscles still tensed. I still wasn't sure that us dating was the smartest idea. Not that this fake dating turned real fling was wise either. But it was easy to lose my head with Derrick. He was right. Saying goodbye was going to suck, whenever we said it. We might as well postpone it.

But I had noted that he was only postponing the inevitable. Neither of us were claiming this was a forever-after kind of love. Long-term wasn't for us, but I was also as reluctant as him to say never again.

So dating it was.

However, I still didn't want to leave the bed. "You're too cuddly to leave."

"And so are you, but we both know that gong is about to sound and we're not packed." He tickled my ribs lightly before he sat up.

"Okay, okay. I'm going." I finally rolled out of the bed as he started the packing. "There better be a coffee. And a donut with sprinkles left."

"I'll hunt you down one," he promised.

"My hero." I faked a swoon back onto the bed only for him to haul me upright. "Fine. Be the adult. I'll pack."

"Me too." He was far neater than me about it, folding even his dirty laundry and neatly organizing his bag whereas I more haphazardly made mounds of my belongings.

"Oh, hey, we never played my dice game." I shoved the

game along with my chess set into the middle of my bag. I'd sort it all out later.

"We could play it tonight?" he offered absently as he folded a shirt. "After I drop you off?"

"You're dropping me off?" That was news to me, but he snorted like it was a foregone conclusion that he'd take me into Seattle proper, a prospect that added a fair amount of drive time for him.

"I'm not going to make you take the ferry and buses." He had the same commanding tone as he had when he'd promised my favorite kind of donut. On anyone else, I'd find the caveman alpha act too much, but on him it was endearing, the way he made taking care of me a personal mission. "Besides, I want to see your place."

"It's not much," I warned.

"That's okay. I'm used to the barracks remember?" He reached over to rub my neck. "You don't have to impress me."

"Good. It's typical shared apartment chaos, but there is a decent TV. You can come up." I was still slightly dazed that he wanted to, but I wasn't going to turn down either the ride or more time with him.

"Okay." That settled, he zipped up his bag and tossed it near the door.

"Wow. Look at us making plans," I joked to cover how weird this actually was. "Guess we *are* dating."

"Yep." Waiting for me to stuff my bag closed, he then added it to the pile by the door.

"Next thing you'll offer to cook for me." I was only teasing but he nodded all seriously.

"I *can* cook, actually. Basic stuff mainly, but Grandma made sure I could do more than boil water."

"Well, aren't you full of surprises?" I took a last look under the bed to make sure neither of us was leaving something behind.

"See? Dating will be fun." Coming out of the bathroom, he threw my toothpaste at me. I stuck it in the front pocket of my bag, then crossed over to him and looped my arms around his neck.

"Yeah it will." Feeling decidedly more hopeful about this whole dating decision, I gave him a kiss that quickly had me plotting to tumble him back onto the bed.

Gong. Gong. "Donuts are going fast," someone called as they passed by our front window.

"Fine. Guess I'm ready." I wasn't really, but there was no choice other than to follow him out of our cozy little cabin. "I'm going to miss this place."

"Me too." He grabbed my hand. "We'll have to find you another tub."

"You do that." I let the fantasy of another vacation carry me to the dining hall. Maybe no relatives, but some pretty place with another tub for two. That would be nice.

"I'm going to find you that donut," Derrick said quickly as my mom headed our way.

"I see how it is." I waved him away right as Mom reached me, a cup of coffee in her hand and a far too upbeat expression on her face.

"And he fetches coffee. Arthur, don't let this one get away."

"I'll try." I could no more hold on to Derrick than I could capture the lake in my hands, but at least I'd have a little longer with him, and the side benefit of a pleased mom wasn't a bad thing.

"You do that." She squeezed my upper arm. "I've never seen you as happy as I have this week."

"Really?" Despite my crankiness around outdoor family reunions, I was known for being a pretty upbeat guy. As a kid, I'd been happy in my little music-and-trivia bubble, and I'd been pretty content in college and graduate school. Was this the happiest I'd been? I dug my teeth into my lip, dangerously afraid she was right.

"Really," she confirmed before taking a sip of her coffee. "And he's nuts about you."

"Oh, we're nuts all right." Nuts to ever think we could pull this thing off without some serious collateral damage.

Mom's eyes narrowed, undoubtedly picking up on my dry tone. "Are you okay, sweetie?"

"Yeah." Mindful of her coffee, I gave her a quick hug. "Typical end-of-camp blues."

"Ha. I know you. You can't wait to get back to the city."

"Not this time. This was pretty special." Glancing away from her, I tracked Derrick to the food table where he'd been waylaid by Aunt Sandy. Even at this distance, he still made me smile, everything from how he balanced two plates and two coffees to how he managed to seem super interested in whatever Aunt Sandy was saying.

"See?" Mom called my attention back to our conversation. "I told you you're happy."

"Maybe." Oh, why keep denying it? I exhaled hard. "Yeah, I am. He makes me happy."

And now my brain was back in the tub with Derrick telling me how happy I made him and me believing it. Top ten moment of my whole life right there.

"Good. You deserve it." Mom waved to Oliver's family as they came into the dining hall, Oliver and Stacey looking even more bleary-eyed than Derrick and me.

"Thanks."

"And maybe now that you're happy you can call your mother occasionally, hmm?" Her narrowed eyes said that that point had been her objective the whole conversation. Which was typical of Euler family goodbyes. We couldn't part without guilting each other into the next get-together and more contact.

"I'll try." I was struck by the sudden urge to ask her how she did it, loving Dad all these years, coming in second to the navy. But before I could work up the courage, she was tackle-hugged by Taylor and the twins.

"Help," she squeaked, pretending to flail under the assault.

"Think you're on your own," I said even as I pried the kids off her.

"Found your donut." Finally free of Aunt Sandy, Derrick returned with a triumphant grin.

"You're the best." I accepted the chocolate donut with sprinkles and the coffee, which he'd perfectly doctored to the butterscotch color I preferred. Perfect fake—wait. Perfect *real* boyfriend. That switch was going to take some getting used to.

"He is," Mom agreed.

"You promised we could see your car," Taylor reminded Derrick.

"Yup. Come on." Derrick grinned at his fan club.

"We're going to miss you." Seth sighed dramatically before diplomatically adding, "Both of you. Not just Derrick's car."

"It's a pretty sweet car." I rubbed his shoulder. Seeing the kids all dejected at saying goodbye reminded me of being their age when the time between visits with cousins seemed to stretch on and on.

"Dude. Cheer up," Vince demanded. "They'll be back next year. And Derrick better bring the car. I'm gonna want to drive it someday."

"Easy there." Derrick laughed, but he also shifted his weight from foot to foot, undoubtedly uncomfortable at the assumption he'd be back. Would he? My chest clenched. I wanted that. So badly. And yet, what were the chances?

"Arthur better pick some good songs again next year. I can't wait to see what I win!" Taylor bowed like there was an imaginary cheering audience in front of him.

"Me too." Derrick glanced my direction and the ache in my chest intensified.

Maybe. Maybe we'd get next summer. It was the most my hope-impaired heart was willing to wish for, but as the kids danced around us, I also resolved not to give up too soon. Derrick said we could figure things out as we went and perhaps that could mean delaying goodbye until we never had to say it. A guy could dream.

Chapter Twenty-Nine

Derrick

"Finally free." Arthur waved as Oliver's and Roger's SUVs loaded down with kids and luggage departed the parking lot. "Love the kids, but man, I thought they were going to insist you perform an oil change to delay leaving."

I could also remember being their age, not wanting the fun to end, so I'd been happy to answer their endless questions. And it was easier answering car questions than ones about when they would see us again. Taylor had somehow managed to get a *maybe* out of me in response to an invite to his birthday, but I'd dodged other requests and invitations and tried to keep their attention on the car.

"Hey, it was nice to have fellow car geeks showing enthusiasm for my ride," I joked to get rid of the tightness in my chest as we watched the others drive away.

"I show enthusiasm for your ride." Arthur gave me a look so hot it was a wonder the finish on my car didn't bubble up.

"I know and I love that." We were one of the last cars left in the lot, so I felt safe giving him a fast kiss. "Speaking of your enthusiasm, you want to drive until we need gas?"

I figured that was about as long as I could play passenger, but he had asked on our way here and I was feeling way more amenable these days about Arthur touching all my things, car included.

His eyes went almost comically wide as he stuck out his hand. "You're going to let me drive your baby?"

"Sure." I passed over the keys. Worst that might happen was something to the clutch if he hadn't driven a stick in a while, but he was worth a new clutch if it came to that.

"Damn." Arthur whistled low as he slid behind the wheel, leaving me to head around to the passenger side. "I would have given you the fake-to-real boyfriend upgrade sooner if I'd known this was one of the perks."

"Go easy on me." Taking a steadying breath, I buckled up. "I'm trying to be less of a control freak."

"I noticed." Adjusting the seat and the mirrors, Arthur smiled at me in the rearview. "Living for today, having fun, and letting me drive? You're a new man."

"Trying. You inspire me."

"I do?" He sounded genuinely surprised, and that humility was part of what I really liked about him. He seemed unaware of how damn *good* and special he was, making it a new mission of mine to show him appreciation.

"Sure you do. And yeah, the kids might have been all over my car, but they adore you. Look how many drawings and camp crafts you collected."

"A fair number, yeah." His cheeks were bright pink before he carefully backed out of the parking spot. "I like being the goofy uncle. And a number of parents told me they enjoyed the show, so maybe my message got through."

"Keep at it," I said firmly. Stretching, I tried to loosen my jaw and spine and trust his driving. "You've got an important lesson for them."

"Thanks. You believing in me, that means a lot." He had

a little smile as he expertly turned from the lake road onto the rural highway.

"I do." Sitting easier now, I managed to suppress a sigh of relief. "And you weren't kidding. You actually can drive a stick."

"I know my lack of aptitude for outdoor activities adds to the whole hopeless-nerd persona, but all those hours playing video games honed my reflexes." Proving his point, he smoothly changed gears. "And cars are closer to instruments than kayaks."

"True." I had to chuckle. And truth be told, watching him drive was turning me on a little. "I wanna see you make music sometime."

"That can absolutely be arranged. A week without work has me majorly jonesing for my equipment."

I snorted. "A week without your equipment would have me craving something too."

"Dork." He tilted his head my direction. "If you hook my phone up to the stereo, I made a playlist for the return trip."

"Of course you did." Charmed, I queued it up. This time instead of water being the common theme, the songs all centered on driving and roads.

"I think you purposefully chose things I might know," I said several songs later after we'd both harmonized our way through some road trip classics.

"Guilty."

I liked this, liked the way he'd thought about me and guessed right, liked hanging out and singing with him, even liked being the passenger more than I'd thought I would. By the time we stopped for gas, I'd stopped being antsy to drive and was actually surprised at how fast the time had passed.

"Your turn to drive," he said while I paid at the pump with

my credit card. "You still sure you want to burn all the extra gas going the long way back?"

"I don't mind extra drive time. I don't get enough chances to take the car out, and I'll take the extra time with you."

"If you need someone to exercise the car next time you're away, let me know." He was lounging against the car and his voice was casual, but I still tensed.

"Will do." It meant something that he'd offered, that he seemed to think we might still be together or at least friendly through my next deployment. Luckily that was likely a ways off because I was less than certain how he'd cope with that separation.

However, I wasn't about to ruin our drive by dwelling on that topic, and as we got back underway with me driving, I made a concerted effort to keep the vibe light, telling Arthur more stories about Grandma's friends. Swapping stories and singing along with his playlist served us well, including for the wait for the car ferry until we approached the northeast Seattle neighborhood where Arthur lived.

His demeanor markedly shifted as we started navigating the city streets. "I probably should have warned the roommates I was bringing someone back."

"Oh?" It hadn't occurred to me that he might not be out or might have roommates who would be less than accepting, but I probably should have considered the possibility before inviting myself over. "Is it going to cause issues for you?"

"I didn't mean the boyfriend factor." Grabbing his phone, he typed quickly on it. "They'll find it hilarious that I found someone to put up with me. I meant more that I can't guarantee they aren't having a video game marathon in their underwear."

"Consider me forewarned." I could deal with those sorts of nerves much easier, and while we were at a red light, I gave him a fast pat. "And stop being so nervous. You forget that I squash in with a hundred guys for weeks at a time."

"I know." He shifted around in his seat as I finally found an acceptable parking spot. "I just... I want you to like spending time there. Like really like it."

"You're there. I will. Promise. And even if your roommates are the most obnoxious dudes on the planet, I'd still want to spend time with you." Unbidden, my vision of the little blue house and his dream of a music studio crept back into my head. I wished I could give him a situation he liked better than this one. I'd be fine hanging out with him wherever, but I wanted him happy, like truly happy. As I handled paying for the parking, I sent up a quick wish that maybe I could be the one to make him that way.

We made our way to his apartment building, an eighties-era tan collection of apartments and townhomes on a tree-lined street, not far from the hustle of the bigger streets. Arthur's place was a typical three-bedroom setup with white walls, beige carpeting, and teeny kitchen with newer cabinetry but cheap appliances. And two rather gawky roommates who were indeed playing some game on a large, wall-mounted TV in the living area. But they were clothed and pleasant enough.

They paused the game to chat with us, but I kept getting distracted by the catchy tune of the game music.

"What game is this?" I asked.

"It's not released yet. We're beta testing it for friends. But Arthur did the music."

"Oh? It sounds amazing." I smiled at Arthur, enjoying the way he blushed and dipped his head.

"Thanks. How about I give you the rest of the tour?" Glancing down the hall, he seemed eager to escape the scrutiny of his friends.

"Sure." I waited until we were away from the seating area to lean in and whisper, "Show me your room first."

"This way." He led me to the room at the end of the hall. All that time in the car had been nice, but it had also been hours since I'd kissed him, and I needed to rectify that at once.

"See?" I said as he closed the door. His room was cluttered with dozens of instruments, an impressive computer setup along one wall, and a small bed that was going to be a tight squeeze, but I was still game to try. "This place is nice. Lots of light. And meeting your roommates wasn't so bad."

"Yeah. They're good guys. I just wasn't in the mood for much small talk." He offered me a shy smile that only upped his kissability factor. "Should we think about food? We skipped lunch, but we can order something."

"Later." I pulled him to me.

"Later?" His smile widened.

"Does your door lock?" I whispered right before I kissed his ear.

"It does." Inhaling sharply, he broke away long enough to flip the lock. "For what it's worth, I can also be quiet. Very quiet."

"Good." I kissed him then, loving the way he melted into me. Maybe this dating thing was going to be easier than I thought.

Chapter Thirty

Arthur

"So you're dating now?" Sabrina looked up from her iced coffee as we lounged on my microscopic balcony. The Seattle summer was really starting to heat up, and below us a crew of sweaty-but-ripped graduate students were moving into one of the lower units. Sabrina had spied them on her way in and had insisted we take our drinks out here to appreciate the view. "Like actually dating? No bet?"

"Why is that so hard to believe?" I took a sip of my drink, which she'd brought from our favorite local place. All the sweetened cold-brew goodness still didn't taste as good as the slushy half-melted coffee had at Lake Crescent.

"No reason." Twirling her straw, she was the picture of innocence. "But you were the one who was rather loudly opposed to such a prospect."

"I know." I groaned and made a vague gesture. "But Derrick's rather..."

"Hot as hell?"

"I was going to say *persuasive*, but yes, that too." I glanced down at the guys moving in. Objectively, they were quite possibly as hot as Derrick. Tall. Muscular. Deep voices and great laughs, but I still wouldn't take any of them or all three together in place of Derrick.

"Look at you, all dreamy." She tapped my outstretched leg with the heel of one of her gold sandals. "When do you see him again?"

"Tonight." My tone came out a little guilty because I should have been catching up on work, not doing coffee with Sabrina, and also I'd purposely scheduled her for now so that I could have Derrick all to myself without the interrogation. "He's on duty until three and then has twenty-four hours off, so he's coming here to hang out."

"Hang out." She gave me a pointed look over the top of her jeweled sunglasses. "Yes. Because that's worth the ferry ride."

"It's not all sex," I protested. "I'm going to show him the composition I've been working on."

"Uh-huh."

"But speaking of him coming over, I should probably change my sheets. Good host and all."

Snorting at that, she sloshed her coffee around in the cup. "You need a bigger bed."

"Or a smaller computer setup." Getting a small bed had made sense when I was the only one sleeping in it and when I seemed destined to die a virgin, but these days I was spending a lot of time debating how many monitors I truly needed and whether my next contract should go toward a new mattress.

"So what happened with you and that ensign?" I asked, eager to change the topic from Derrick and me and the dating that still felt new even though it had been a couple of weeks now.

"Oh, sailor boy?" She made a dismissive gesture, sunlight glinting off her metallic nails. "That was a one—okay, *four*-night deal. Nothing serious."

"Did he know it was that casual?" I teased. Below us, the guys moving in were good-naturedly bickering over where a couch went. Sabrina had undoubtedly already picked out which of the trio was her next target. "You probably broke the poor boy's heart."

"Says the guy who's going to break Derrick's heart." She tapped my chest with the sharp tip of one her nails.

"I am not. This isn't that serious!"

"Does he know that?" Pulling her sunglasses down this time, she gave me the full force of her skeptical glare. "Because this dating thing sure sounds like he's after more than just a repeat hookup."

"He knows it can't last," I said weakly because she had a point. The sex might be a good motivator, but Derrick wasn't coming over here whenever he had time off simply to get laid. We watched movies, ordered takeout, played chess and my dice game, and talked until we were too sleepy to do much more than make out clumsily in my too-small bed. "Damn it, why do I have to like him so much?"

"Because he's a catch?"

"Says the one who practices catch-and-release fishing like she's going for a tournament record." I tapped her right back, lightly poking her arm.

"Hell, sweetie, if I landed a Derrick, I think I'd put away my net for good."

"Me too," I said miserably, a mood that carried me all the way through Sabrina leaving and Derrick arriving. I liked him too damn much and that was a fact, and yet I still couldn't stop the thrill that raced through me as I opened the door.

"Hey." I tried to sound as casual as I'd told Sabrina this thing was, but my heart was busy tap-dancing over how damn good Derrick looked. It had only been a few days since I'd seen him, but he'd had a haircut since then and his black T-shirt stretched over his chest in an extra-sexy way. I narrowly refrained from licking him in the entryway.

"Hey." He sounded as dazed as me, and we just stood there

stupidly grinning at each other until he held up a white bag. "I picked up bread from the bakery by the bus stop."

"No car?"

"Nah, not worth the car ferry and parking hassle when the bus option is almost as quick." He shrugged and let me shut the door behind him. "Anyway, I was thinking I could make soup if you didn't want to order out again."

"You want to cook for me? I'm not turning that down." I smiled at him. And yeah, the bread alone was proof this wasn't strictly casual, but I couldn't be bothered to care. Derrick wanted to cook for me, and dating him—hell, just smiling at him like this—felt so damn good. "But we should probably be nice and make enough for the other guys when they come in."

"They're not here now?" His smile widened.

"No. Liam mainly telecommutes, but he had an in-office meeting today. They should both be back pretty soon, though. And you just missed Sabrina."

"We'll have to hurry." He grabbed my hand.

"Hurry?" I made a surprised noise as he hauled me down the hall. "Wait, where are you taking me?"

I had a good feeling, but making him say it was fun too.

"To that tiny bed of yours." He winked at me as we reached my room.

"Sorry. I know it's crowded." Locking the door behind us, I pulled him to me. The room definitely felt smaller than usual with him in it, and his nearness combined with the yummy scent of his aftershave made him the focal point instead of my musical clutter.

"I'm used to it. Besides, I like crowded with you." He gave me a soft kiss, a greeting that had me sighing with its sweetness. "And at least in your bed, we don't have to strap in."

"You have to strap yourself in on the sub?"

"Yep. Every time unless you like concussions and broken

collarbones. Everything gets strapped down." Eyes flashing devilishly, he pulled my shirt loose from my shorts. "At first it was hard to sleep so confined, but now I'm used to it. And as it turns out, it was good practice for you."

"I'm not the one who turns into a baby koala in his sleep." Laughing, I helped him remove my shirt, then turned my attention to his clothing.

"Maybe I was just trying to get back the covers you stole." After shrugging out of his shirt, he neatly draped it and mine both over the back of my office chair.

"I miss the bed at the cabin." I used his belt loop to pull him back to me so that I could kiss him again.

"I miss that tub." He kissed me longer this time. By now he knew exactly how to heat us both up, but somehow the familiarity of his mouth was even sexier than it had been brand-new. "But this room is nice too. It's got you. And later, you're going to show me your music. Couldn't do that in the wilderness."

"True. But I did play your instrument rather nicely there…" I blatantly grabbed for his fly. He'd wanted to hurry and my body was all over that plan.

"You are rather gifted—*damn*." He ended on a low groan as I freed his cock.

"You were saying?" I kept my tone casual even as my pulse raced.

"There's nowhere I'd rather be than right here with you." Cupping my face, he gave me a kiss so tender that I forgot all about the plan to be fast and simply clung to him.

"That type of sweet talk will get you whatever you want."

"Show me." And I did, pushing him onto my bed. As we kissed and moved together, I hoped that what he wanted was me and that I had it in me to give him everything he needed, body and soul, because he deserved it.

Chapter Thirty-One

Derrick

Arthur had me well-trained. Right as I exited the chow hall, my phone buzzed and right on schedule, my pulse purred like a newly tuned engine even before I saw Arthur's picture on the message.

It's your lucky night. Or rather our lucky night. Liam just left on an emergency business trip for Portland, and Craig said this morning that he's sleeping over at his girlfriend's house. So just us. All night. As loud as we want.

I laughed aloud. Alert the neighbors, I texted back. I have to check on a few more things here, then I'm all yours.

"What's so funny?" Calder came loping up from the opposite direction.

Crap. I quickly pocketed my phone. We'd been on different shifts most of the time since we returned from family camp, and I could fully admit that I'd been avoiding him as much as possible the rest of the time. I'd been dreading the big talk that we needed to have.

"Oh. Hey, man. Nothing much." I smiled at him, but my face felt too stiff, like the air had dropped thirty degrees.

"I hear you're getting out of here early today." Calder raised an eyebrow, his intense scrutiny making me shuffle my feet.

"Uh. Yeah."

"You can stop looking so cagey. I already heard from my mom that you and Arthur are going to that thing for Oliver's kid this evening."

Well, hell. I should have known that the gossip network would get back to Calder eventually. I rolled my shoulders, trying to avoid the guilty look he was accusing me of having but probably failing. "It's Taylor's birthday. He asked back at family camp if we'd attend. I said maybe, but my schedule worked out so that I can go. You coming?"

"Nah. I've got plans." He waved his hand in a vague way before his eyes narrowed even farther. "And speaking of plans, exactly how long are you two going to carry on this charade? You got Steve all jealous, got a vacation you definitely needed out of the deal, but what's keeping you guys from breaking up already?"

Time to pay the piper. Looked like we were having that big talk whether I wanted to or not. But I wasn't going to lie nor was I going to dodge the question. "It's not a charade."

"Say what?" Calder tilted his head, mouth pursing like I'd given him a super-sour candy.

"I mean it was. But not now. I like him."

"I knew it." Calder pulled off his hat, slapped it against his thigh. "I had a feeling you were hooking up with him. You've avoided me for weeks, and you were a little too convincing at camp about being into him."

"I'm sorry. I should have talked to you sooner." I'd been too busy having fun with Arthur, heading into Seattle every chance I got, and living in a happy bubble where I didn't have to royally piss off my best friend to spend time with my guy.

I hadn't wanted to deal with Calder's hard stares and harder questions, and he was right to call me out on it.

Calder shook his head, expression nearly identical to my grandmother's the few times I had gravely disappointed her. And like then, the disappointment was worse than anger ever could be. I'd take a punch over the heavy self-loathing bearing down on me.

"It's not me you should apologize to," he said at last, voice tight.

"No?"

"You're both going to be sorry. You're going to break each other's damn heart."

"We're *both* adults. We know what we're doing." *I hope.* A group of young midshipmen headed toward the chow hall, and I stepped off the sidewalk to allow them to pass. Calder followed me onto the grass. His let-down expression made my voice even more defensive. "And what makes you so damn sure?"

"Arthur might be twenty-five, but he's flighty as hell." Calder made a dismissive gesture. Maybe it would have been better had he slugged me because then I could hit him right back for his attitude about Arthur. "And he doesn't even have a real job. No way is he sticking around for you to play house with."

"He has a real job." By some miracle I managed to keep my tone even and my hands fisted at my sides. "He got a new contract last week. He's really good at what he does."

"He might be good at it, but talent isn't the same thing as job security. I had to bail him out with bills a couple of times when he was in Boston. That's probably a big part of why he agreed to the fake homecoming stunt."

That stung. I'd been under the assumption that Arthur had agreed out of the goodness of his heart, not guilt and obligation to Calder. And if he had money worries, I wanted to hear about it from him, not Calder. However, I wasn't going to let Calder undermine what we had built either.

"Maybe we were both in it for crappy reasons to start, but now I care about him." More personnel exited the building, so I kept my voice to a low but firm whisper. "For real. And his financial security or lack thereof isn't relevant to how I feel about him."

"This is what I mean." He huffed out a breath. "He might not intend to, but he'll break your heart. I guarantee you that if he gets an offer for a contract that requires him to be in LA or Vancouver, he'll take it."

Another topic I hadn't exactly covered with Arthur. We were both excellent at avoiding any mention of the future and any plans later than my next day off. "So? It's not like we don't travel for work ourselves."

"Exactly." Calder pointed at me like he'd caught me in a lie. "Because he's always been absolutely adamant that he's never ever doing long distance. I'm not sure exactly what sort of kiss-drunk spell you put on him to make him temporarily forget he hates the navy, but emphasis on *temporarily*. He's not suddenly gonna get okay with the military. You're going to break his heart right back with your next deployment."

And there Calder went, hitting my biggest fear. It didn't matter how hard I fell for Arthur. My job would always be the stumbling block to a future together. Eventually Arthur would stop being patient, and that goodbye I was already dreading would come. But I also couldn't let Calder see that dread.

"You don't know that. And besides, we're still working things out as we go. Long-term is a bridge to cross when we get to it." *Or a bridge to avoid.* Maybe if we continued to take things one day at a time, we could bumble our way into long-term. Accidentally uncover a way to have forever. It could happen, and I tried to make myself believe the lines I was feeding Calder. "Right now we're having a great time together, and he makes me happy. Really happy."

That part was true, a little too true. Arthur made me happier than I could ever remember being. Everything from cooking for him to lying awake talking to him to listening to his latest composition made me happy. And that really was the bottom line here. I wasn't going to give that happiness up before I absolutely had to.

"That's something." Calder's shoulders slumped like I'd deflated the big guy with a single pinprick. "And I want you *both* happy. I do. I simply don't think you're right for each other. And someone is gonna get hurt."

"Let me worry about that," I said with more conviction than I felt. His words slithered through my brain, like spec ops troops infiltrating a target, undermining my defenses. He'd hit on another of my big worries, namely that while Arthur was perfect for me, maybe I wasn't the best thing for him and that I was being selfish in keeping our relationship going. Me getting hurt was inevitable and a price I was willing to pay, but Arthur hurt was a whole different story.

"Like you worried about Steve?"

Another dart, right to the chest, but I only gritted my teeth. "Arthur's not Steve."

"No, he's not. Unlike the cheating snake, he's a good guy who's not gonna double-cross you. But you're on the rebound, vulnerable, and I'm worried you're seeing a future that's just not there because you're trying to make up for what you lost."

Fuck. Was Calder right? Was this all simply me on the rebound? Not real emotions? I didn't want to believe that. "I didn't lose anything with Steve. We were never going to make it, and I see that now. What I feel for Arthur is different."

It was. I'd never felt this intensely about Steve, never lain awake plotting what I wanted to talk with him about the next day, never raced to be able to send him a single text, never rearranged things simply so we could have a few extra hours together. That wasn't a rebound fling, it was—

"Chief Fox." Grammer, one of the newer guys from our boat, dashed up to us. "Senior Chief is looking for you. Some sort of meeting."

"On it." Whatever the emergency was, the churning in my gut said it wasn't going to be good.

Chapter Thirty-Two

Arthur

"Do you want to tell me now or later what's bugging you?" I finally asked as we approached the exit for Oliver's neighborhood. He'd been quiet and moody ever since I'd met him by the ferry, short answers to my questions, and flipping on the radio as soon as we'd hit traffic, not even joking about my playlist selections. "Because if I can tell that something's the matter, my mom will for sure be able to sense your mood, and she'll ferret it out of you. Not to mention the kids."

Bringing up the kids was something of a low blow, but I was desperate for him to talk.

"Later." Derrick gave me a strained smile. "I'm sorry. I know I'm terrible company right now. You deserve better."

"You're not terrible. I like being with you even when you are quiet and grumpy. I'm worried about you, though. And I'd help if I could." Sabrina's point about how this was more than sex pricked at me. This was more than casual, way more, and Derrick being upset made me upset, made me want to fix whatever it was for him.

"I know you would." Derrick patted my hand at a red light. "And I appreciate that, more than you can know. But can we talk after this thing? Please?"

"Okay." Like I could deny him anything, especially with

his current wet-kitten expression. It was still summer, but he looked cold and miserable and in need of a hug. To that end, I waited until we'd parked outside Oliver's ranch-style rental close to his base in Tacoma before I rubbed Derrick's neck.

"That feels good." He stretched into the contact.

"Bet I can make you feel even better later," I bragged, putting more oomph into my efforts. "I'll search massage how-to articles on the way back to my place."

"You do that." His smile was still at half-power, but there wasn't a ton I could do here in Oliver's driveway, especially if Derrick wasn't ready to talk.

"I'll get the presents," I offered as we exited the car. "But first I'm going to hug you because you need that."

"Yeah, I do." He sagged against me more than usual when we embraced. I hugged him as tight as I dared for as long as he let me. He breathed in and out, tension ebbing with each exhale only to return on another sigh. Whatever was wrong was more than a simple bad day, and my own back stiffened. I hoped I could solve this or at least make it better for him.

"Uncle Arthur. Uncle Derrick." Taylor raced out of the house followed by assorted siblings, dogs, and friends.

"Hey, kiddo." Pulling away from me, Derrick pasted on a smile and greeted the kids. After grabbing the presents, we made our way through the happy chaos into the house. We were greeted with a flurry of hugs as soon as we got in the door. Stacey whisked the presents off to a towering gift table and pressed sodas into our hands in short order.

I didn't have as much time to worry about Derrick with the party in full swing. There were several wet and silly games to keep the kids occupied. Not surprisingly, Derrick proved to be a menace at water balloons, and the kids utterly loved his participation, dodging and squealing and making him laugh.

"You certainly earned your cake," I teased, handing him a towel.

"That was fun." This time his smile was almost normal. Maybe whatever was bugging him wasn't so bad. Or at least was something we could deal with, emphasis on *we*.

"Cake!" my mom called from the deck, assembling the troops. We dutifully dried off and made our way inside to sing "Happy Birthday" to Taylor. Everyone got big slices of chocolate cake.

"Look! Chocolate sprinkles. Your favorite." Derrick's expression was so tender that it made my chest hurt as he scraped some of his icing and sprinkles onto my plate.

"Thanks." Him remembering meant even more to me than the sharing. I wanted to get back to the cabin, to who we'd been there, easy and free and falling—

Oh hell no. I might be able to admit this was more than sex, but I wasn't ready to go *there*.

"Presents!" Stacey gathered everyone around the table where Taylor opened many video games and assorted merch from those same games.

Finally, he arrived at our gift. "From both of you?"

"Yeah." My skin heated. It was a very established-couple thing to do, more so even than showing up together.

"It was a team effort," Derrick explained. "I had the idea, but Arthur hunted it down and made it happen."

"Nice wrapping job." Mom winked at me.

"Oh my gosh!" Taylor crowed as he tore the package open. "It's Derrick's car! But Legos! Vince and Seth are going to be so jealous."

He hopped around the room with the box, big grin on his face. It had taken some major searching, but I'd found a model version of Derrick's car that Taylor could build.

"That's until you're old enough for driving lessons." Derrick ruffled his hair. My heart squeezed hard. So much want bubbled up in me that I couldn't even name it all. All I could do was grab Derrick's hand under the table, hope he knew what he meant to me.

Eventually the party died down, kids carted away by tired parents, and Mom and Stacey boxing up the leftovers.

"You want a beer?" Oliver asked. "You're both welcome to crash here if you don't want to deal with traffic."

"Nah." Derrick darted his gaze to me. "We have…"

"Plans," I supplied. Derrick wasn't getting out of talking to me that easily, and bunking down on Oliver's family room floor was hardly conducive to the sort of evening we both needed.

"I see." Oliver chuckled. "Suppose I should go all big brother and—"

"Please don't." I laughed, but also I really didn't want a lecture for either of us.

"Okay. Okay. Be safe. And don't be strangers. The kids love you."

I supposed that was his stamp of approval, so I nodded before we all exchanged backslapping hugs.

Once out of the house, Derrick immediately checked his phone, sighed, and slumped into the driver's seat, resting his head on the steering wheel.

"Okay, now you're going to talk," I ordered, done asking nicely.

"Sorry. There was no news. That was a relieved sigh, not a sad one," Derrick said as he put the car in gear.

Not mollified, I made a frustrated noise. "No news about what?"

"I don't know for sure yet—"

"I'm okay with uncertainty," I lied. Uncertainty sucked. I'd spent large chunks of my life uncertain—when was Dad's deployment ending, where would we be stationed next, who would be my friend. "And if you tell me, then we can be uncertain together."

"Fine. Not being alone in my head sounds good." He gave me a grim smile before heading out of the neighborhood and back to the highway. "Right before I came to meet you, my commanding officer and chief of the boat called me in."

"Never a good sign." My stomach sloshed around, dread gathering, but I tried to keep my voice even so he'd keep talking.

"Yeah. Somehow I knew I wasn't going to like it. And it turns out there's a situation on another sub. Their sonar chief is sick and likely needs a medical evac. They need a replacement ASAP if they pull the chief."

"Oh." The sick feeling intensified, like a little kid on a roller coaster with a too-full stomach.

"Anyway, this is a situation they're monitoring, waiting to see what develops."

"Isn't there anyone else they could ask?" I knew even before he shook his head what the answer would be.

"The navy doesn't ask. They order. They're looking at a few options, including other chiefs, but honestly I'm probably the most likely candidate. If the brass says I'm going, I'm going."

"Yeah. That's how it goes." I took a deep breath, which helped not at all. "You've got to follow orders."

"Yup." Derrick nodded sharply, ever the good sailor, making my jaw clench. "Also, on a personal level, I know what it's like being down someone key. It sucks. I feel bad for that crew, and if I can help, I want to do that."

"I know. You're a good guy." I watched the traffic out the window rather than his face. Typical Seattle traffic—we'd be rolling along only to come to an abrupt halt, not unlike what was happening here inside the car.

"I try. But I know it sucks for you—for us—too." His voice cracked on *us*, a sharp noise I felt deep in my gut. "I really thought I'd have more time stateside."

"Me too." My sinuses burned but I couldn't cry, couldn't add that burden to whatever he was already feeling. His face was pale and his mouth a harsh slash across strained features. He didn't need my tears. "How long will you be gone if they send you?"

"I don't know." Derrick tapped his fingers on the steering wheel as traffic slowed. "Likely weeks. They don't do an evac like this lightly. There are all sorts of complicated logistics for an extraction and arranging the rendezvous to take on the new personnel."

"Makes sense," I said flatly. There wasn't much else I could say.

"I'm not going to lie, though, it could be months, and I don't get a say in that either."

"I know." In front of us, the city lights twinkled, the usual hustle and bustle continuing unabated.

"I'm sorry." There was a whole universe of meaning in Derrick's voice, the sort of deep nuance I could work on musically for weeks and never completely convey. I wasn't sure how to reply either. I couldn't say it would be okay because it so clearly wasn't okay.

"I'm sorry too," I said at last because that at least was true. I was sorry for the other chief and for Derrick and for myself too. And for us, for the time we'd thought we'd have and now likely wouldn't.

"Do you want me to just drop you off?" he asked quietly. "I can if that would be easier."

"No. Nothing's going to make this easier." And being alone was going to bite. The idea of trudging up the apartment steps on my own, him headed to God knew where, had bile rising up my throat. "But do you have to get back?"

"Not yet. They haven't called. When they call, I'll have to go, but it could be hours or days yet. My commander said to stand ready, get my things in order, but to keep going about my life until we know more."

"Waiting sucks." I shifted in my seat and stared out the window again.

"Yeah, it does. I'd rather wait with you, have the night I promised you, but not if you'd rather be alone. I get it. You didn't sign up for this. And I'm probably not the best company tonight either."

"I don't want you to be alone," I said softly, hating the vision of him driving back alone as much as the one of me alone in my cramped room. "Is it bad that I just want to pretend this isn't happening?"

"Me too. But it is." Derrick's tone was tight and miserable as we approached my neighborhood. "However, maybe more talking isn't what either of us needs."

"I still want you to come up," I said before he could offer again to not. "Let's have tonight. We don't need to talk."

Chapter Thirty-Three

Derrick

Not talking seemed like my best idea ever. There was a ton unsaid between us, but as we made our way to his apartment, holding hands and staying silent felt far better than the serious discussion we should have been having.

The apartment was blissfully empty, and it felt like a lifetime ago that he'd messaged about the roommates being gone. What had seemed like an opportunity for naughty fun now felt like a blessing because I was so not up for small talk. We didn't even bother with the living room lights, heading right back to Arthur's room, where he flipped on his low desk light rather than the harsh overhead. The soft glow was calming as he hugged me from behind, burying his face in my neck.

"Tighter," I urged, pulling his arms snugger against me and leaning into the embrace. His hug in Oliver's driveway had been so steadying, and that was exactly what I needed.

"Whatever you need." He snaked a hand under my shirt to rest on my abs, and the warmth made me hum contentedly.

"Want to lie like this." Shameless, I pulled up my shirt so his other hand could find skin too.

"Excellent idea." Arthur tugged my shirt the rest of the way off before removing his own. Then by some wordless agreement, we both shed our pants. Naked, we curled up on his small bed, him behind me still.

"Good?" he asked as he held me close.

"Yeah." Lying down like this, I could rest my head against his, our legs a happy tangle under his covers. Usually I felt taller and bigger and liked that contrast, but at that moment Arthur seemed stronger, and I was more than happy to wallow in that strength and let him squeeze me tighter. His arms flexed and his thighs tensed as he surrounded me with his warmth.

"It's okay if this is what you need tonight," he whispered after a while. Minutes or hours. I was no longer certain. "We don't have to do anything else."

I laughed then, a low rumble in the quiet room. The more his warmth seeped into my bones, the more other parts of me woke back up.

"I'm not ruling it out. Just taking our time." I tipped my head back so we could kiss. It went without saying that we didn't truly have time to take, but damn it, I was going to make time. I'd will the universe to give us this.

Our mouths met, a symphony better than anything Arthur's genius brain could dream up. We kissed until my neck protested, and then he smoothly rolled us so he was on top and we could kiss even easier. He tasted sweet and familiar, and he knew exactly how to use his agile tongue to heat me up further.

I kissed him back with a desperation I hadn't known I possessed, clinging to his shoulders and back as we kissed and kissed. Our hard cocks butted against each other, but that need wasn't as urgent as the one to keep kissing, keep him close as possible. Eventually though, our bodies started moving on their own.

"Like this?" he asked, hand roaming down my side.

"Mmm." I was tempted, but there was something I wanted more. "Would you want to fuck?"

"Sure." Affable as ever, he rolled over to retrieve supplies from the nightstand.

"Do you want to top?" My pulse sped up. We hadn't done it this way yet, but I craved it right then.

"Depends." His face went serious. "Are you offering because you feel guilty about maybe leaving and think you should? Or because that's what you need?"

"That's what I need," I whispered, admission not coming easily. It was always easier to focus on him than to articulate my own needs and wants. "I want it because it feels good and because nothing else gets me out of my head quite like being fucked. And because I want to be close to you, share that together."

"I can't guarantee I'm any good at it." He gave a shaky laugh.

"I'll talk you through it." I pulled him close for another kiss. Being his first was another motivation, one that made sweet warmth spread throughout my torso. I liked being able to give him that first, to know that it was me, no matter what happened next.

But I wasn't thinking about next, only this moment and this night with this guy. We kissed more hungrily now, hands more active, bodies surging.

"Tell me what to do," he panted against my lips, stroking a hand down my torso. I was way too tightly wound for much of that, so I batted his hand away and reached for the lube.

"Let me." I was good at efficient prep. Arthur's heated gaze and hooded eyes as I touched myself ramped me up even more, and I softly moaned.

"I want to help." He bit his lip as he reached a hand out.

"Yeah." I dragged his hand next to mine, showing him

what I liked. Directing him like this made my cock pulse, more so as I moved my hand aside so he could play on his own. Proving himself a fast study, he kept up the deep, insistent rhythm I loved.

"Fuck. You're so tight. Hot." The reverent look in his eyes was almost enough to get me off on the spot. Almost.

"More." I rocked my hips up toward him.

"Like this?" He angled his fingers perfectly, and I could only answer him with a moan.

"Oh. You do like that." Grinning slyly, he did it again. And again.

"Enough." I groaned. "Now. Please."

"Now?" Arthur didn't sound in nearly enough of a hurry.

"Now," I growled, shoving the spare pillow under my ass. I wanted to watch his face as he experienced this for the first time.

"So bossy," he chided while reaching for a condom.

"And impatient." Not wanting to wait for him to read directions, I rolled it on him and slicked him up. "Go slow at first."

"I can do that." Shifting to kneel between my legs, he lined us up and moved at the speed of an arthritic turtle.

"Not that slow." I rocked my hips upward, trying to chase more contact.

"Complaints, complaints." In addition to the tease though, he did put a little more force into pushing forward. I groaned as my body remembered how to yield, the stretch intense but not unwelcome.

"Doing okay?" His voice was breathy, and knowing I was having that effect on him made me even harder.

"More," I demanded.

"Trying. Slow," he gritted out. The cords of his neck muscles stood out and his mouth was a thin line of intense concentration. "Want it good for you."

"It is. So good." I bucked my hips, urging him deeper. "Tell me what you feel."

"Feels so good. Tight. But smooth and slippery too. The way you grip me…" He trailed off on a gasp as I intentionally clenched harder. "And close. I feel so close to you."

"Me too." In fact, it felt like my heart couldn't take much more, I was so full, the intensity of my feelings for him there in every thrust, every gaze, every brush of our hands. I'd never felt so deeply before or so in-tune with the other person. I couldn't give voice to things in my heart, yet they were right there reflected back in Arthur's eyes, which were soft and tender in contrast to the tension in the rest of his body.

"Derrick…" he panted, a world of meaning in the syllables of my name. He sounded so close to losing control. "So good."

"Yeah it is." I reached for my cock with my still-slick hand. "Go as hard as you need to. I can take it."

"Don't want you to take it." He frowned, pausing his motions, still buried deep in me. "Want you to love it."

"I do," I assured him, painfully close to admitting I loved him even more than this act. And it meant a lot that he saw the distinction between taking and giving, enduring and loving. But I couldn't burden him with my overwhelming emotions with everything else going on. It wouldn't be fair to him, so instead I held his gaze, trying to memorize his face in this moment, the flashes of pleasure, the taut muscles from holding back, the flushed skin and shining eyes.

I let my body do the talking for me, moving with him, meeting every thrust, encouraging him deeper and faster, until we were nothing more than a chorus of moans, a concert of bodies striving together, urgent rhythm driving us onward.

"Oh." His eyes widened, the exact instant his control

snapped reflected there. His jaw went slack and his careful thrusts lost their finesse.

"Yeah, that's it." I reveled in his wild expression, stroking myself faster now, as done holding back as he was.

"Gonna come." He made a desperate noise that went straight to my cock.

"Do it. Please." My head fell back. This was what I'd wanted, my body hurtling away from me, no thinking, only doing and feeling. Even my moans sounded farther away now, the expansiveness of my climax pushing everything else out of my head.

"*Yes.*" One of us said it, the who no longer mattering, because I was coming, deep body-wracking shudders as I shot over and over. And so was he, hammering hard before grunting and going stiff as he made a low, guttural noise so full of pleasure it coaxed one last spurt out of me. My eyes stung, sweat or tears. I couldn't be bothered to care which.

"Wow." His voice was all wonder, shifting to concern as he stroked my face. "Oh fuck. Did I hurt you?"

"No. All good. Too good." Keeping my eyes shut, I rode out the last of the sensations. Even the aftershocks were overwhelming in the best way possible.

"Damn, I had no idea…" He still sounded all dreamy as he gently untangled our bodies. His touch was feather-light on my skin as he flitted his fingers down my chest, over my stomach, through the streaks of come there, glancing across my still-sensitive, almost buzzing cock, and brushing lightly across where we'd been joined. The reverence in his touch was enough to make my eyes sting anew. He'd taken care of me in a way I wasn't sure anyone ever had before. I'd been fucked, but this was something else, something more.

I wanted to say something profound, but words continued to fail me as he cleaned us both up. Curving his body around mine, he cuddled me close, like earlier but different now too. There was a peace between us, an inner calm that went beyond post-sex bliss.

I wasn't about to ruin it with idle conversation, and he must have felt the same way because he simply lay there and held me and breathed with me.

"I don't want to sleep," he whispered at last.

"Me either." I snuggled more securely, a yawn belying my words. "No tub here for a midnight bath, sadly."

"Yeah. Guess we'll just have to stay here in bed forever." He kissed my temple.

"Sounds perfect." I yawned again, but in the end, he was the one whose breathing evened out first, sleep claiming him in little huffs and soft snores. I watched him sleep until my eyes burned every bit as much as my heart. He looked younger and more vulnerable in his sleep, silky red hair tumbling across his forehead. I wanted to keep him like this forever, stay here like this for all eternity.

That was the thought I too faded away on and the one I came awake to, hours later when my phone buzzed and my heart sank. I *knew*.

Chapter Thirty-Four

Arthur

I knew as soon as I heard Derrick shuffling around what was happening. And even half-asleep I hated it and wanted to bury my head in my pillow and pretend to sleep through him leaving. But I couldn't do that to him. To either of us really.

My muscles still protested as I sat up, body rebelling against this middle-of-the-night intrusion of our cozy nest. I'd rather drift on memories of the amazing sex, but if Derrick had to do this, then so did I.

"The call came?" I asked even though it so clearly had.

"Yep." His mouth and eyes were violin-string tight. "I've got a couple of hours to report, but I can't risk getting caught in morning rush hour."

"Yeah. Traffic will be brutal," I said inanely. Next we'd be discussing the weather.

"Ferry shouldn't be that bad." Derrick pulled on his pants. "I've got someone meeting me at the station."

"Ferry?" I pulled the covers closer around me. "But you drove."

"I'm leaving you my keys." He tossed them next to me on the bed. He'd removed the car keys from his other keys, and he'd left the car ones on a fob with a dangling beaded charm one of the kids had made at camp. My chest contracted hard.

"What? You can't leave me your car!" I protested, not making a move for those keys. Hell, I didn't even want to look at them or think about what it meant, him leaving them for me.

"Sure I can. You like driving it." Derrick shrugged before bending to retrieve his shirt. "I'm leaving you the contact info for my buddy who garages it for me in case you don't want to keep it in this neighborhood, but maybe you can do me a favor and take it for a drive or two?"

"I can do that." My voice was thick. That was all the confirmation I needed that this separation was likely to be weeks or months, not days.

"Good."

"I'll keep your baby safe." I tried to smile but probably failed miserably. "Will I know when to have her ready for your return?"

It was a roundabout way of asking if there was any hope of news. I knew chances were slim of him having many opportunities to send messages, but I wanted something to cling to.

Derrick nodded sharply. "Hope so. I updated my contact info to make you my next of contact so you get all the notifications. One of the liaisons in the ombudsman or family services office can likely help if you need to get word to me in case of an emergency on this end."

"Thanks." I licked my parched lips. That was big. Like way more than friends hooking up sort of big, and it underscored all the overwhelming emotions I'd been battling all day. As much as I didn't want this to be happening, I liked being that important to Derrick. Made me want to offer him something in return. "I'll be there when you return if they get me notice."

"You don't have to." His face was as solemn as I'd ever seen it.

"What? You're leaving me your car. You're adding me to your contact list. Of course I'll be there." I simply couldn't fathom a world where I wouldn't want to see him again. I'd never wanted to be in this position, but hell if I'd send him with anything less than an assurance that I'd be there.

"Yeah, I am doing those things," he said evenly as he finished dressing. "But not because I want you to feel obligated or guilty. I want you to have options and at least a small way to contact me."

"Thanks. Knowing something, anything, will help the wait. And I will be there. You can count on that." Wrapped up in the blanket, I left the bed to stand next to him and put a hand on his shoulder.

"I don't want to." His eyes were as hollow as his tone.

"What do you mean?" I asked in a small voice, hand tightening on his shoulder. "You don't want me?"

"Of course I want you. I'm always going to want you." He put a hand over mine.

"Then what's the problem?" My tone was demanding, my resolve to not give him additional stress slipping.

"I knew going into this that eventually you'd need to say goodbye." His sigh echoed through the room.

"But not now," I protested. Hell, simply letting him go was going to suck. No way could I cope with a permanent goodbye. My opinions on long distance aside, I refused to break up moments before he had to deploy. That wasn't fair to him. Or me, really.

"It could be." He peered deep into my eyes, deeper than I wanted him to. "This could be goodbye, and what I'm trying to say is if it is, if this is goodbye, I'm okay with that."

"Well, I'm not," I snapped back. "I'm not okay with *goodbye* in any sense of the word. This isn't over. I'm not done."

"You say that now." He smiled sadly, his all-too-wise tone grating on my last nerve. "And that's why I added you to my contact list. Because you should have the choice. And that's all I want. Seeing me after I come back has to be your choice to come, not an obligation."

"Because you're okay if I don't," I said miserably. He had shoes on now, and we were moments from him leaving, and this was not how I wanted this to go at all. When I'd first woken up, I'd intended to send him off with an upbeat attitude, nothing heavy, and fall apart later on my own. That he was forcing me to think about the hard stuff now made me angry. At him. At myself. At the situation. I kicked at the carpet, welcoming the abrasion of the rough rug against my bare feet.

He cupped my face in both hands. "You make me happy. Happier than I've been maybe ever. I don't regret a thing about any of this, and if this is goodbye—because it could be—it was worth it to be this happy, and to have had you even for a while. I want you to know that, to feel it."

Not sure I could speak, I nodded.

"If you do come when I return, I want that. I do. I want more time together. But if you can't be there, I understand, and I'm grateful we had this time."

"I'll—"

He cut me off with a finger to my lips. "No promises, okay? You know I want you there, but no promises right now because I can't make you any. I don't know how long this will be and neither of us knows how this will go."

"I'm not your ex," I said stubbornly.

"On that we are very clear." He pulled me even closer, the friction of his clothes against my skin another reminder of how close he was to the door. "I never felt for him what I do for you."

"I've never felt like this before either," I admitted. No crush or fantasy could ever rival what I felt for Derrick, and in that moment, I hated it. It wasn't fair to find this and then have to risk losing it.

"I know." He brushed my face with his thumbs. "And that's why I'm trying to give you space for however you feel when I'm back."

"You are coming back." I said it like the sternest of orders, channeling every military relation I had. I simply refused to entertain a world where Derrick wasn't okay, where we might not have a chance to make this right.

"God, I hope so." And then he kissed me like the world was burning down. His mouth was hungry and urgent and tender all at once. Even knowing he had to go and that time was ticking away, I still clung to him. The blanket I'd been holding with one hand fell away and still I kissed him.

He might not want me to make any promises, but I wanted to, wanted to offer him my assurances. Wanted to bind us both to that promise, honestly. I didn't need room to think, and I was more than a little afraid what I might find if I dug deep enough into my psyche. I didn't need space. Just him. But already there was an entire ocean between us.

Chapter Thirty-Five

Derrick

"Well, you certainly know how to make an entrance, Fox." The senior chief regarded me carefully as we settled for our daily report meeting. He had a shaved head, Southern drawl, commanding features, and a piercing stare that had a way of seeing every uncertainty. So I drew myself up taller and gave a firm nod.

"Yes, sir." *Entrance* was one way to put the harrowing foggy medical evac that had required coordination from multiple teams including the shore-based doctors, the ship the sub had had to rendezvous with, its helicopter crew, and various levels of mission command. Being on deck during a sunny homecoming had nothing in common with navigating the slick surface in choppy conditions with limited visibility. It was only thanks to tireless training that the operation had gone off without incident. "You should be proud of your crew."

The sub's young medic had had to help negotiate the sub's tight passageways with his patient on a litter while the deck crew had to coordinate closely with the evac helicopter.

"They did fine work." This senior chief wasn't the type to smile much, but the warmth in his voice said even he was impressed. "Glad they got you on that bird."

"Me too. We cut it close." I'd narrowly made the helicopter

rescue flight, a mad dash alongside the crew following a long flight out to that ship. Not counting time zone changes, I'd been awake over twenty-four hours by the time the evacuation was complete. But Command hadn't wanted the submarine to have to surface more than once, and time had been of the essence once the sick chief's condition had deteriorated. "Do we have an update on Gordon yet?"

"Stable. He's a fighter. Higher-ups can't share specific medical information, but prognosis was sounding good last I heard."

"Excellent." Everything I'd heard about the ill chief was glowing. I had big shoes to fill on this mission, that much was certain.

"You settling in?" The senior chief did another of those hard stares, but I had years of practice schooling my expression. This was not a moment for complaints.

"Yup." The senior chief didn't need to hear that I had a rattly bottom bunk with a restless snorer above me and an intense longing for my boyfriend's cramped-but-cozy bed where at least I had Arthur as a pillow and the sound of his heart for white noise. Senior Chief also didn't need to know that I hadn't slept any of the trip to the sub because I'd been replaying that final kiss with Arthur over and over. All my boss wanted to know was that things were on automatic, not that I was lovelorn and homesick. "Good crew here. I'll be up to speed in no time."

"That's what I like to hear." Predictably, he nodded sharply and didn't ask follow-up questions. "Now, do you have that report for me?"

"Absolutely." I pushed thoughts of Arthur from my head. I had a job to do and needed to prove to both the senior chief and the personnel under me that I was more than capable of meeting the challenge. "I analyzed the last few days of data."

I rattled off my report, focusing on the minor discrepancies I'd found, my plans to study them further, quality control procedures in place, and possible conclusions that could be drawn from the sonar data we had available. This was the part I was good at, and my confidence showed in my decisive tone.

"Damn." The senior chief whistled low. "You do know your stuff. Brass said you were one of the best."

I stood a little taller at that. It didn't matter what was happening in my personal life. My ego still enjoyed the praise, and I had too many years of training to let my funk impact my ability to do the work that was so vital to the sub's navigation. "Thank you, sir. I try."

"Reputation like yours, you'll be coming for my job soon enough, I reckon." The senior chief stretched, arms hitting the side of the tight compartment we were in.

"Oh, I've got some years left before that." Any other previous deployment and the comment would have buoyed me for days. I wanted to be where he sat, chief of the boat, commander's right-hand personnel and responsible for so much of the daily operations. It was a level of responsibility I'd aspired to my whole career. But lately, I kept having this little voice in the back of my head going *what if*, and me not sure how to answer it.

"Ain't that right." His Southern drawl intensified when he was relaxed, and like every senior chief I'd had, he might joke about retirement, but he knew damn well he was an institution. "I've got a few more deployments in these old bones before y'all put me out to pasture."

I laughed because I'd heard that a time or two. "I bet."

"You let me know if y'all need anything, you hear?"

"I've got it on automatic, sir." I had what my department needed to run smoothly. What I needed personally was way more of a question mark and not something the senior chief could provide for me.

★ ★ ★

"Your move." Weiss, the grizzled chief across the narrow table from me, grinned as he slapped a card down.

We were playing a mindless game, too brain-dead from back-to-back long shifts for anything else. Hot sludgy coffee sloshed around in a half-full cup in my hand. A couple of weeks into my deployment now, I missed Arthur's coffee-snob brew and the mismatched mugs at his apartment even more. Missed his narrow bed every time the snorer above me tossed and turned, and Arthur himself most of all. I tried not to think about him when on duty, but in quieter moments like this it was hard not to. Arthur was a better card player than Weiss, who while usually sharp had left me an opening for a quick trick and easy points.

"Nicely done. Wasn't sure you were even paying attention at all." Weiss was jovial enough, no censure in his voice as he considered the cards in his hand.

"Sorry."

"Don't be. Happens to all of us. My brain keeps wandering too. It's my oldest's birthday today." His voice took on a faraway tone.

"How old?" It went without saying that I was sorry he wasn't there, and that was the type of sentiment we tried not to dwell on down here. It sucked to miss things, and we all knew it.

"Eleven today. My ex will make sure there's a big party and lots of pictures. She's great about details like that."

"Good mom." I nodded, waiting for him to finish his turn. "Did you leave a present?"

"Did I ever." His smile went from wistful to bragging. "Tickets for when we're back. Gonna take her and my younger one to LA. Do all the theme parks, and I scored passes to the birthday girl's favorite tween comedy for a taping and tour.

Big surprise for the kids and hopefully a nice break for my ex. She deserves it."

"I'm sure. And I bet the kids will love the trip." I smiled as I collected some more points by throwing down another pair.

"I hope so. Gotta give them some incentive to make it through this latest deployment."

"Yeah." My jaw tightened. Had I given Arthur any incentive? Use of my car hardly counted. Weiss was smart, giving his kids something concrete to look forward to. Myself, I'd been so sure that Arthur wouldn't wait that I'd been hyper-focused on giving him an easy out. But should I have given him more of a reason to wait? He wasn't a kid I could bribe with Disney, but I also hadn't given him anything to pin his more adult hopes on.

"You doing okay?" Weiss asked, leaning forward. "I know you'd just finished one deployment. Back-to-back with a tight turnaround sucks. I've been there."

"Yeah, it does." I rolled my shoulders. "I'll be glad to be home, that's for sure."

"Got someone waiting?" Weiss wasn't a gossip, but I still hesitated, more out of my own mental muddle than any other reason.

"Sort of." My mouth twisted. "It was still pretty new when I had to leave."

"Ah." He gave a crusty chuckle. "This life is hell on relationships, that's for sure, and I have the alimony to prove it."

"I bet." I joined his laugh. "But it sounds like you got two great kids out of it."

"Oh yeah." He smiled more tenderly. "And a number of good years with their mom. Don't regret that for a second."

"That's great." I'd told Arthur I was happy with whatever we got together, but that wasn't quite true. I wanted longer. Any finite block of time was never going to be enough, but had I prematurely tried to hasten the end rather than appreciating what we could have? With each passing day, I grew less and less sure.

"Will your ex bring the kids to the homecoming?" As it had worked out, I'd been assigned to this sub for the remainder of its deployment. I tried not to add up the total weeks in my head but at least it wasn't measured in months.

"Hope so. Depends on if her new husband can get time off. He's a firefighter down in Portland, but they usually try to drive up. How about you? This new person going to be there?"

"Maybe." If I hadn't talked Arthur out of it with that parting speech. I hadn't told him not to come, but I'd also made it easy for him to make that decision, hadn't begged him to be there. And there we were back to incentives. I'd told him he made me happy, but I also hadn't done very much to ensure his happiness, nor had I translated that feeling into any sort of commitment or permanent emotion. Hell, I'd all but shook his hand and wished him well on my way out the door even though my heart had been breaking.

"For your sake, I hope you get a big welcome." Weiss stretched lazily. "But, man, lifers like us, I just don't think civilians get it."

Lifers like us. Huh. He wasn't wrong there. I'd always said I'd be in as long as they'd have me. I'd come in with something to prove, eager to make rank, hungry for the structure and recognition. But then I'd spent time with Arthur, discovered what it felt like to be around someone whom I didn't have to prove a damn thing to. And I still found satisfaction in my job, but hell, I missed that comfortableness with Arthur something fierce too.

"Heard you'll be up for senior chief next year. Maybe chief of a boat soon, huh?" I kept my voice even for Weiss's sake, thinking of all the years Calder and I had been driven by rank and advancement, same as him. I'd never wavered from that path, never considered alternatives, even when I'd been with Steve. I had no room for doubt in my life.

Except for lately when doubts were my fucking constant companion and answers few and far between.

"Yup." Weiss nodded definitively. "My old man made master chief. I'm not doing any less."

"Good for you," I said even as that little *what if* voice in my head said *maybe*, and more of those doubts I'd always kept out came rushing in.

"Eh. This is all I'm good for, you know? I don't know anything else." He shuffled the cards in a crisp rainbow.

"Yeah." For years, I'd tied my own worth to my rank. What else did I have to offer? I simply didn't know. "And the navy's family. I've been with a couple of folks since sub school."

"Yep, exactly. Another round?" He dealt us each a fresh hand.

I picked up my cards, studied them. Funny how with cards there was always a fresh start if you waited long enough, a chance to try again, hope for better luck. Sure, you had to play the hand you were dealt, but you could also wait for the better hand. Strategy.

"Speaking of sub school, they keep trying to get me to accept an assignment to Groton." Weiss gave a harsh laugh. "But no way. Long as I'm fit, they're not getting me off a boat."

He sounded exactly like the senior chief and every other sailor I knew determined to make rank.

"Yeah, you're a lifer all right." I played a jack, the impish face reminding me of Arthur trying to get his way about something. God, I was such a fool. I missed him so bad I ached from my teeth down to my toes. And there was nothing to do about it but wait—

Wait.

That was it. My eyes widened as I drew another jack, my luck shifting. Fresh hand indeed. I might actually win one off Weiss, who despite not being the most strategic of players did seem to have the damnedest of luck.

Or maybe his care-not attitude was his strategy, all part of his plan. Maybe he made his own luck.

And maybe I could too.

"Hey," I said, keeping my voice casual. "You got any talent for getting a message to the surface?"

"Hell, yes." Weiss puffed up his chest. "Been at this enough years, I know all the tricks. You need something?"

"I just might." I nodded slowly. Maybe my luck was about to change for good.

Chapter Thirty-Six

Arthur

"This family takes birthdays way too seriously," I complained to Oliver, who was manning the grill. We'd all gathered for my dad's birthday. Even Calder, who was still stateside, had come. It made me irrationally angry to see him, not Derrick. His crew was on extended shore time, but not Derrick, who was at the literal bottom of the ocean and not here with me where he belonged.

Meanwhile, there was Calder drinking a beer and laughing with my dad and giving me a very noticeable wide berth. If he was upset over Derrick and me being a legit thing, that was on him. But if the distance was more because he didn't know what to say to me, that I could understand. I didn't know what to say to me either. I missed Derrick more than I'd ever imagined possible. I'd thought I'd known what separation felt like, but I'd been wrong. And what I'd felt as a kid was far different from this adult reality.

I'd always assumed I'd be lonely and angry. But I didn't feel abandoned, even if I was still unhappy with how we'd parted. Derrick didn't have a choice here. I, however, did, and I spent most of my time obsessing over what to do, the choice he'd left me with.

"You're cranky." Mom passed Oliver a platter of uncooked

burgers before coming to stand next to me. "You need a distraction."

"A distraction?" Frowning, I leaned back against the deck rail.

"Something to take your mind off the wait," Mom said patiently like I hadn't tried every new show on my various streaming apps as a way to make it through the way-too-quiet nights.

"I sew," Stacey volunteered.

"I tiled two bathrooms last deployment," added Roger's wife, Veronica.

Oh. I was in this club now, partners left in limbo, united by a shared understanding of exactly how awful waiting was, and I wasn't sure I wanted membership. Or advice.

"I don't need a new hobby." I crossed my arms. "I've had several new contracts the last few weeks. Work keeps me busy."

What I didn't have, however, was a Derrick to share all that news with, and no amount of keeping my hands busy could help with that.

"It's okay to admit you're sad and that you miss him." Stacey patted my tense shoulder. "But he wouldn't want you all cranky."

Wouldn't he? That was an excellent question, one I didn't have an answer to. Derrick had put up with me cranky at family camp, had seemed to understand my bad moods in relation to my family and never tried to jolly me out of them. But on the other hand, he'd all but given me permission to move on. He clearly assumed I couldn't hack this separation, so why was I making myself so miserable? Perversely, his lack of faith in my ability to stick it out made me that much more determined. But it didn't make me any less cranky.

"I bet you had a nice drive up at least." Stacey nabbed a fresh drink from the cooler.

"Eh. Car needed exercise." Driving alone had only reminded me how fun driving with Derrick was. But maybe Stacey had a point in that I could try to find joy in the few things I got to do for him. And I had found satisfaction in cleaning the car to his standards, getting it ready for the drive here, and I had felt close to him while driving to a playlist I'd made for him prior to his deployment. Maybe I didn't need a hobby, but I could afford to get over myself a little more. Inhaling, I made an effort to sound less pissy. "I'm glad he trusted me with the car."

"Of course he trusted you." Mom passed me a bowl of chips. "He loves you."

That remained to be seen. He hadn't said the *L* word, but then neither had I. And he'd said I made him happy. And left me the car to watch over. If actions spoke louder than words, every touch, every look, every kiss had revealed both of our hearts for weeks. But was that enough? I wished I knew.

I shook my head at the offer of chips. "Sorry. Not hungry. And sorry I'm such crappy company."

Sparing them more of my crankiness, I paced off into the yard, beyond where the kids were playing. Watching them made me remember the talent show and Derrick's unbridled joy and pride. I sank down on a nearby bench. I wanted more of Derrick's happiness, wanted reasons to make him smile, wanted to feel his pride, wanted to share every success with him. But damn, waiting was *hard*.

"You're not crappy company," my mom said, plopping down next to me on the garden bench.

"I don't think I'm cut out for this," I admitted, dropping the attitude and getting real for the first time all afternoon. Much as she drove me up a wall, I also couldn't lie to Mom, and she had a way of making me admit hard truths.

"Oh, honey." She put an arm around me. "None of us are."

"You are. You were always so cheerful, managing Dad's absences, living your life without him around, being super mom and never complaining."

"That you think that means I did a good job with you boys, but maybe a little too good."

"What do you mean?"

"I wasn't some sort of cheery zombie who never missed him and never got frustrated. But we had a plan, and I believed in our plan."

"Oh?" Now it was my turn to frown.

"My job as a parent was to make things bearable for you kids, but your dad and I were a team." Her tone stayed patient even in the face of my surliness. "We decided on each re-up together, considering all the factors. It wasn't something he decided and I simply put up with."

"Oh." *A team.* Why hadn't I thought of it that way before? And, more to the point, could I be that with Derrick? Team us. "But even though you were a team, it still sucked, being without him?"

"Yeah, it did." She squeezed me closer. "But at the end of the day, I wanted to be on his team, with all that meant, even if it was hard."

"Because it was worth it?" I'd heard her say similar things enough times, but this time I really let those words settle deep in my soul. That she thought the sacrifices she'd made were worth it was more than clear, but I'd always seen her as misguided in that belief, settling for less than she should have. I hadn't seen the team at the heart of their marriage. I'd always focused on who she was without him, but maybe a better inquiry was who she was *with* him.

"I think it was." She nodded, her gaze going distant as she glanced over at the kids. "But that's a question only I can answer for myself. I can't say if it's worth it for you."

"You can't?" I wrinkled my nose. There was a whoop of laughter as the kids tossed a big beach ball. "You're not here to tell me to buck up and soldier through for Derrick's sake?"

"Nope." She shook her head. "You've got to make that choice for your own sake, no one else's."

Choice. There was that word again and I hated it, hated that Derrick had left me with one instead of extracting a promise from me. Making it through as martyr would be so much easier than having to choose to be here. I made a frustrated noise.

"I know you think he's good for me. The mature and responsible option, unlike my career aspirations." My voice was bitter as my head churned, so much static filling my brain.

"He is good for you, but not if being with him makes you miserable."

"Huh." Did it make me miserable? I was doing an A+ job of convincing everyone around me of that, apparently. But inside, I wasn't so sure. I didn't *want* to be miserable and I didn't think Derrick wanted me miserable either. But what if my attitude was the real choice all along, not whether or not to choose to love Derrick? I'd been struggling because I couldn't seem to control my emotions about Derrick. But I could control my reactions and that was exactly what I had not been doing.

Mom brushed my hair off my forehead. I was in desperate need of a trim, and the gesture made me feel like I was ten again. "Being with you at family camp, I was reminded how special you are, how remarkable your gifts are."

"I don't fit in, though." Even as I said it, I knew that wasn't quite true. I had fit in with Derrick, had never felt out of place around him, and through that sense of belonging, I'd felt more at home around the family than I had in years and years. He'd centered me in a way that I couldn't really make sense of, even in my own head.

"No, but you sure do stand out." Mom laughed as loud as she had all day. "And as you'd undoubtedly say in a better mood, why fit in when you can be a star? Stand out. Do you."

"You did listen." I blinked. All that work at family camp had been worth something. She'd heard.

"I always listen. And that's your challenge now. Be yourself. Don't do something because we all expect it."

"What if what everyone expects is the right thing to do?" I countered right as the bouncing ball landed between us. I batted it back to the kids. "What if the right thing for someone else is the wrong thing for me?"

She signed and leaned forward. "I wish I had an answer, Arthur. Do you, but doing you has consequences."

"I guess the key is figuring out what consequences I want to live with," I said at last.

"That's all we can do," she said as Oliver called from the back. "Oops, time to check the food. You okay?"

"Yeah, I think I am." I exhaled as she walked away, but I didn't budge from my spot. No easy answers, even from Mom. No one to tell me what to do. No—

My phone buzzed, interrupting my muddled thoughts. I checked the message and suddenly my weeks of deliberating and dithering over choice seemed silly. I'd known all along what I was going to do. And I didn't need Derrick or my mom or anyone else to tell me. *Do you.* If I wanted to be the best Arthur I could be, and indeed the happiest me, there was only one real course of action. I'd been inching toward the answer all day, and now the universe had sent me confirmation, and I knew precisely what I had to do.

Chapter Thirty-Seven

Derrick

It would have been easy to say that I was the most eager sailor on the sub for homecoming day, but the truth was that I had been a late arrival and most of the hundred-plus souls on board had been deployed far longer than me. Many like Weiss were parents and as the day approached, I'd learned names and ages and seen cherished photographs. So, the truth was that we were all eager, not simply me.

A young nuke won first-kiss honors, and Gomez's choked-up reaction had my own eyes smarting. That morning, as we approached base, the sub was a flurry of activity, mirrored by my rapidly spinning brain and the rising hope in my heart. After weeks of not being sure what to hope for, I'd turned a corner after getting Weiss to send my message, and now I knew precisely what I wanted and what I was willing to do to get it.

But wanting and hoping weren't the same as getting, and as I did a submarine shave and donned my dress uniform, my spine tingled, nerves causing weird pins and needles because I kept holding my breath.

Please, I asked the universe. *Please.* I hadn't asked it for so much in a very long time, hadn't thought my own needs that significant. *Be selfish,* Arthur had urged me at family camp.

Be selfish. Want something solely for my own benefit. Because damn it I was worth it. We were worth it. I didn't have to prove anything or earn it. I finally believed I deserved Arthur, but that didn't mean he'd be waiting.

"Fox." The CO stopped me in the passageway. "You went above and beyond, filling in on this tour. You want to be on deck?"

Be selfish. My pulse galloped, even my ankles wobbling. Yeah, I wanted to be up there, be among the first to see the crowd.

"Yes, sir." I nodded at him. "I'd be honored."

I joined the others heading on deck in getting into safety gear and rigging. My heart rate increased more with each buckle and tightening of straps until I felt ready to run a 10K. Finally, we got the go-ahead, and the harbor was gloriously in sight on a sunny fall day with a warm breeze ruffling our hair and rustling the big flag we unfurled. As we rose up, my footing had never been more sure. No way was I slipping now, not when we'd come so far, and we were so close. As we neared the pier, I caught a glimpse of the crowd, still too far off to hear, but getting closer, the signs and clumps of families coming into view.

Red hair. I started scanning the murky shapes. *Come on, red.* Holding my posture, I continued to search. And hope. So much hope my heart hurt from holding it all, and the rest of me ached from keeping my other emotions in check. I understood now why a lot of sailors cried at homecoming, and I felt the symbolism of the first-kiss ritual on a whole new level. Having someone waiting meant that damn much.

We were close enough now to hear the clapping and cheers, our able crew navigating us into our berth as we waved to the waiting crowd. Still no red hair. As usual the crowd was held back by a barricade, and it was hard to make out faces, but still I looked.

A sign. *Show me a sign,* I asked the universe. *Please.*

And then as those on deck started getting antsy to disembark, restless chatter as we waited for Gomez to get his first kiss, and right as my hope started to flag for the first time all day, I saw my sign. And I knew exactly what was waiting for me.

Chapter Thirty-Eight

Arthur

"We'll get you there on time." Sabrina drove like a menace, navigating Seattle-area traffic like her social media status was on the line to make it to the base before the buses to the pier departed. She was a demon behind the wheel, with her flame-colored hair flowing, but even she hadn't been able to account for a ploddingly long car ferry ride. She had gone with autumnal colors, burnt oranges and reds that would look garish on anyone else, and the look added to her fiery driving once we were free of the ferry.

"I can't be late. If I'm not there, he'll think I didn't come. He'll assume I wasn't waiting—"

"Breathe," she ordered. We were in her car because Derrick's car was safely stowed at his buddy's. Parking in my neighborhood was too ridiculous, so I'd been keeping the car there other than drives like the one to Dad's birthday. But if Derrick heard about the car being there and saw me not on the pier, he might assume the worst. My thoughts were maybe not the most rational, which was undoubtedly why Sabrina ordered me again. "Inhale, exhale. And here's the community center. And lordy, look at the hunky sailor loading the buses."

"I thought you were done with navy personnel." Now

that we were here and the tension in my spine was ebbing, I could tease more.

"I'm feeling a change of heart coming on." She laughed wickedly as she finished parking. "Now let's run."

"You're in heels," I reminded her as I grabbed my stuff and she fluffed out her hair.

"If I fall, that nice petty officer will be obligated to pick me up," she huffed as we trotted across the parking lot.

"True that." I lugged my sign under one arm and readjusted the balloons.

"We made it," she crowed as we managed to be the last two on board before the bus doors closed.

"Arthur, over here!" a familiar voice called. "We saved you a seat."

"Mom?" I had to blink and blink again. But sure enough, she and Dad were there near the front, having saved seats. "What are you doing here?"

I sank down next to her while Sabrina ended up beside my befuddled father.

"We love Derrick too," my mom said brightly and squeezed my arm. "I didn't want you waiting alone."

"I'm not alone," I said, still slightly dazed.

"I didn't know you were bringing Sabrina," Mom said apologetically as the bus started to move. "I still would have come, but—"

"No, I mean, I haven't been alone this whole time." I spoke slowly, puzzling deep thoughts out, same as when a music composition finally started to come together on paper for me, moving from vague awareness to deeper understanding.

"Of course not." My mom shook her head like she might check my temperature next. And maybe she needed to, because it was only now hitting me that I hadn't been alone this whole time. I'd had Liam and Craig distracting me with the game they were beta testing, Sabrina bringing me coffee, Mom calling to check on me, Stacey sending me cookies, Roger's wife spamming me cat memes, and the rest of the Euler clan pinging me on social media. I'd been lonely, but not alone. Like at Dad's party when I'd realized I was part of some new club, but now I actually understood that club had been there all along. It was part of what defined us as a family, the teamwork that went into the service at the heart of our identity. I'd always been a part of it. Even when I'd stood out, I'd still belonged.

I hadn't been alone, but more importantly neither was Derrick. Maybe this right here was one of the things I could bring him.

"We're family." My voice was still woozy, like I was recovering from a gut punch.

"We are," Mom assured me.

"I'm ride or die with you, bestie." Sabrina reached across the aisle to touch my arm. "Silly sign and all. Which if he doesn't appreciate, he's an idiot."

"Oh, let me see." Mom peered around me. I BET ON LOVE my sign read. Frowning, Mom tilted her head. "But you hate bets and wagers."

"I also hate long-distance relationships and yet here I am, going all-in on one." My voice was way less cranky than it had been at Dad's party. The long distance was less a roadblock and more a fact, like the weather, something we'd have to deal with but not insurmountable.

"I'm proud of you." Putting an arm around me, Mom squeezed me tight. "But not because you chose this particular outcome. Because you figured out what you wanted and you're going for it."

"Derrick's a lucky guy," my dad added, making my throat go winter-sweater thick.

"Thanks." Glancing away from all that parental approval, I tapped my sign. "I'd be here regardless but he sent me a message, so I'm sending one back."

"Oh? Do tell! What did it say? Was it deeply romantic?" Sabrina leaned forward, eyes flashing and thick eyelashes fluttering.

"More like highly private," I countered, then softened my tone. "But yes, romantic."

I'd long since memorized every word. *I love you. Maybe we can tie? I'm betting on us.*

I had already known deep inside that I'd be here today, but his message had sealed the deal and ensured that I was filled with so much hope that it was a wonder I hadn't floated through the remaining separation. Of course, I hadn't had a good way to get Derrick a non-emergency message, but my fondest wish was that he knew and was similarly hope-filled instead of as despondent as we had both been when we parted.

This was better, so much better, and this was the part that was a choice. I was choosing hope.

As we exited the bus, that buoyant emotion lifted me even higher. My anticipation was so different this time, new nerves that had nothing to do with creating a public spectacle, and my focus was way more inward. Fuck going viral or an audience. All I needed was that ship to appear.

And then it did, at first a distant shadow, then closer, personnel on deck in gleaming uniforms, flag flapping in the breeze. Sabrina had learned from our last outing and brought opera glasses.

"Hey! I think Derrick's on deck!" Bouncing on her heels, she shoved the little gold binoculars at me. She was right. As the boat drew closer, I could see him standing with other chiefs, proud and tall. My own posture straightened, muscles tensing with worry for the sailors on the slick deck as the sub was moved into position at the pier.

The wait was down to minutes, but each minute felt like hours, dragging on and on, each step closer to disembarking happening in slow motion. My internal soundtrack was full of dramatic pauses and rising emotion, a musical countdown, and my toes tapped along impatiently. I held my sign and balloons high, but there were so many other signs and people that the chances of him spotting us were slim.

An utterly adorable young couple got first-kiss honors, the woman's dress with little chili peppers on it making Sabrina snap pictures and rave about the duo's adorableness. But for all their cuteness, they weren't Derrick and me. The universe needed to hurry up and get to *my* kiss, damn it.

However, I tried to find some patience for the new dad who sobbed his way through meeting a tiny blue bundle. Then finally more crew disembarked. Not Derrick, not yet.

"He's coming," Sabrina assured me, tugging my sleeve.

"I know, I know. Sometime this decade." Sighing, I looked down at my shoes. Sabrina had dressed me again, and my boots were more club than hiking. Too new. Too stiff.

"No, I mean he's coming right now. Right—"

"Here," I breathed out as I looked up and all that waiting came to an end. And now he was *here*, and hilariously, I felt woefully unprepared for his presence.

He was here, looking resplendent in his white uniform, sun glinting off his medals and ribbons. He even smelled familiar, the aftershave I hadn't caught whiff of in weeks. The few times I'd sensed it on a stranger, I'd been wistful and filled with longing. But now it was really Derrick right here in front of me, this very second, and I didn't know what to do or say first.

He licked his lips, looking uncharacteristically uncertain. He wasn't smiling, and my nerves reached epic levels. My inner soundtrack hit a warning note. What if he'd changed his mind? What if he no longer meant—

"Hey."

"Hey," I said back. *A+ communicator, Arthur. Good job.*

"You came." The wonder in his tone hit me right in the heart. Maybe he too was simply too overwhelmed to smile.

"I did." I managed a smile or at least I hoped I did. My face muscles weren't exactly responding to my brain.

"I want to kiss you. Can I kiss you? Please?" That he thought to add the *please* was adorable, and finally my mouth muscles resumed working and I grinned broadly.

"You better."

Chapter Thirty-Nine

Derrick

He came. Arthur really came. And he was grinning at me and waiting for me to kiss him.

I didn't realize how scared I'd been that he wouldn't be there until I saw his sign, and relief so intense flooded me that my knees legit shook. Not the best thing when standing on deck of a moving sub, but somehow I stayed upright and made it through the last bit of waiting.

Now my shaky legs had carried me here, to him, and as I pulled him to me, I swore one of those mental soundtracks he was always joking about swelled like an orchestra was among our audience. But beyond that, I didn't register much of our surroundings as I claimed his mouth. I wanted to go slow, remember each second of the contact, but my body kept sprinting ahead of my brain.

In some ways it felt like our first kiss all over again, new and special, and in others it felt like we'd never paused, like I'd been gone an hour not weeks and weeks, a comfortable familiarity there that hadn't been there that very first kiss.

He tasted like a memory, like mint and tea and a hint of sweet coffee too. His lips were every bit as soft as I remembered, and his strong arms clutching me lived up to my memories as well. He was solid and real and there and we kissed and kissed.

Behind us, I heard some whoops and the sound of cameras flashing. But still I kissed him.

"Welcome home," he murmured against my mouth.

"You're my home." I sucked in a big lungful of air, even oxygen tasting better now. Or maybe that was still more relief, more tension bleeding away so I could breathe easier.

"Can you go viral twice?" Sabrina mused next to Arthur, holding up her shiny phone. "Who says we find out?"

"I'm too happy to care." Arthur laughed.

"Me too."

"Bet that ex of yours will have kittens if he sees," Sabrina crowed as she clicked something on her phone with a long orange nail.

"Let him. I don't care." And it was true. I wasn't jealous anymore, if I'd ever truly been. I'd been hurt and embarrassed, but I'd never wanted Steve back, even in the beginning of this whole thing. I'd hated how inadequate the breakup had made me feel, but the intervening time had healed a lot of those more petty feelings.

And from the very first kiss, I'd wanted Arthur. He, not Steve, had consumed my thoughts for months and he was truly all I cared about.

"He lost out." Arthur tugged me closer for another kiss, this one way more possessive and showy. Laughing, I kissed him back.

"You're cute when you go all caveman," I said to him.

"I could say the same thing to you." He beamed at me. There was so much more I needed to say to him. Simply him being here was amazing, but it was a start not an endpoint. I was ecstatic, but not deluding myself into thinking everything would work out from here onward.

However, right then, I only wanted to kiss him more, bask in his realness and there-ness. True conversation could wait.

"You got my message." I pointed at his sign. He'd had balloons too, but those seemed to have escaped at some point.

"I did." Eyes deep with meaning, he nodded. "Thank you for sending it. But I was coming anyway, and I want you to know that."

"For real?" I met his intense gaze, trying to suss out whether he was simply being nice.

"For real and also not because you left me your sweet ride." His chuckle was as welcome as his words and smile. "I was coming for me."

"Good." I grabbed his hand because I couldn't not touch him. Around us, people were chattering, hugging, taking pictures, a chaos I was so happy to be a part of. And for maybe the first time ever, I did feel part of the festivities, not removed and watching at a distance.

"Welcome home, Derrick." Arthur's mom gave me a hug.

"You both came too?" I finally registered the presence of Arthur's parents on the other side of Sabrina.

"Wouldn't miss it. You're practically an honorary Euler at this point. Good work, son." That was maybe the longest I'd heard Arthur's father speak at one go. My chest went so tight, it was surprising that my uniform didn't crack.

"Thank you, sir." I maybe should have been a little embarrassed that Arthur's parents had had to witness yet another highly enthusiastic kiss between Arthur and me. But this one had been real, not fake, and there was no ruse about my feelings for their son. Also, I was a little too giddy to care overly about shocking anyone right then.

"Dad's right. You're one of us now." A deep voice I'd recognize anywhere came up behind me, and I whirled. Except for this guy. Maybe I did care a little more than I'd thought about shocking or pissing Calder off. He was wearing a work uniform and was slightly out of breath, like he'd jogged across base.

"Sorry, man. I almost missed it. Finally got free." He clapped me on the shoulder hard and his expression was difficult to read. Not affable like normal, no easy smile, and his usually sparkling eyes were cloudy, but there was also no anger there. And he'd come. That had to count for something.

"You sure you want to claim me?" I asked, a quiver running down my legs. Losing his friendship would suck, and his approval meant possibly more to me than even Arthur's parents'. I was doing this thing regardless, but I couldn't deny wanting to keep Calder in my life too.

"Dude. I'm always gonna claim you." Calder regarded me solemnly. "You kissing my brother doesn't change anything between us."

"Ride or die," Sabrina supplied.

"Yup. And if you want to put up with this guy, you're welcome to him. Man, he was the king of misery at Dad's birthday. I didn't think he could miss anything that much. Guess it is the real deal." Calder shrugged, all relaxed now, but my back tensed.

"I wasn't that miserable." Arthur made a pained face at Calder. "He's overstating."

"No, he's not. You sulked—"

"Sabrina," Arthur said sharply.

"Oops." Sabrina giggled. "Sorry, Arthur was the picture of patience. All zen and chill."

She offered me a winning smile, but I wasn't convinced. "That so?"

"Don't worry about it." Arthur squeezed my hand tight. "Not now. Please?"

"Okay." I agreed because this was neither the time nor

the place, but I also added it to my mental list of conversation topics.

"I know exactly what you both need." Arthur's mom had an alarmingly wide smile.

"Oh?" I kept my voice upbeat even though I was almost certain that the answer involved a Euler family dinner. Which would be fine and fun and eventually, some century, I would get Arthur alone and we could have the first of what promised to be several important conversations. Maybe we'd get lucky and Liam and Craig wouldn't be around tonight. At least I had a few days' leave and an Arthur to spend them with.

However, instead of announcing a dinner, she dug in her purse. "Here." She held up a piece of plastic that for a single horrifying second I thought was two condoms, but then realized had the name of a local chain of hotels on it. "Now you don't have to do the ferry tonight and you can be alone that much sooner."

"Oh wow." My jaw went as slack as my brain right then, but Arthur was faster, plucking the card from his mom's fingers.

"Thank you. You shouldn't have, but wow is right, and boy am I glad you did. Sabrina—"

"Like I was ever going back with you?" She rolled her elegant eyes. "Don't worry, honey. I already got the number of Petty Officer Helpful from the bus."

"Excellent." Arthur gave her a high five. "I suppose we should do dinner first…"

"Your father and I have reservations." His mom continued to beam. "For two. I cashed in a bunch of airline miles. Dinner for us, hotel for you. Oh, and I asked for a late checkout time."

That last bit made both Calder and his father turn pink and look away.

"Thank you," I said, perhaps a little too heartily because Arthur's dad's blush worsened.

"You're the best." Arthur gave his mom a fast hug. "Calder? Were you counting on Derrick for dinner?"

A strange look flitted across Calder's face. Perhaps he was thinking about all the times he hadn't made an effort to include Arthur. "No," he said at last. "He's all yours."

"He is at that." Arthur linked arms with me. I wanted to say something else to Calder, a thank-you at least, or touch his arm, but he was already striding away, murmuring something about getting back on duty. It might take a little time for our friendship to get unweird, but him showing up meant a great deal.

"Ready to go?" Arthur asked. "I'm more than ready to kiss you without going viral or risking indecent exposure."

"Me too." Talking. We needed to talk, with words. And sentences. Lots of them. But hell if I wasn't wanting more kissing too, the indecent kind especially.

Chapter Forty

Arthur

"I love my mom. Like really love my mom." I was all but dancing as Derrick let us into the darkened hotel room.

"Yeah, she's pretty great." He flipped on the light. Basic hotel room decor greeted us—two queen beds—like we'd need the second—white linens, beige walls, bland seascapes over the beds, and a view of the parking lot. But it was ours and it was blessedly private. He tossed his bag on a bed.

"I think we're alone now," I hummed to Derrick, pulling him close.

"We are." He gave me a short but all-too-fast kiss. "But don't you think we should talk?"

"Talk is overrated." I pulled at his shirt. He'd stopped by the barracks to hang up his dress whites and grab a change of clothes. "Does wearing civies feel weird now?"

"Rather." Laughing, he tilted my chin up. "And I can tell you want them on the floor."

"Really? What gave me away?" I batted my eyelashes at him, Sabrina style.

"Ha. I'm dying for a real shower."

"With me?" I had zero chill.

"Yes, with you." He slid a hand up the back of my close-fitting shirt. Sabrina had dressed me in a nice shirt with slinky material and skinny jeans. I looked ready for a club or for climbing Derrick like a tree, which was definitely the more fun option.

But Derrick was frowning. "But don't you think we should—"

"Talk. Yes. Later." I made an impatient noise. "Right now isn't it enough to say that I'm in this thing—whatever it takes—and you are too?"

"Yeah, I am." He used his hand on my back, warm and strong, to guide me even closer until our torsos were flush together. "And I meant what I said. I love you. I should have said it before I left."

"Yeah, you could have." I bumped his chest with mine. "A message, Derrick? Really? With me not able to respond?"

"Sorry." A rare rosy flush crept across his cheeks and his eyes shifted nervously.

"But it's okay." I looped my arms around his neck, meeting his uncertain gaze. "I love you too. And that's why talk can wait. We love each other. The rest is all details."

Derrick pursed his mouth as if he were preparing a list of objections, then exhaled hard. "Okay. And really? You don't have to say it back."

"Yeah, I do." I kissed him then, hard and long, and tried to let my lips do the convincing. I loved him. So much. And he loved me. That was what mattered. Well, that and the fact that we were both still wearing too many clothes.

"Shower. Now." I released him long enough to push him in the direction of the nearby small bathroom. "Damn. Now I really miss the cabin. That tub in particular."

"Ha. This is paradise compared to the head on a sub. And two beds? Luxury."

"Let's use them both." I laughed wickedly as I shrugged out of my shirt. "After I wash you all over."

"Yes, please," Derrick gasped as I pulled his shirt up enough to stroke his bare sides. He leaned in for another kiss, this one full of dirty promises I intended to hold him to. We both wiggled out of our remaining clothes. After we were naked, I set the water to hot and grabbed the soap and shampoo from the sink.

"Don't be alarmed if the water turns gray," he joked as he climbed in the shower, groaning like we were already having sex.

"If it does, I'll just wash you again." I climbed in behind him and shut the curtain as he made another orgasmic noise. "That good, huh? Going to trade me in for a showerhead with decent water pressure?"

"You have no idea." He turned so his back could get some spray. It was a cramped fit and I wasn't getting very wet, but hell if I was going to complain. Instead, I unwrapped the soap and started sudsing up his chest.

"How are you more muscled after weeks under water, not less?" His already impressive chest was possibly even more firm and his biceps seemed bigger too.

"Nothing to do but work out." He groaned and stretched into my touch. "Damn that feels so good. Entirely possible I might get off simply from soap bubbles and your touch."

"Please don't," I said sternly. "I have big plans for you."

"Big plans, huh?" Stopping my lathering with his hands on mine, he found my mouth for another kiss so hot that I stopped caring about chilly air and lack of water. I gave myself over to his mouth until we were both panting, hard cocks brushing against each other, hands clutching.

My back had goose bumps but not only from the cold. His lips were like a large cold brew after days without caffeine, and I sucked down everything he gave me like it was the last drink on earth. And somewhere between thirsty kisses I managed to soap his arms and back.

"You too." He stole the soap from me and proceeded to lather me up.

"Hey! I had a shower this morning," I protested as he moved so I could rinse.

"Yeah, but I didn't get to do the scrubbing." He gave a wolfish grin.

"Well, in that case…" I stretched my arms so he could have his fun.

"Missed you." His tone was almost reverent as his hands skimmed down my torso. He didn't touch my cock, but it strained toward him nonetheless.

"Missed you too."

"Parts of you more than others?" he teased.

"All of me." My voice was all breathy as he soaped my ass. I rinsed then angled myself so he could have more hot water. "Damn, this is cramped."

"Don't talk to me about tight spaces." He made another of those near-sexual groans again before shampooing his hair.

"I was going to do that for you!" I pretended to scold him, which was really simply another excuse for a kiss.

"Sorry. Getting desperate to try out one of those beds."

"Who needs a bed?" I moved closer, cock dragging against his side. I'd be more than happy to get him off now then work on a repeat later. But right as he dipped his head to kiss me, the hot water sputtered, leaving us with a tepid spray.

"On second thought, bed. Now," I ordered.

"Aye, aye, Captain." He saluted me before flipping off the shower. We sped through drying off, giggling like teenagers as we raced to the closest bed. Tumbling onto the bed next to his bag, we landed in a happy pile of limbs and towels.

Sprawled on his back, Derrick tugged me more fully on top of him, moaning softly as I settled against him.

"Okay. Totally on board the no-talking plan now." He gave a tight laugh as he encouraged me to rock against him, grip firm on my hips.

"Me too. Shut up and kiss me should be the new plan."

"I like it." Bucking upward to meet my rhythm, he found my mouth for another blistering kiss.

Not satisfied with our mouths having all the fun, I broke away to pepper his jaw and neck with kisses, rediscovering some of my favorite spots on him, the ones where his aftershave still lingered and the ones that made him gasp and writhe.

As I explored, he did too, hands roving all over my back and ass. He traced my crack with devious fingers, making me need to move faster. And making me need something else too.

"Seriously regretting not packing lube in my pocket this morning." Even my laugh was strained.

"I grabbed some when I went up to my room to change." Derrick fumbled for his bag.

"Bless you," I said as he came up triumphant with a small bottle.

"Kiss me." Slicking up his fingers, he proceeded to torment me on dual fronts, mouth hot and needy against mine and slippery fingers teasing me open.

"Not enough," I groaned as I grabbed for the bottle and moved enough so that I could coat his cock.

"Fuck yeah." He tipped his head back against the pillows only to raise it as I adjusted my position to line us up. "Whoa. Condom?"

"Do we really need it?" I made a frustrated noise both because I was that impatient, but also I had a whole new set of fantasies where Derrick was concerned and I was desperate to fulfill this one. "I mean, I was a virgin and you were tested twice. Nothing's changed there."

"Nothing?" He studied me carefully. "I would understand if—"

"I wouldn't," I growled, capturing him for a possessive kiss. "Nothing's changed other than a new wish list item for going bare, and a sore left hand from all the solo jerking. I want this with you."

"I want this too." He stroked my face. "I've never done it without a condom. But I trust you."

"I trust you, too." I kissed him lightly and finished slicking him up, jacking him slowly as I levered myself more upright.

"Do it," he ordered, like I needed encouragement.

"Yeah." Slowly, I sank down. Even with his earlier play, I was still tight, and my body was reminding me how very long it had been. The blunt pressure made me gasp as I tried to relax.

"Easy." He caressed my sides before dancing his fingertips over my nipples.

"Do that again." I took a little more of him. It still wasn't the most comfortable, but it was getting better especially when he tweaked my nipples.

"This?" He repeated the motion before dropping one of his hands to my cock. "Or this?"

"Definitely that." And definitely easier now, the fullness and heat of him exactly what I'd been craving.

"You feel so good." He leaned up to press a kiss to my neck before falling back onto the bed with a moan.

"Different?"

"Yeah. Intense. Slicker. Hotter." His eyes closed, face tensing. "So good."

"Awesome." I loved being able to give him something new, something we could share together. He'd been my first for so many things, so it made my insides even warmer to get to be a first for him too.

"More." He bucked his hips. "Whatever you need. Whatever feels good to you."

"This good?" I asked, finding a shallow angle that hit where I most wanted it, sparks of pleasure racing up my spine. "You want me to get myself off on you?"

"Please. Use me." His shoulders and chest were stone boulders under my hands, and he met my every movement with low, needy noises. He was the hottest thing I'd ever seen, struggling for control like this, letting me ride him however I wanted.

Drunk on power, I moved faster, keeping that same angle but taking him deeper. It felt like we shared an electric loop, his heart hammering under my palm, the pulse reverberating all the way to my ass. He stroked my cock and I felt it everywhere, pleasure finding my abs and thighs, even my tense neck and calves. We moved together, urgently now, and unlike him, I kept my eyes wide open, waiting to see the exact moment he shattered.

"You're so fucking gorgeous." He popped his eyes open to catch me staring at him. "What?"

"So are you. I could watch you forever."

"Not sure I can last forever." He gave a half moan, half laugh. "But I can try."

"Don't want you to try. Want you to fall apart." I rode him harder, seeking his shattering even more than my own orgasm. I was merciless, reveling in each of his sounds. It felt like his pleasure was my due for all this waiting, a prize I'd earned and I was damn sure going to claim it.

"Arthur…" His face scrunched up. "Please."

"Do it. Come for me," I demanded, still in ruthless mode.

"You too." He tightened his grip on my cock, matching

my rhythm. Devious, but I could be too. I flexed my spine, rolling my hips more, and clenched my ass.

"Fuck." *Bingo.* His next moan seemed pulled from the depths of the Pacific. His cock pulsed, even harder if that were possible. Lips falling open, his whole face went slack.

And I felt it, felt him come in a way I couldn't with a condom. Everything became slicker, turning me on in some primal way, feeling him that deep in me.

"Derrick." And then I was coming too, crying out as his fist milked my cock. I shot all over his stomach, marking him like he'd marked me. Simply that dirty thought was enough to get one final spurt from me.

Spent, I collapsed against his chest. He smoothed a gentle hand down my back and pressed soft kisses against my face.

"Love you," he whispered. "Love you so much."

"Me too." My voice was husky and I buried my face in his shoulder. "Love you. That was…" I trailed off because I lacked words.

"Yeah, exactly." He chuckled. "I think it will be a week before I can feel my legs again."

"Good. I'll keep you right here until then."

"We'll starve." He gave me a dopey smile.

"Nah. I can still reach the phone. I'll feed you pizza."

"Such caring." His laugh rumbled through both of our bodies.

"I try."

"We're going to need a second shower at some point as well." He stroked my sweaty back.

"We're a mess," I agreed. "Still staying right here."

"Okay." He went silent, so still I almost thought he might doze off, but he seemed to be deliberately syncing our breathing. It was some sort of joint meditation, and it was almost as good as the sex, being joined to him like this.

"Love you," I whispered a long time later, breaking the silence because much as I loved lying like this, I was a little hungry and clammy and not all that sleepy.

"Me too." He kissed me tenderly on the mouth before uttering my least favorite sentence. "We should talk."

Chapter Forty-One

Derrick

Arthur did not want to talk. That much was clear from the stubborn set of his chin as well as his delaying tactics—another shower, ordering some food for delivery to the room, putting on clothes so we didn't shock the delivery person, and eating said food. However, I drew the line when he wanted to check the news.

"You never follow the news." I plucked the remote from his hand. "And you can critique whatever bad music reality shows you want after we talk. Really talk."

"Okay." Defeated, he flopped next to me on the bed, one arm over his eyes. "I'm not convinced there's that much to talk about. You were gone and it sucked, but I made it through it. Rather, *we* made it through it, and now you're back and I just want to enjoy you and be happy."

"I know. Me too." I peered down at him. God, I loved him, obstinate streak and all. "But how miserable were you? Everyone seemed to think you were doing terribly."

My stomach sloshed, pizza dinner not sitting particularly well. I didn't want him miserable, and if he was, I needed him to be honest so that we could figure out a solution together.

"I coped. I wasn't wasting away. Sabrina and Calder were

overstating it." He managed a bored tone, but I wasn't buying it.

"So you weren't lonely?" I frowned at him.

"I had work. Got some new gigs I can't wait to tell you about."

"That's awesome." Despite my frustration with him, I still managed a smile and patted his arm. "I'm proud of you. So work was a good distraction?"

"I didn't take up a new hobby like Stacey and everyone told me to, but yeah, work helped. You know me. I get in the zone and suddenly it's been a week and I'm starving and in massive need of a shower."

I laughed a little at that. "No other distractions? Not even a new instrument?"

"Damn. You do know me well. I got a replica of this twelfth-century stringed rebec, and I've been fiddling with it some."

"I want to see." I stroked his thigh. "And I don't want you sad and depressed and needing to escape into work. Maybe Calder and Sabrina were joking, but you being happy, that matters."

"Thanks." He dropped his arm from his face and held my gaze. "You happy matters too."

"I'd like to tell you that I'll be stateside for a while, but we know how well it went last time I promised that."

"I know. There will be other separations. I get it. That's part of this gig." He sounded so resigned that my heart clenched.

"It doesn't have to be," I said softly.

"We are not breaking up." His stern tone would have been comical under other circumstances. "You're not getting rid of me simply because the being together is hard and separations are a challenge."

"No, no." I held up a hand as he glared at me, his arm back

down by his side, fist balled up. "No breaking up. I mean I don't have to be in the navy forever." Swallowing hard, I had to work to keep my voice steady. I'd rehearsed the line in my head, but saying it aloud still felt big. "This whole time we've both been assuming that I'll stay in as long as possible."

"They don't hand civilians chief-of-the-boat duties." He cocked his head to one side, regarding me coolly. "You've had a dream, Derrick. Same as Calder. Same as me, really. It would be like asking me to give up music."

"You're my music," I countered, resolve stronger now. It might be big and scary to visualize a different future, but I couldn't ignore my recent realizations either.

"What?" He wrinkled up his face.

"You're the thing I'm most passionate about. The thing I think about first in the morning. You and building a life with you. For years, the navy gave me what I didn't have—a family and a purpose. But for the first time I've got a passion that doesn't have a rank attached. With you, I don't have to prove anything, and that's a feeling I want more of. I want a life with you. A home. A family."

Arthur's already fair skin paled further, freckles standing out more starkly. "Wow. Just…wow. Warn a guy before you do a speech like that."

"Sorry." Hoping I hadn't gone too far, I shifted on the bed.

"No being sorry." Sitting up, he leaned in to brush a kiss across my mouth. "I want those things too, but you can have those things and stay in. I'm not going to make you choose. I want to be your family to come home to whether you're gone eight hours or eight hundred."

"Wow." Now it was my turn to be gobsmacked out of words to describe how wonderful he was.

He found my hand, held it between both of his. "I get you *and* music. You can have me and the navy. Promise."

"You deserve a full-time partner." I finally brought up the ravine that had always separated us, even when we'd carefully avoided its mention. "It's what you've always wanted. And I want you to have that."

Arthur quirked his mouth. "It's true I always had a certain type of guy in my head as being what I was holding out for. But it turns out that what I was waiting for was *you*."

"Okay, you're pretty damn good at speechmaking too." I kissed him hard and fast.

"You had a point back at camp that I probably could have found someone sooner, especially if I'd been willing to tone down my crazy hours and musical obsessions. But I wasn't. I didn't want to compromise."

"You shouldn't compromise on being you," I said firmly.

"Exactly. And you shouldn't have to either. I don't love you in spite of the navy, Derrick, I love you *because* of it."

"How so? You hate the navy," I reminded him.

"I love you because you are loyal and disciplined and a great leader. Sure you'd be amazing in whatever career you want after the navy, but you're also amazing in this one too and I don't want to take that away from you."

"It seems so unfair, asking you to make all the sacrifices." I sighed and dropped his hands so I could scrub at my hair.

"See, that's what I always thought. I figured that the people at home were the ones sacrificing most, but you're sacrificing too. You give up a ton, and not only for me, but for others as well. So no, I'm not making all the sacrifices."

I let out an audible gulp before digging my teeth into my lower lip. I was not going to cry, damn it. "Feels like I've already given up a lot. We both have. And I want to give you a home. The music studio you want."

"Amazingly, that is possible whether you stay in or not. I'm not so high-maintenance that I can't make my music studio dreams happen in base housing. And maybe you want to give me a place, but I want to give you the feeling. *Home.* We can be that for each other."

"Yeah." It was the only word I could get out, I was trying that hard not to let the tears fall. "I want that. And I am going to work on ways to be around more. Stateside assignments. Plans for if I don't re-up or for after I hit my twenty. But not for you—or rather not only for you. For me. There's a lot I don't want to miss out on, including my own life."

"You deserve to find your passion, Derrick." He gave me a sweet kiss on the cheek, and that was it. A rogue tear escaped despite my better efforts to hold it back. "And it can't only be me. You're right about that. It has to be you too. Maybe it's enough right now to say that we can be a team, figure out a future together. But finding your passion should be a part of it."

"Kind of like you tell the kids—do you." My voice was all choked up now and the temptation to bury my head in a pillow was high. Emotions were hard. "I want to figure out what it means to be Derrick, but I do think you're key."

"Good. And that's what I've been trying to say too. I like who I am with you. It's not who I am without you, but who I am *with* you and because of you." His eyes were shining. Maybe I wasn't the only one fighting to hold things in.

"But if you're miserable—"

"That's also a choice. I was kind of wallowing in self-pity at first. But then I discovered that I'm stronger and more resilient and less alone than I thought. Neither of us may choose the separations, but we can choose our reaction to being apart. If I had a bad attitude at first, that's on me."

"Well, maybe a little on me for such a crappy goodbye." I bit the inside edge of my mouth.

"Perhaps that's on both of us." He was way more generous than my behavior merited.

"I could have said that I love you and that I want a future together and that I'm going to do whatever it takes to get that future."

"Okay, yeah, that's a nice speech." He kissed my cheek again. "How about you try that next time instead of assuming that I'm going to bolt?"

"I don't deserve you."

"Of course, you..." Arthur started a flip response then trailed off as he frowned. "Wait. You're serious. You think that you, best person I've ever known, guy my parents would happily trade me for, doesn't deserve me?"

"Good things never last," I whispered, bunching up the comforter with my fist.

"Yeah? Well, this one does." Arthur used his hand to make me look at him. "And you, Derrick Fox, are one hundred percent deserving of being happy. You. Not because you made chief or because you qualify for a mortgage, but *you*. You are worth this."

And then I, Derrick Fox, decorated naval chief, really was crying. I'd been afraid to hope for so long, afraid to trust in a future that might not be here for me. I'd almost lost my shot at a future I could have, if only I was brave enough to reach for it.

"Oh, fuck. Now I've made you cry." Arthur wrapped me up in a big hug.

"Didn't even take sex this time." I took a big breath, trying to use the joke to steady myself.

"I love you. You need to love you too." Arthur was apparently not done being serious, and his solemnity made my eyes sting all over again.

"I'll try," I promised. "You make me want to try."

"Good, because you're worth forever."

"So are you." I found his mouth for a sloppy but heartfelt kiss. "Wait, you're crying too."

"You started it." Laughing, he poked me in my chest. "And are you sure I'm the one you want? I mean I do come with this big, crazy family..."

"I love your big crazy family." I kissed him hard. "But I love you more."

"Good. And that's another thing I love about you. You kind of helped me to love them again. To see that maybe I did belong even when I assumed I didn't."

"You did belong. And you'll always belong with me." I pulled him more fully against me.

"Well, being in your cabin does have certain perks." He winked at me. "But I'd share a canvas yurt with you. Truly."

"I'm not going to hold you to that." I chuckled and tumbled us both back onto the pillows. "I'm good for indoor plumbing at least."

"You're the best fake boyfriend ever." He kissed my nose. "And the last *real* partner I want to have."

"There's nothing fake about how I feel for you." I hugged him close. My favorite blanket in the world was his warm weight on me.

"Me too. I love you. And I'm always going to be waiting. Always."

"I'm gonna do my best to make it worth it." My voice was thick again. Knowing he would be waiting made me want to come home that much more. He was my home, my purpose, the thing I didn't even let myself want. He was home, and as I kissed him, I knew I'd spend the rest of my life coming back to him.

Chapter Forty-Two

Arthur—Winter

"Are you sure you can make it for breakfast?" Mom asked, voice crackling like she was in a store. Outside my window, a dank gray Seattle winter day had settled in for another long week of rain. But inside, my heart was sunny, and I smiled as I leaned back in my desk chair.

"We'll be there," I assured her. "Derrick's due here any time now, and I'll set double alarms if I have to."

"Good. I can't wait to have everyone together again." The family was gathering for Calder's birthday, and a weekend brunch had worked out the best for multiple packed schedules.

"I know. And Derrick doesn't want to miss it either." Things were less weird with Calder these days. He and Derrick had recently hung out with other friends from the base for a night of cards. I'd been invited, which Calder seemed to be making more of an effort to do lately. I appreciated Calder cutting way back on the teasing, but I'd still sent Derrick without me both to meet a deadline on my latest project and to give them some friend time alone. We'd picked out Calder's present together, though, and neither of us was about to bail on family breakfast to see him open the handheld poker game we'd found.

"I hope it doesn't snow. Oliver and Roger are both driving so early," Mom fretted.

"It won't snow. Just more rain, but Oliver and Roger are great drivers, regardless."

"I know. I only want a nice day for Calder. He's seemed subdued lately. I want to see him happy. Maybe he needs to date more." There was a rustling noise on the phone, and I laughed softy to myself at the notion of her shopping for dates for Calder, like flipping through a rack of choices.

"Mom. You finally get one kid happily partnered and then you start on the next. Let Calder find his own path, whatever that may be."

She sighed. "I know, I know. Let Calder be Calder."

"Exactly. Do you need me to sing you a song about it?"

That got a hearty laugh. "No, but you and Derrick better both be at family camp this year. The kids are counting on it, and I can't wait to see the musical numbers."

"I know. We're planning on it. Derrick's put in for the leave, but a lot can change as you well know."

"Yes, I know. I'm crossing everything that everyone can come."

"I'm sure—" I cut myself off at the sound of the door and Craig talking to someone in the hall. "I think he's here. Can we finish this talk at breakfast?"

"Of course, honey. Have a nice night." We ended the call right as Derrick appeared in my doorway.

"Hey." He said it all casual, but his wide smile gave him away. He might have a killer poker face for Calder and his friends, but for me he was an open book, and I loved that about him. He was way less broody these days, and as I tugged him into the room, there was lightness to his step that hadn't been there a few months ago. Leading him over to the bed, I stopped to give him a kiss.

"Hey, yourself. You taste minty. Did you get a peppermint mocha on the walk from the bus without me?"

"Yours is iced and on the counter in the kitchen, Mr. Cold Beverages in Winter." Eyes twinkling, he gave me another kiss. "And you're the one who got me hooked on the drink. And you."

"Awww." That got a third kiss before Derrick perched on the edge of the bed. I moved to join him, then stopped. "Should I go rescue our drinks?"

"In a minute." He pulled me to sit next to him. "First, I've got news."

My pulse sped up. *Thump. Thump.* We'd been waiting for this. And waiting. "News?"

"Yup. Orders came through early this morning. Groton, here we come. Got the instructor billet."

"Oh my God. Finally." I wasn't sure whether to laugh or cry. Ever since Derrick put in for the instructor position at sub school, we'd both been on edge. It was a big, huge change. For both of us. But it would mean him stateside for a few years. I was all for that as long as it made him happy.

As for me, I'd be close to the East Coast Eulers and all my Boston friends from college. It would be fun seeing them again, and even the snow would be a nice change and worth the hassle to be with Derrick. Really with him. Team us. We'd made this decision together, and I felt good and excited about it.

"Wait. You found out this morning? And you didn't text?" I fake pouted. "I would have had a celebration waiting. Cake."

"You Eulers and cake," he teased. "We'll order some later. Promise. And I was busy."

"Busy?"

"Yeah." He pulled out his phone. "I scored a last-minute phone meeting with the housing folks at Groton."

"Oh?" All of a sudden, the lack of a text seemed less important. "And?"

"And I spoke to a great transition specialist. She thinks she has the perfect place for us. She sent pictures. Do you want to see?"

"You have to ask?" I made a grab for his phone, but he held it out of reach.

"Here, I want to show you."

"Okay. But hurry." I leaned in, his arm around my waist, anchoring me, as he called up the pictures he'd saved.

"So it's a freestanding house." He showed me an exterior shot of a small blue home of indeterminate age. The picture was clearly from the summer—no hint of snow or cold and there were cheery flowers out front.

"No apartment? No neighbors to complain about noise?" I liked the place already.

"Neighbors, but hopefully not close enough to hear you scream." He leered at me.

"Counting on it." I leered right back. "And maybe you'll be the one screaming."

"Yes. Please." A faint pink flush spread up his neck. "And here's the inside pics. Lots of windows. Kitchen's bigger than I expected."

"Oh, that's nice." I admired the white cabinetry and the appliances I'd have to put some effort into learning to use. "You can cook me lots of things there."

"I will cook you all the things." He kissed my forehead.

"I can't wait." I bounced lightly on the bed. "Show me more. One bedroom?"

"No. That's the best part. Two." He flipped to a new picture, this one a large, sunny L-shaped room. "Monster second bedroom. All yours. We'll wire it all up for your studio, put some instrument hooks up..."

"I love it." I kissed his cheek. "And heck, that's so big, I may have to add to my collection."

"We'll hang extra hooks." Laughing, he lightly tickled my ribs. "And here's the bathroom."

"A tub!" I beamed at him like he'd tiled the damn thing himself.

"I knew you'd love that detail."

"I do. Tell me you told her yes." I knew full well how fast good base housing options could go.

"I did. But there's a tiny catch."

"Oh?" I frowned. This couldn't be good.

"I said we were engaged." His voice was soft but even, not joking.

"Derrick." I scooted away from his arm. "We're not doing a fake engagement to get better housing."

"Not a fake engagement. A real one."

"Is this…" I trailed off because Derrick was sinking to his knees like this was a movie. My eyes went so wide, the stretch hurt. "You're serious. Like this is actually happening?"

He nodded. "Arthur, will you marry me?"

"So we can get a sweet housing upgrade?" Even my jokes were shaky, but it was that or cry my way through a yes.

"No. So I can get a life upgrade." He pulled out a little box. "I actually got these two weeks ago. I was going to ask you transfer or no transfer. You can see the receipts."

"I trust you." My eyes smarted anyway, the teasing not enough to keep my emotions at bay.

"Good. I wanted to marry you even if they sent me back out on a sub. I was only dithering over how to ask. Flash mob? Going viral?"

"We definitely don't need to go viral." I leaned down to kiss him. "I don't need an audience. Or a sweet house. Or a transfer. Only you. This is perfect."

"So..." he prompted.

"Yes. Yes, I'll marry you." Words tumbling out, one after the other, I put us both out of our misery.

"You sure you don't need to see the rings first?" His eyes were shining and his mouth wobbled as he flipped open the box to reveal two silver-colored rings that, knowing Derrick, were probably some special indestructible metal. Simple, but elegant. Probably more elegant than my nerdy self could pull off.

I carefully picked up the slightly smaller band, slid it on. Yup, instant class upgrade. "Wow."

"Looks great." Derrick slid his on, then placed his hand next to mine.

"We match." My voice was giddy.

"We do. We can get them engraved if you want before we do this for real." He put his hand over mine, making the rings touch.

"What do you mean *real*? You said this wasn't fake. This is real and I'm never taking mine off."

"Okay." He gave me an indulgent kiss. "Sounds like a plan. And it *is* real, but maybe we can make it official soon?"

"I love that idea. I mean my mom and the aunts are gonna have kittens if we elope, but yeah, let's do it soon. I don't want to wait." We'd both waited long enough. Rushing on this felt good. Right.

"Me either. And they can come. I'm not depriving your mom of an excuse for another Euler family gathering."

"You're so much nicer than me." Tired of leaning down to kiss, I hauled him up next to me.

"I am." He kissed my temple. "She's going to freak out tomorrow, right? Moving *and* an engagement?"

"Tom—oh! The breakfast. Oh my God. Calder's gonna have a fit, us upstaging his birthday."

"Eh. He won't mind the distraction. And he knows." Derrick added that like it was no big deal when I knew it was. "I told him I was going to ask you."

"Oh." I wasn't entirely sure how I felt about that. Like asking Calder permission would be weird, but I also understood that they'd been friends over a decade now and not telling him would have probably also been weird. "What did he say?"

"That he's happy for me. And you. For all of us. And that it wasn't his plan, but maybe it should have been." Derrick squeezed my side.

"Ha. Of course he wants to take credit."

"He also welcomed me to the family." Derrick's eyes sparkled as if he already knew my reaction, so I played into it with a horrified expression and loud groan.

"Oh God. You're a Euler now."

"This calls for cake," he deadpanned, and I bopped him with a pillow.

"At least there's no contest involved. Wait. Should I be worried about whether there was a betting pool on us getting engaged?"

"Everyone wins here." He found my mouth for another kiss. "Especially me."

"And me. I win too." I grinned at him, joining our hands again simply to feel the rings brush. "I can't wait to spend the rest of my life with you, Derrick Fox."

"I love you, Arthur. I can't wait to come home to you."

"You already did," I said right before I kissed him. Wherever he was, there would be home and the one place where I truly belonged.

★ ★ ★ ★ ★

Author Note

Every time I undertake a new series, the research is one of my favorite parts. For this book, I got to immerse myself in the world of submarines and what it's like to serve on one. Even the title stems from research into submarine jargon! I spent a lot of time on blogs, message boards, and with other first-hand accounts, but even as I tried for authenticity, a certain amount of liberties were taken for the sake of the story and ease of understanding. Likewise, I got to explore one of my favorite areas in the country, the Olympic Peninsula along with the Bremerton, Washington, area. I tried to include a lot of local flavor, and historic camps like the one used by the Euler family do dot the peninsula, but the exact camp used here is a fictional creation. I love this area of the country so much, and I can't wait until travel is more possible again. I wrote *Sailor Proof* while the quarantine for Covid-19 continued, and it was so nice to escape to a world without the virus where family reunions and big gatherings like homecomings were still possible. Accordingly, you won't see mention of the virus or masks in the series, and that's an intentional choice to provide readers with the same escape I so badly needed myself.

Acknowledgments

My amazing readers are the reason *Sailor Proof* came to be. I asked my readers what they wanted more of from me, and the overwhelming response was more military romance. Readers adored the Out of Uniform SEAL series and wanted more like that. In brainstorming with my team at Carina, I decided to go for a lighter military vibe, one with more time away from base. I also wanted to explore another elite job classification in the navy, and thus *Sailor Proof* and my submarine heroes for the Shore Leave series were born. So, thank you, readers, so much for loving my military romances and wanting more! Your support via social media, reviews, notes, shares, likes, and other means makes it possible for me to continue to write stories that mean the world to me, and I don't take that for granted!

As with all my books, I am so grateful for the team supporting me, especially at Carina Press and the Knight Agency. Kerri Buckley at Carina had such early enthusiasm for this idea and that made a huge difference. My editor, Deb Nemeth, is always the blend of support and critique that I need, and her encouragement means the world to me. My entire Carina Press team does an amazing job, and I am so very lucky to have all of them on board. A special thank-you to the tireless art department and publicity team and to the amazing narrators who bring my books to life for the audio market.

My behind-the-scenes team is also the best. My revisions were also assisted by invaluable beta comments from Abbie Nicole, Layla Noureddine, and Edie Danford.

Extra special shout-out for Abbie Nicole, who is the best PA I could ever ask for.

I wrote the end of *Sailor Proof* during a nine-day power outage. My family showed amazing resilience through that natural disaster on top of everything else the past year plus has thrown at us. I am so grateful to my spouse and children for their support. My life is also immeasurably enriched by my friendships, especially those of my writer friends who keep me going with sprints, advice, guidance, and commiseration. I am so grateful for every person in my life who helps me do what I love.

Falling in love is the biggest gamble of all.

Navy Chief Calder Euler loves to win big, and his latest score is a remote mountain cabin. His luck turns when an injury and a freak snowstorm strand him there with two girls and their silver fox father, who claims the property is his. Felix Sigurd is on a losing streak, with his ex gambling away his property to a hot guy now trapped in the cabin with him...

Keep reading for an excerpt from
Sink or Swim *by Annabeth Albert:*

Calder

"You seriously won a whole house? Man, you are the luckiest fucker I know." Max's voice crackled over my car speaker. My signal kept fading in and out the farther outside Seattle I drove, but his skepticism came through loud and clear.

"Cabin. And yeah, it's probably my biggest score yet." I couldn't help doing a little bragging as I navigated a curve on the country highway that kept advising travelers of their elevation and the distance to Mount Rainier. "I lucked into the invite for this high-stakes poker party and this one idiot kept going all-in. Totally out of his league. But he wasn't drunk or otherwise impaired, so his loss is totally my gain."

"Hell, yeah. So when do we get to come for a ski weekend?" Max sounded predictably eager to get away from base. "Cards and ski bunnies sounds pretty damn good right now. Not that you have anything left to play for."

"There's always something to play for." I had to slow for an RV plodding along. I was relying on some sketchy directions and my GPS to get me to this place. Now that I'd left the Seattle suburbs behind, the terrain had turned decidedly mountainous, little towns with folksy sort of names fewer and farther between long stretches of evergreen trees marching up and down scenic vistas. "You can come soon, but I need to check the place out first. For all I know it's a shack inhabited by a family of elk. This guy wasn't especially high on the place, but I figured what the hell. Even if it turns out that calling the place a ski chalet is pushing it, property is property."

"Yup. And knowing you, you weren't about to walk away from the table with a winning hand either." Max snorted, then coughed, like he'd inhaled some of his ever-present diet cola.

"Too true." I wouldn't take bets I couldn't win, but I also wasn't one to back down from a challenge either. A passing lane finally opened up, and I seized the chance to pass the RV. "If the cabin is too much of a dump, I'll unload it in a quick sale as soon as I get the paperwork straightened out. But in the meantime, having my own getaway sounds pretty sweet."

"Sure does. And hell, the way Seattle real estate prices are going, some sucker's gonna be willing to buy it to attempt the crazy-ass commute."

"Exactly." Those same ridiculous prices were a big reason why I kept living in the barracks. As a chief I had options, but in the Seattle area all those options required more bread than I was willing to part with. For all that I loved the thrill of winning a bet, I was also notoriously tight with my money. My brothers liked to joke that getting a loan out of me required three signatures and collateral, and they weren't that far from the truth. Saving cash by staying in the barracks made sense, but all the regulations, cramped spaces, and constant drama of other sailors got damn old. Having a place to escape to and bring my buddies was going to be awesome.

As long as the place wasn't falling down. Even I wasn't enough of a risk taker to bring the gang to a cabin that wasn't structurally sound. I'd take this weekend, inspect everything, make it as clean as possible, and draft some to-do and to-buy lists. Then I could set a date for the weekend away I'd been promising my crew. Traveling alone wasn't usually my style and my car had felt too quiet until I'd dialed Max, but I didn't want anyone around to laugh if it turned out I'd been had and the key didn't even work.

"So, how's the new duty assignment going?" Max asked, voice too careful to pass off as totally casual. Fuck. Maybe calling him hadn't been so smart after all.

"Awesome," I lied. "Shouldn't be too much longer before I'm out from behind a desk."

"Good to hear it. Couldn't pay me to get chained to an office." Max was a crane operator at the pier and possibly even more outdoorsy than me. Another reason to not have him along. If there were things I had to figure out, like lighting a tricky woodstove or something, I preferred to get it right before I had an audience eager to swoop in and help.

"Quit reminding me how much I wanna be back out there," I grumbled right as the phone crackled again. "Damn it. Signal's dropping again."

"No worries. I should probably run anyway. I've got a date tonight. Maybe you're not the only one with some recent luck." Max's warm laugh made me a little less grumbly. "This hottie swiped right and slid into my DMs with some killer pics."

"Have a good time. Hope they're not actually some pimple-faced kid." I kept my tone light, the sort of ribbing we gave each other all day.

"Hey, that only happened one time." The static increased, garbling whatever else he was trying to say until the call dropped completely. For once though I wasn't cursing the trees and lack of cell towers. Max had been wandering into territory I didn't want to think about, so I cranked the stereo rather than attempt a call back.

Without passengers I could indulge the musical tastes my brother the composer called hopelessly basic. Whatever. I liked what I liked, but I'd barely gotten two songs in before the GPS bleated that it was time to turn onto an even smaller side road and then another, each road more narrow and less maintained than the last. They'd been plowed at least, but not well. My sports car had all-wheel drive and was rated decent for winter, but I was still glad the forecast called for only a light dusting this weekend.

A rogue flake danced across my windshield. Probably an escapee from a nearby snowbank and not an omen. *Here's hoping.* Finally, the GPS led me up a gravel drive to a red mailbox beside a large carved wooden bear holding a cheery sign that read Dutch Bear's Hideaway. Hmm. *Hideaway* could be anything from a shed to a tree house, and a weird Christmas-morning-level excitement gathered in my gut as I made the turn. The house wasn't immediately visible from the road, and when the driveway turned to reveal a red Swiss-style cottage with white trim hidden among the trees, I couldn't help grinning.

This I could work with. It was older, sure, probably fifty years at least, and humble, but it looked sound, no saggy roof or missing windows. Its footprint was a basic rectangle with deep eaves, and a little white balcony indicated there was a second story tucked under the sloping roof. I went ahead and followed the drive around back to where it ended at a little outbuilding painted the same red as the house. Tim, the guy at the poker party, had made it sound way shabbier than this.

True, it was remote, with no neighbors that I could see, but as long as that chimney worked and we had something resembling electricity, this could be a nice bro hangout. Like the little clubhouse we'd had in the backyard at one of Dad's duty stations. Man, I'd loved that place. Maybe I'd change the sign to something more me. Keep the bear. He was cute and homey, kind of like the place itself.

After I parked, I started exploring on foot. A little fire circle with carved wooden benches and an ancient hot tub on a deck lurked behind the house. The hot tub might have to be replaced, but there was plenty of firewood in the little outbuilding, and lo and behold, one of my keys opened the white door to reveal snow shovels and other winter supplies. Not a bad start.

When I ducked back out of the outbuilding, a few more snowflakes fluttered over my face. Luckily I wasn't planning on going anywhere before morning, and I'd have wood and the food and supplies I'd brought if nothing else. The rear patio door next to the hot tub didn't take the first key I tried or the second or the same one as the outbuilding either. But then I went back to the first key, jiggled the knob a little, and the lock turned.

"Who's got the magic touch?" I crowed to the empty woods before opening the door. It let out a loud creak but would be an easy fix to put on my list. The door opened into a hallway with a neat row of hooks for coats and a mat for shoes and boots. Taking the hint, I took a second to take off my boots so I wouldn't track mud and snow all over the house. I left my coat on until I could assess the heat situation. The hallway led me past a modest bedroom with what looked to be a queen and bedding already on. *Score.*

A breaker box hung on the wall between the bedroom and bathroom. The electric was already on, so I tested the light in the bathroom. Worked. The bath was cramped with a cracked vanity, but I'd done multiple submarine tours. The tub/shower combo was practically palatial compared with the head on a sub. And after a brief pause with a gasp and sputter, the sink turned on. A little hard to turn and the water was rusty. However, I could let it run later, and I'd brought bottled for drinking, anyway.

"Running water! We're in business now." Happy, I hummed to myself as I continued down the hall, which opened into a U-shaped kitchen. Old appliances, but neat and tidy. Like the bath, it was cramped, but it opened to a living area, making it appear bigger. I could already picture games of cards at the built-in eating nook. It'd be a tight fit for my build, but I could always pull up a chair.

The living area was dominated by a stone fireplace and woodstove. I'd come back to that in a moment, but first the stairs beckoned me. I felt like some storybook character exploring a fairy-tale cottage. So far, everything was just right.

"Come on, Goldilocks. Let's see what's upstairs." Talking to myself was helping me feel less alone, especially when the third stair creaked like a horror movie. I'd brought a portable speaker for my phone. Maybe I could play some music while I messed with the woodstove.

The upstairs had a sleeping loft with three twin beds all in a row made up with identical quilts. "Wow. This really is some fairy-tale shit."

My nieces and nephews would go nuts for this space. My adult-sized pals were gonna be a tight fit in those beds, but it beat making them bunk down on the floor, and there was also a small room with crowded bookshelves, a rocking chair and a small desk next to a teeny half bath tucked into the eaves.

"Nice." Giving the space one last look, I turned to head back downstairs. For a second, I thought I heard the echo of children's voices. Damn. All this aloneness really was getting to me. *Click.* I thought I heard another sound, but the noise didn't repeat. Still, I hastened my trek down the stairs.

Whoosh. A rush of cold air made my whole body tense, every sense on red alert as the front door burst open.

"What the—" Whatever curse I'd been about to bellow was cut off by an ear-piercing shriek as a young girl appeared in the door. If I'd tried to conjure up an actual Goldilocks, I couldn't have done much better than her pale blond curls, pink cheeks, old-fashioned wool coat, and startled expression.

"There's someone here!" Her alarmed shout echoed off the wood walls.

"Wait," I called out right as my sock slid against the stair step. "Whoa!"

I thrust an arm out, but it was already too late and I was tumbling down the last three steps, landing on my ass in a heap at the bottom. *Ouch.* Trying to figure out what I'd injured, I was still catching my breath when another form appeared in the front doorway, this one adult, male, and mad as a grizzly.

"Who the hell are you and what are you doing in my cabin?"

Don't miss Sink or Swim *by Annabeth Albert,*
coming soon from Carina Adores.
www.CarinaPress.com

When an unexpected snowstorm strands two art historians in Madrid together, an old crush turns into a weekend fling...but can it turn into more? In this sexy, sophisticated romantic comedy, two women juggle romance and career across continents.

Keep reading for an excerpt from
Meet Me in Madrid *by Verity Lowell!*

Chapter One

Madrid, Charlotte pondered. There had to be someone she could call on short notice in Madrid.

She was sitting alone waiting on the bill in the rather stuffy restaurant belonging to her rather stuffy hotel near the Academia de Bellas Artes. Again, the middle-aged man at the bar turned around to look at her with an alarming lack of subtlety. And again she busied herself with her phone, hoping to give the impression she was waiting for someone.

It was just after 10:30, a perfectly typical time to finish dinner in a city that sleeps even less than New York. She'd had an excellent three-course meal including a lobster bisque, cardoons with salt cod, and four kinds of mushrooms a la plancha, plus a generously poured glass—make that two—of tasty Rioja. She was well-fed and tired, but given the time change, a little restless, too.

The best thing about Charlotte's job at the museum was the travel. The worst thing about Charlotte's job at the museum was the travel. It was as if someone gave you a Porsche 911 Turbo with all the bells and whistles (and horses) and said it was yours as long as you never did more than drive it under the speed limit to the local grocery store and back—without stopping anywhere along the way. And as long as you left *right now* and came back ASAP.

That was what a courier trip felt like.

Most people didn't think about how priceless works of art got from one museum to another for a blockbuster show. Which was why her job chaperoning American paintings and sculptures to the Prado or the Louvre or the National Gallery in London sounded so glamorous when she explained it: she was the one personally responsible for making sure the Mary Cassatt or John Singleton Copley loaned by her institution arrived at its destination without a scratch.

So, yes, her job description required travel, usually business class, to great museum cities around the world. And yes, "all" she had to do was ride along, drop it off, and show up for work the next day. And yes, she liked to think of her role as a cross between Secret Service agent and sexy librarian. But in reality the trips abroad were usually just plain head-buzzing, eyes-feel-like-they're-bleeding, weak-kneed exhausting.

Across the Atlantic and back in three days, door-to-door, and she would be once again drinking coffee in her cubicle in New Haven.

The upside? Once in a while, maybe every third trip or so, something went delightfully sideways. Mishaps usually boiled down to logistics. Bad weather, schedule mix-up, house registrar out sick, striking preparators. These were the flies in the ointment she pinned her hopes on. Unexpected delays translated into extended stays, and that, in a city as vibrant and sophisticated as the Spanish capital, was just what she wanted.

Thank God for saints.

James, Charlotte's museum colleague in operations, was a dapper, some would say needlessly fussy, fellow who had handled travel at the museum for two decades. It wasn't at all like him to miss an official foreign holiday. But somehow in the process of carefully piecing together Charlotte's hour-by-hour itinerary, even perspicacious James hadn't factored in the Immaculate Conception.

Nor could he have planned on the arctic squall that unexpectedly descended on the city the very day of the Marian festival in early December.

Someone or something had conspired to keep her in Madrid just a little longer.

But what to do with the unforeseen gift of free time?

She'd go out, obviously. But that was easier said than done well in a city she'd only visited once. The most annoying thing about these junkets was that she actually knew (or knew of) some attractive and intelligent people in many of the places she was sent to. If only she'd been given the time to see them.

In anticipation of her first-ever courier trip last year, Charlotte had written well in advance to one of her dissertation advisors at Yale, who was visiting at Oxford. Sadly, their planned pub crawl in King's Cross never happened. As she'd sat backstage at the V&A counting the elapsing minutes, a forklift's transmission gave out and the crate containing the full-length Eakins portrait in her care couldn't be opened and inspected until several hours after her predicted quitting time.

This had been Charlotte's initial schooling in the futility of trying to add pleasure to a business trip.

But now that the wine had started to ease away the day's stresses, a local contact hovered just beyond the tip of her mind. Madrid or the Prado or the Thyssen or the city's other important museum, the Reina Sofía, had come up in a quasi-recent post in one of her personal feeds. Or was it someone she followed? Or had it been a tweet?

Charlotte oscillated between platforms, scrolling and searching until she found what she was looking for. Adrianna Coates. The name alone filled her with a delightful little charge in what James would jokingly call her "nether regions." And it had been a minute.

The last time she'd seen her, Adrianna was wearing her

newly issued robin's-egg blue academic regalia, rising in turn with the other would-be professors to receive her doctoral degree under a crowded tent in one of the grassy quads. Though somewhat older than Charlotte, Adrianna was only four years ahead of her in the doctoral program in art history. They'd actually met when Charlotte was still an undergrad at Yale. Adrianna had been a graduate TA in one of Charlotte's last big lecture classes. Adrianna had been new to teaching but she was every bit as intimidating as the full professor she was there to assist.

As PhD students, they'd only had one seminar together— in Adrianna's final year. Charlotte had put herself *together* for those beyond-daunting weekly class meetings, dressing as she might for a job interview, if not a first date. With Adrianna to impress up close, she'd read more thoroughly and carefully than for any other class. The paper she wrote that term was the reason she'd received honors. It was published the year she graduated, helped get her a museum job—and was the last original scholarship she really felt good about.

She still remembered the first time they'd run into each other socially. It was Charlotte's third year in the program and she'd gone out to celebrate the end of her first term of teaching—Corot to Manet—with her all-male entourage of grad student queer boys because "real lesbians don't study the Impressionists," as they were fond of telling her.

There were still one or two actual old-school gay bars in New Haven in those days. The most storied, One Fifty-Five Lancaster, a two-roomed garden-level cave with a great patio, was practically across the street from the art history department. Although it had to have been close to eight years ago now—she must have been about twenty-five—Charlotte could summon that night to mind as if it was last week.

She and the boys were sitting around a big table near the

bar when Adrianna came in trailing some extremely hot and considerably younger student type. The two of them, arranged precisely in Charlotte's sight line, had hardly ordered their dry martinis before they started making out at the bar like prom-goers in the back of a limo. It was dark to begin with, and they were in the back corner. But there was something about the way Adrianna, always so formal and frighteningly whip-smart in the classroom, had allowed the woman's hands to slip inside her blazer. Something about the way her kiss seemed to deferentially answer to the younger woman's aggressive advances had stayed with Charlotte; all these years later, she vividly recalled what it felt like to watch them. It was funny and a bit sobering to realize she was now probably about the same age Adrianna had been at the time; she'd have to be in her early forties by now.

But here were the Instagram photographs Charlotte had been thinking of. Carefully composed, really quite sensual imagery of lipstick-stained espresso cups on marble café tables; of the hems of women's skirts, their legs tucked underneath; of stray cats regarding each other across the pebbled paths of the public gardens. If Adrianna's moody snapshots were taken in Madrid, it was not the city Charlotte had yet discovered.

Cross-referencing them with Adrianna's Facebook page, Charlotte determined (she preferred to think of it as good spycraft rather than stalkery behavior) that Adrianna was currently residing in Madrid on a prestigious sabbatical fellowship. According to her latest posts, she was there to document a group of objects housed at a convent near the palace. Made up of paintings, elaborate jewels, and tapestries, the collection had originally belonged to a seventeenth-century nun who spent her life assembling art in a cloister of royal women.

All very interesting. But did she dare send *La Reine des*

Glaces—the Ice Queen—as they used to call her, an after-dinner message on a snowy night?

Adrianna Coates had had a long day. She'd spent the morning at the National Library ordering up baroque manuscripts and poring over them in a very cold and crowded reading room. She'd then gone to the dismal basement cafeteria for her usual late lunch: a crust of hard, saltless bread, a few pieces of chorizo, and a *pincho* de tortilla—as Spaniards referred to a narrow slice of cold potato, onion, and egg pie. A demi glass of cheap white wine was her reward.

After the sun went down, she'd Metro'd to the city center in anticipation of a tiresome but mandatory dinner meeting of her fellow fellows in the loud, smoky bar next door to one of the city's oldest restaurants.

She had quickly come to hate these monthly gatherings. Of a group of fifteen, she was, and would continue to be, the only woman of color and, as far as she could tell, the only queer person. It was a true boys' club. The two other women were a pompous sexagenarian emerita from Columbia who continually asked her where she was "really" from and a mousy blonde from Dartmouth in a constant state of anxiety (understandable, Adrianna granted) over the well-being of her three-year-old twin sons still residing with their overwhelmed father back in New Hampshire.

It was always a two-stage affair. The Ivy that funded their fellowships was fond of following the fellows' interminable happy hour "reports" with the same kind of vaguely narcotic, drawn-out fish-and-cream-sauce dinner the restaurant had been serving since—and maybe during—the Spanish Civil War. She never got through all the courses but she always left feeling like a snake who had swallowed an ostrich egg.

The thing dragged on forever, and as it did, hands and conversation began to wander from the scholarly to the salacious, none of it tasteful or even funny, with alarming speed.

Adrianna waited until the discussion took an especially off-color turn, which it inevitably did, to excuse herself for an unnecessary trip to the powder room. En route, walking the long wood-paneled hall to the back of the building, she felt her phone's vibration through the sides of the Goyard bag that accompanied her everywhere.

She didn't receive many communiqués at this time of the night. Most people stateside would assume she'd be either out for a late dinner or asleep. Adrianna was curious enough about the sender to plop down on a bank of tufted leather benches outside the W/C and have a look. In any case, it wasn't like she actually had to go.

Charlotte Hilaire.

Now that was a blast from the past. What in the world might cute little Charlotte want—contact info for a colleague, perhaps, or a good word for a job?

How striking she must be as a grown woman, Adrianna mused. With an ease that surprised her, she could conjure up Charlotte as she was when they'd first met, a formidably intelligent, tennis-playing type who'd gone straight through to grad school and couldn't have been more than twenty-two. A wearer of sundresses. Small-boned and curvy with olive skin grown deeply tan from days at the beach or on the courts. Freckled. A shy but devastating smile.

Supremely shy. In fact, if memory served, outside of the seminar, they'd barely spoken to each other. The one exception might have been a few ridiculously chaste coffee dates provisionally arranged to discuss "professional development" or suggested revisions for Charlotte's brilliant, as Adrianna recalled, thesis on "The Color Line and Impressionism in New Orleans."

Wasn't she *from* New Orleans? Some old-guard Creole family?

Adrianna realized all this reminiscing had played out even before she clicked into her instant messages to see what, if anything, Charlotte Hilaire wanted from her.

She'd forgotten they were Facebook friends. But there it was.

Hers was the kind of stilted, charmingly awkward correspondence Adrianna sometimes received from younger, though usually queer, female scholars who hoped she would read their incipient articles or participate in a panel at a conference.

Dear Dr. Coates, it began. The remainder of the paragraph said in four or five multiple-claused sentences what she might have led with: I'm in Madrid on a courier trip with a couple of extra days on my hands due to the storm. Might you have time for a drink?

Don't miss *Meet Me in Madrid* by Verity Lowell, out from Carina Adores!

Discover another great contemporary romance from Carina Adores

April French doesn't do relationships and she never asks for more.

A long-standing regular at kink club Frankie's, she's kind of seen it all. As a trans woman, she's used to being the scenic rest stop for others on their way to a happily-ever-after. She knows how desire works, and she keeps hers carefully boxed up to take out on weekends only.

Then Dennis Martin walks into Frankie's, looking a little lost. April just meant to be friendly, but one flirtatious drink turns into one hot night.

When Dennis asks for her number, she gives it to him.

When he asks for her trust, well…that's a little harder.

For the Love of April French by **Penny Aimes** is available now!

CarinaAdores.com